END

"On a warm summer evening in 2012, I was fortunate enough to be at a dinner, where Charles & Marie Therese were present. Initially, I believed I would hear Charles speak about his experiences while stationed at Nellis Air Force Base. He was kind enough to recount his days and nights while on the ranges, but to my wonderful surprise, also detailed events which paralleled my own personal experiences as a child growing up on a small farm in rural Canada. Until that night, I believed I was one of few people who had seen things and been witness to events and life which others dismiss as imagination or fantasy. An area of discussion which had always been taboo in my family was now openly spoken about without judgment or ridicule.

If you've ever had a known truth in your life which you've had to keep buried as a secret, you will understand when I say the emotion of finally having someone unknowingly acknowledge all your experience has been real was so overwhelming it brought me to tears. Listening to Charles, many of my own blanks were filled and I was finally able to connect dots to otherwise pieces of fragmented memories.

Charles, Marie Therese and I had never met until that night and neither of them could have known, for me that evening would feel like a burden finally lifted. Our visit turned into an unforgettable truly enlightening weekend, as it spilled over to the following day when Charles continued to relive stories he has written in earlier books in the Millennial Hospitality series.

In Millennial Hospitality V, The Grays, readers will find further accounts of the existence of extraordinary life, and for those already aware, better understand their own experiences.

CLP"

Also by Charles James Hall

Hall Photon Theory, Jan 27, 1998
Copyright TXU836-663

Millennial Hospitality

Millennial Hospitality II
The World We Knew

Millennial Hospitality III
The Road Home

Hall Photon Theory,
Explores Force Fields Which Enable Travel Faster Than The Speed of Light.
September 19, 2006 copyright TXu1-317-919

Millennial Hospitality IV
After Hours

www.millennialhospitality.com

Millennial Hospitality V

The Greys

Charles James Hall

authorHOUSE®

AuthorHouse™
1663 Liberty Drive
Bloomington, IN 47403
www.authorhouse.com
Phone: 1-800-839-8640

Although names of people and places have been disguised, everything in this book is a true account of the personal experiences of Charles James Hall while serving as an enlisted airman in the U.S. Air Force during the mid 1960s.

Published by AuthorHouse 12/14/2012

ISBN: 978-1-4772-9787-2 (sc)
ISBN: 978-1-4772-9786-5 (hc)
ISBN: 978-1-4772-9789-6 (e)

Library of Congress Control Number: 2012923259

This book is printed on acid-free paper.

Dedicated to the greater glory of God
Who created All, Extraterrestrials included.

Foreword

When Charles began telling me of his two separate TDYs among the Grays, I reminded him, I'd heard him say, the Grays were not at Indian Springs, and he never wanted to meet them. My question, and that of readers who heard him as well, would be: Why the contradiction? Why write about them now?

While Charles had an up close and personal relationship with the Tall Whites, he was never as close to the Grays. The place he was sent for these TDYs, is even more closely guarded by the military than Indian Springs. Nervous as Charles was, when writing about the Tall Whites, he was even more cautious, as he considered writing about his experiences among the Grays.

The time is drawing very near, when all will know, extraterrestrials are real, and, are here. There remains no compelling reason, not to write about Charles' terrifying and unique experiences, while serving our country in the mid-sixties. Therefore, it is with great pleasure that we present Millennial Hospitality V, The Grays. Seeking Truth in all things, is a worthy life-long quest. In the meantime, there are many people who are being bothered by the Grays. We believe, they in particular, may find comfort in reading this book.

In late 2005, Charles & I were able to pursue our dream of traveling to Italy. While in Rome, we left a presentation of Millennial Hospitality series for Pope Benedict, along with a letter, explaining, disclaimers aside, everything in the books was true, and happened to Charles. To our pleasure and surprise, we received a letter from the Vatican, dated February 16, 2006, from the Secretary of the Vatican state, as directed by His Holiness Pope Benedict XVI, acknowledging the letter and the books, as well as his appreciation for the sentiments expressed in the letter. It is interesting to note, there was an article in L'OSSERVATORE ROMANO, in 2008, stating, it was perfectly all right for people to believe in extraterrestrials.

As always, our books are dedicated to the greater honor and glory of God, who created all, extraterrestrials included.

Marie Therese Hall
Veterans Day, 2012

Contents

The Greys

BOOK TWO
DISASTER AT ROSWELL

Remembering Martha

Then the wolf
shall be a guest of the lamb,
and the leopard
shall lie down with the kid
The cow and the bear
shall be neighbors,
. . . Isaiah 11:6,7

It was early afternoon in the summer of 1950. The well kept fields of fully grown hay, ripening corn, recently harvested oats, densely forested woods and hills and pastures that comprised my grandfather's two dairy farms, lay serene, majestic, and idyllic in the warm Wisconsin summer sun. The 430 acres or so of my grandfather's two farms, along with the neighboring 200 or so additional acres he sometimes rented, on the edge of the little town of Fitchburg Corners south of Madison, seemed like a little Garden of Eden, lost in time. To me, my father and his father before him—to all of us, it was home—a near perfect Wisconsin paradise. None of us realized that one day the State of Wisconsin would declare our little town of Fitchburg Corners to be a State Heritage Site and seek to preserve it—to keep it looking forever just the way it was on that beautiful summer day.

My father worked the smaller of the two farms and helped his father and his two younger brothers work the larger, along with the additional rented farmland. That day my father was helping his father and his brothers bring in the harvest of newly baled hay. He, my Grandfather, and I were alone together, down in the large hay field by the marsh on the big farm. We were waiting for one of my uncles to return with more empty wagons. I was five years old that summer. I would be starting first grade down at Maple Corners school in the fall.

"Pa," you should see how smart my son Jim is," my father said proudly to his father. "He's already taught himself how to read. I taught him a little. I got him started. He just seemed to set his mind to it and then he did it, all by himself!"

My Grandfather didn't appear to be particularly impressed. "Jim? Is that what you're calling him these days?" he gruffly responded.

"Yes," said my father proudly. "Because his name is Charles just like mine, we decided to use his middle name as a nickname, so everyone could keep us straight."

"That will just confuse him," replied my Grandfather sternly. "After a while, he will forget his name is Charles. You should have named him Jess, after me, like I told you. Hell, the way you're raising him, soon he won't even know what his name is."

"But you should see him and how quickly he learns," replied my father proudly. "I wanted him named after me because he is so intelligent."

My Grandfather eyed me slowly for a bit.

"He don't look that bright to me," stated my Grandfather with a final, impatient tone in his voice. Then patting me on the top of my head, he stated forcefully, "Jimmy boy, you better get in the habit of learning from others. Watch the other men around you and see how they do things.

Then do just like they do. Don't go getting any big ideas of your own. You ain't that bright. Every day of your life, you better get up in the morning, look around, and say to yourself, 'Today I need to learn something from others.'" Then my Grandfather stomped away up the field towards my uncle, the oncoming tractor, and the returning empty hay wagons.

A few days later, I was over at the big farm standing outside the screen door on the front porch. It was another lazy summer day. I had decided it would still be a few hours before the usual afternoon thunderstorms developed, so I had walked barefoot over from the little farm by myself. I wanted to play with my older sister, Martha. She was alone inside my grandmother's kitchen, cleaning up after the noon meal. "Martha," I spoke to her quietly. "I thought I would come and play with you. We could play with your dolls on the back porch, or under the apple trees in the orchard the way you like."

"I would love to, Jimmy," she answered quietly. "But I have a lot of work to do. I have to finish doing the dishes and cleaning these aluminum cooking pans. Then I have to clean up the floor and everything else in the kitchen."

"I'll help you," I responded. Quietly, I opened the screen door and went inside. Together Martha and I finished washing the dishes. Then we cleaned the cooking pans, and cleaned the top of the wood burning cook stove that my Grandmother used for all of her cooking. The two of us were laughing together as we washed off the top of the kitchen table. I began mopping the floor while she began cleaning the kitchen cupboards. Suddenly, without warning, one of our aunts came into the room. She was one of my father's younger sisters. She was very angry with us. "Jimmy!" she exclaimed. "What are you doing here? These are Martha's chores. And Martha! What are you doing letting Jimmy help you clean the kitchen? He should be back up at the little farm helping his father. Jimmy is already turning into a sissy. You're just making him worse!"

Then my aunt sternly ordered me outside, slamming the inner door behind me. As she was doing so, Martha was saying, "Come back when I finish my chores, Jimmy, we can play together then."

I waited outside in the fields and pastures for the rest of the afternoon, but Martha never came out. Her chores never seemed to end. Later, as I was walking back home in the late afternoon rain, I noticed that through it all, my aunt had seemed afraid of me. Through it all, she had never once laid a hand on me.

I spent the next few days playing by myself on the smaller of my Grandfather's two farms. I was playing along the western line fence, next to the road that passed by the front of the farm. The road was known as Adam's road. After passing by our farm, the road continued west. past the 200 acres of land owned by two unmarried sisters. It also passed by the large 250 acre gentleman's farm owned by the Adams, for whom the road was named. Adam's farm was located diagonally across the road to the northwest of our farm. The sister's land was on the same side of the road as our farm. My grandfather usually rented more than 400 acres of land from those two neighbors. He would have bought either one or both of the farms, if either had been willing to sell. The sisters had inherited their land, and the Will had forbidden them to ever sell it. As for the Adams farm, my grandfather told me there was little point in asking. My grandfather said he could still remember the cold snowy January night when their only child, a son, had died. The Adams were both wonderful people. Their many riches only allowed them to turn the huge wooded area just over the hills in the back, where my grandfather said their son had played, into a secluded, park-like place. They now spent many warm summer evenings walking alone—sometimes singing quietly to the Lord with tears in their eyes—sometimes walking silently in prayer. Their wealth couldn't bring back their son. I enjoyed playing in the park-like place, and the Adams seemed to enjoy seeing me playing where their son used to play.

The sister's land was just across the line fence from where I was playing on this day. The sister's owned perhaps a thousand acres scattered over a wide area. Their land next to ours contained only a few corn cribs for buildings. Consequently, no-one actually lived on their land next to us. Their line fences were usually in poor condition.

For many years Adam's road had been a narrow tree-lined gravel road that passed through an unusually large grove of huge, impressively beautiful, ancient oak trees. The road had just recently been widened and paved. In order to widen the road, against my father's wishes, the highway department had chopped down most of the large oak trees and hauled them to the dump to be burned. Only a dozen or so oak trees remained, along with a large number of ancient stumps. The stumps sat open and exposed along the western line fence, and along the new fence which ran alongside the newly paved road. I was teaching myself to count to one thousand by counting the tree rings on the exposed tree stumps. Although most oak trees live only 400 years or so, these trees appeared even older. Cutting them down seemed a terrible waste, and my parents were particularly disappointed when they disposed of the wood. We could have used it in our wood stove for many years.

A day or so later, my father and I were finishing the noon meal at my Grandparent's house on the big farm. One of my uncles was with us. The four of us were otherwise alone in my Grandmother's kitchen. "Pa," began my father forcefully, "I want to talk to you and Ma about my daughter Martha."

My Grandmother appeared to become very nervous. "Should we do it in front of Jimmy, here?" she asked. Then she turned to my uncle and said, "Take Jimmy outside and feed the goats. He spends so much time playing alone in the woods and fields, he needs to start doing things with others. Charlie never puts him to work. I've even seen him playing out in the fields and woods alone at night, hours after his bedtime. He doesn't seem to be afraid of anything, even the darkness. He's getting older now. It's time he started doing more work around the farms."

"Yes, Ma," replied my uncle. He got up from the table and headed towards the front door. "Come with me, Jimmy. We'll feed the goats. We just got them last week. Have you ever fed a billy goat?"

"No," I answered, as I got up from the table and followed my uncle outside.

We crossed the wide northern side of the large loop made by the gravel driveway. Then we headed slightly downhill across the grass in the center, towards the pump house where the small flock of goats were grazing. The goats were running loose and were not fenced in. "You need to get some goat pellets from the feed bag just inside the machine shed over there." stated my uncle. "There's a pail next to the bag. Go get a large pail full of goat feed."

"Yes," I answered. I continued walking on across the narrower southern part of the driveway. Reaching the end of the first long machine shed, I entered its darkened interior through the already open doors. Several large bags of goat pellets were sitting inside, and one of them was open. I took the pail that was sitting next to one of the bags and filled it, probably three quarters full. That made it about as heavy as I could carry. Then, with pail in hand, I headed back across the driveway to where my uncle was waiting.

"Good job, Jimmy," laughed my uncle. "Now go feed it to the goats. Start with the Billy goat. Just take a handful, walk right up to him from the front so he doesn't kick you, and feed it to him."

Leaving the pail with my uncle, I took a big handful of goat pellets. Holding the handful out in front of me, I slowly approached the Billy goat. I stopped when I was still perhaps 20 feet from him. He continued grazing and didn't appear to notice me.

"Don't be afraid," exclaimed my uncle. "Just walk right up to him and feed him."

"He'll see me in a few minutes," I responded. "He'll smell the food and start looking around. Then he'll see me here and come over to where I am. It's a lot safer for me if I feed him that way."

"Oh, dam-mit!" exclaimed my uncle. "You'll never get anything done! Sometimes, you drive me right up a wall! You can't waste your life waiting on animals! Just go right out there and take charge of him. Be the boss for a change! How's he going to eat if you don't feed him?"

"But Billy Goats are smart animals," I stammered. "He knows how to eat and how to protect himself. He'll come over and eat out of my hand when he gets hungry. It wouldn't be safe for me to surprise him."

Swearing more oaths, my uncle exclaimed forcefully, "I see what ma says. Your father isn't raising you right. You're about as worthless as teats on a boar hog!" He grabbed the pail, stood up straight, and stomped over to where I stood. He forcefully took the goat pellets from my outstretched hand. Then he shouted, "You're so bull headed, you can't even be disciplined, can you?! You can't even be shouted at or sworn at! Calling you names is just a waste of my time, isn't it?! I haven't even hurt your feelings, have I?! You're not even crying or a damn thing, are you?! Shouting like this, I'll bet I would have all of your cousins crying by now! You're just going to monkey around and do things your way even if it was to kill you, aren't you?! And if I was ever to lay a hand on you or spank you the way you deserve, your father would kill me, wouldn't he?!"

Before I could answer, he continued shouting, "Just go play alone, out in the damn woods where all the other kids are afraid to play. Go play out there, the way you always want to. It's all you're good for! The apples are starting to ripen on those two trees you like to play in, back behind the hills in the corner of the big pasture. I'll finish feeding the goats myself!"

Without saying anything more, I stepped away from my uncle and, skipping as I left, I took off to play in the apple trees.

A few weeks passed. It was morning, just after breakfast, and the beginning of another glorious Wisconsin summer day. My father had just finished washing down the milk house on the smaller of my grandfather's farms where we lived. The 38 dairy cows had already been turned out to pasture. My father seemed unusually lost in thought. Over breakfast he told me intently to stay close by him. He needed me for something, he said. After he finished, he strode down into the basement of the barn where the stanchions for the cows stood. Going up to a hiding place between the stone foundation and the heavy wooden beams supporting the barn, with a practiced hand he took out his 22 caliber rifle and probably 35 shells. He carefully unwrapped the well-kept rifle, checked it, and then carefully loaded it with live ammunition. He put the rest of the shells in his pockets. Turning to me, he said coolly, "Come with me, Jimmy my boy. Today we are going to get your sister Martha."

"Yes, Dad." I responded.

Together he and I set out walking out of the barn, down the driveway, and down Adams road, towards my grandfather's big farm, a mile and a half distant, to the north and east of us.

You see, my older sister Martha, didn't live with us. She lived on the big farm with my father's parents. They had taken her from my parent's care when she was barely two years old and had steadfastly refused to give her back. I had not been told the details at the time.

My father and I walked in almost total silence. My father was lost in deep thought. In a short while, we reached the beginning of the big farmland that my grandfather owned. We turned off the country road and began walking north, through the back lane, the pastures and the woods, towards the barn on the big farm. We would be approaching the barn unseen from the back, from its western side. All my father would say to me was, "No matter what happens, Jimmy, take your sister Martha by the hand and take her home. Always stay beside her and help her. Promise me you'll do that for the rest of your life, no matter what happens."

"Yes, Dad. I promise. I will always stand by Martha." I solemnly responded.

My grandfather was alone in the empty barn when my father and I, unannounced, walked in on him. The cows had been turned out to pasture and he was sweeping the floor with a large barn broom. Looking up at the two of us, my grandfather said, "Hello, Charlie. I see you brought Jimmy with you. What are you doing carrying a rifle? Is the gun loaded?"

"Yes, Pa," answered my father sternly. "It's loaded. I've come to take my little girl Martha back home with me."

Then my aunt, one of my father's sisters, came out of the attached milk house and into the barn. "What's going on?" she asked surprised.

My grandfather turned to his daughter and said forcefully, "Get up to the house and get Martha. Have her pack some of her things in a bag and get her down here as fast as you can. Charlie has come to take her home. Hurry, dam-mit! We don't have all day!!"

My aunt, seeing that my father was carrying a gun, turned immediately and left the barn. Through the open barn doors she could be seen hurrying up towards the big house. My grandfather, speaking slowly and calmly to my father, said, "Let's walk out to the driveway. We'll get some fresh air, while we're waiting for your sister to bring Martha."

Then, as the three of us were walking outside to the large circular driveway, he said to my father, "You know none of this was ever my idea. I have always told your mother that Martha belongs back home with you."

My father, for his part, didn't say anything. He seemed unimpressed. Instead he took up a strategic position across the driveway on its southern side, 50 feet away or so, where he had a clear field of fire. He motioned for me to fall back to his right and down the driveway a ways, next to one of the machine sheds that also bordered the southern side of the driveway.

In a very short time, my grandmother came out of the house holding Martha by the hand. My aunt came with her. My grandmother and my aunt hurried across the gravel driveway with Martha in hand, until all three of them were standing next to my grandfather. They all stood facing us across the driveway. "What's this all about, Jess?" my grandmother asked my grandfather, anxiously.

"Charlie has come for Martha." answered my grandfather slowly. "Do you have some of her clothes and things with you? We can bring the rest later."

My grandmother immediately became very agitated. “Charlie? What are you doing with that gun? It isn’t loaded, isn’t it? You’re not going to take Martha back to that drafty old house of yours are you?” she began earnestly.

“She’s my daughter!” responded my father in anger and bitterness. “She belongs with me and her brother Jim here.”

“But she’ll die up there when winter comes,” my grandmother continued, the emotion showing in her voice. “She can’t take the cold like you and Jimmy can. She’ll get pneumonia or a cold again. Here she has her own room. It’s upstairs and warm. It’s heated by a coal furnace. Your drafty old house is only heated by a wood stove! It’s never warm!”

“Martha is my daughter!” screamed my father in rage. “She should be up with us, playing with Jim. They’re brother and sister. They should be sharing their childhood together. It’s not right that she is growing up over here with you.”

“She was dying when we brought her over here.” shouted my grandmother. “We didn’t take her from you! She was only two and she was dying from the whooping cough. You didn’t know what to do. You had given up on her. That was 8 years ago. Don’t you remember? Have you forgotten already? You wouldn’t even have her if it wasn’t for us! We’re the ones keeping her alive!”

My father hesitated for a minute. Then tears of love and anger began to form in his eyes.

My grandmother continued shouting at him, “What will she do for an education up where you are? Here she’s doing so well in school now. She’s getting all A’s. Why ruin that? Here with us she'll get to go to college when she grows up. You're poor. You don't have any money. If she's up there with you, what are you going to be able to do for her?"

My father began trying to choke back his tears and his rage.

My grandmother continued, now in a softer tone. "If you leave her here with us, we promise to send her out to play with Jimmy whenever he comes over. We won't make her keep working like we did the other day, when Jimmy was over. We'll let the two children play together as much as they want. We'll even let Jimmy help her with her chores if he wants. We promise to send her to college when she finishes high school. We promise to make you very proud of her!"

My father, now starting to shed tears openly, asked Martha, "Are you happy here, honey? Are they treating you right? Do you want to come home with me?"

"No, father," replied Martha shyly. "I'm happy here. I have a nice room and everyone is treating me all right. I just want more time to play with Jimmy."

My father now broke down completely. "I love you, Martha." he choked out. Then he turned to his left and, shedding tears and crying openly, he stumbled sadly back towards the woods and pastures behind the barn. The rest of us just stood, frozen in silence. After a time had passed, I could see my father as he disappeared in the distance into the neighbor's woods and fields and pastures. He was crying openly in grief and despair. He obviously wanted to be alone.

My grandfather, grandmother, aunt, and Martha, all remained standing across the driveway, directly facing me while I alone, remained standing, facing them. After a while, still facing me, my grandfather spoke sternly to my grandmother and my aunt, "Be certain you always keep Martha happy. Be certain you always keep your promise to Charlie. Remember, if Martha had said she wasn't happy today, Charlie might have gunned all of us down. After what we've done to him, there wouldn't have been any stopping him!"

"Are you sure?" asked my grandmother, still in shock.

"I'm certain of it!" answered my grandfather.

"But we're his family," argued my grandmother, "Surely he wouldn't have hurt us. He still dreams of becoming a Methodist preacher. He likes to get up and read from the Bible in church. He likes to preach the sermon on Sundays. Years ago, when he was young, he loved to study the Bible at the Institute in Chicago."

"I know my son," answered my grandfather. "Usually he's like you say. But once he sets his mind on something—once he decides that he's going to stand and fight, you'd rather face an angry fully grown male grizzly bear than take him on."

My grandmother and my aunt both stood in shocked silence for a short time. Then my aunt asked slowly, "What about Jimmy, there? I've always wondered about him. If you're right about Charlie, Jimmy over there might be the same way."

"Why would you say that?" asked my grandfather, surprised. "He's already going on six. I've never seen him stand and fight. He is so damn patient. It looks to me like he's willing to put up with anything. Two weeks ago I saw Jimmy and some of the neighbor's older children playing in the feed shed behind the barn. The other kids were teasing him unmercifully and trying to start a fight with him. He didn't give a tinker's damn what they called him. He just laughed it off and talked his way out of it. Then he went off and played by himself. Later I saw him playing alone out in the big corn field with those two dogs of his. He was at the far end where the other kids are afraid to go because it is so close to the neighbor's woods. Yet, Jimmy was just as happy as a kid could be. He wasn't crying or anything. Just look at the size of his wrists. He's growing up to be one big bruiser. He's already plenty big enough to have beat the crap out of at least a couple of those other boys, and made them take back what they were saying about him. Yet, he was happy to just talk his way out of it and run off and play."

"But he's Charlie's son," replied my aunt. "I think he has got to be the way Charlie is. Like father, like son. You're that way, Pa. Your younger brother Ray is that way. It must run in the blood."

My grandfather paused for a minute as he studied me from a distance. My aunt continued, "You know how you always tell us about the times when you and Ray were kids, after you two had been orphaned? Remember how you two spent five years in reform school over at Waukesha? Remember those baseball games between the children and the guards, and the time you and Uncle Ray beat up that big guard who was playing second base?"

My grandfather smiled, as memories of his younger days slowly came back to him. "Yes, those were some good times Ray and I had back in reform school," he said "We both cleated that big guard, good and proper. He sure had it coming. It was a couple three weeks before he was back on his feet again. But Ray and I were natural born fighters. We never put up with anything. We were always ready to stand up for our rights. Jimmy, there, I've never seen him sass me back or anything. I like to see a young man that will stand and fight, but Jimmy there, is just growing up to be a push-over and a sissy."

"You've never seen him sass you back or stand and fight or anything?" asked my aunt incredulously. "Pa, you're wrong about Jimmy. You and Uncle Ray always had each other. But Jimmy has been standing over there alone and barefoot all this time, just watching and listening to us. He has been standing there, thinking things through, every minute he's been here. His father just threatened to kill all of us with a gun. Then his father just walked off and left Jimmy, to fend for himself. Yet, Jimmy hasn't said a word. He didn't run after his father or call after him or anything. For Jimmy to get back home, he has to survive us, cross through those two large patches of Canadian thistles, cross the pig yard, the pasture and the lane where the bull and the cattle are, and climb at least two barbed wire fences because his father won't be there to open the gates for him. Then he's going to have to walk at least a mile down Adam's road past two of the neighbors' farms with their dogs coming out to bark at him. Think of all of the times he's done that alone this summer, just so he could play over here where his sister Martha is. I'm telling you, Pa, you're wrong. Jimmy has to be better at fighting and handling his fears than you, Uncle Ray, or his father,

Charlie, ever were! It has to be in Jimmy's blood more than it's even been in yours."

My grandfather stood looking directly at me as he thought about what she'd said. Then he spoke slowly to my grandmother and my aunt. "You might be right about Jimmy. I don't know. I'll have to watch him more closely than I have. But I'll tell you one thing I do know. You better not keep him waiting to play with Martha any longer. You better get the both of them up to the house and get them playing together now. Make sure you give them both cookies and milk, or lemonade or something. And if Jimmy feels like playing with Martha and her dolls, or helping her wash the dishes, let him. Don't ever say a damn thing to him about it! And make sure he goes home happy and tells his father. Charlie is still perfectly able to come back here late tonight with that gun of his. He has a key to our house. If he comes back tonight, he could shoot us all in our sleep."

It's A Small World, After All

. . . until we have sealed the servants of our God
in their foreheads.

And I heard the number
of them [those]
which were sealed:
and there were sealed
an hundred and forty and four thousand
of all of the tribes of Israel . . . .
. . . Revelation 7.7-9

It was a year in the mid 1950s, a warm mid summer day in the little town of London, Wisconsin. London was a sleepy farming community which lay some 20 miles east-southeast of the State Capitol of Madison. Madison was named after former U.S. president James Madison. It was the home of the prestigious University of Wisconsin. London was a small town, not nearly living up to the dreams of the people who founded London, Wisconsin in 1886, imagining it would grow to become as large as London, England, its namesake—the place the founders had immigrated from.

London, Wisconsin, sat halfway between the larger and equally beautiful communities of Cambridge and Deerfield, both of which were some three miles away, down beautiful winding Wisconsin country roads. London was a tiny collection of houses and taverns sitting next to the train station on which the hopes of the town founders had depended. It also had a lumber yard, cheese factory, gas station, farm implement dealer, Post Office, Grade School, and country store. It had a small country Moravian Lutheran church of special mention. I was being raised as a Protestant. I had not yet converted to the Roman Catholic religion. The passenger trains to and from far away Madison still ran twice a day.

We moved to London over the fourth of July, 1955. My grandfather had died suddenly from liver problems. My grandfather had become quite rich over the years. The money had allowed him to keep his promise to send Martha to college with a secure college fund. The money had allowed him to purchase many acres of prime Wisconsin farm land, orchards, woods, pastures, the dream collection of dairy cattle, chickens, ducks, geese, hogs, horses, goats, tractors and farm equipment. It had also allowed him to purchase many bottles of whiskey, a ruined liver, a botched up will, a beautiful funeral, and a family burial plot in the nearby little town of Oregon, Wisconsin. He was only 67 years old. Almost from the very first minute he was dead, the beautiful Wisconsin farm land and the botched up will attracted big city lawyers the way berry plants with flowers attract honey bees. Of my grandfather's estimated $2 million dollar estate (in 1955 dollars), my father would receive at most a mere $30,000. He would have to wait many years for it. In the meantime we were hopelessly poor. A number of big city lawyers would later be seen wearing big city smiles—and driving brand new big city cars. A couple of them would later be written up in a major Wisconsin newspaper. They were presented as models of the big city legal community which other Wisconsin lawyers should emulate.

My father had never wanted to move to London but, poor as we were, he had very few other choices. He had been forced off the farms he loved, forced to separate even further from his beloved daughter Martha. He remained heartbroken for many years afterwards. On this day in the mid 1950's, he was struggling to rebuild his life and to remain in touch with his past.

My father did well in choosing London. He knew well the difference between being poor in a small upstanding Wisconsin town like London, as opposed to being poor in a big inner city such as distant Milwaukee, far away Chicago, or the over-the-horizon St Louis—where his father-in-law lived. Although the house my father had chosen to move us into, was little more than an abandoned shack with no running water and outdoor plumbing, its location was perfect. It gave me easy access to excellent schools with excellent teachers, easy access to the Wisconsin labor market, the Wisconsin farm labor market—and walking distance to church.

There was no crime rate in London. The other residents of London were as fine and God fearing as any group of middle class Americans can be. We were the only poor family in a town with many hard working Christians, surrounded by an endless sea of equally hard working middle class dairy farmers. My father understood what fresh air, Wisconsin sunshine, lots of hard work, a good education, a few years growth, intense prayers, careful reading of the Bible—and the help of God—would do as the years passed. My father was down, but not out. Unlike my grandfather before him, my father never visited the taverns across the street from our house. Whatever my father was, he was always beside me and always stone sober.

It was just past noon that nice summer day in July. I was in grade school. School was out for the summer. I had walked over to the small country store which sat on the main street corner in London. I climbed the steps, opened the front door and stepped inside. At the far end, on the right side behind the counter, stood the owner. He was an older man, tall and thin, and one of the nicest older men I ever met when I was still in grade school. On my side of the counter stood another older man, probably in his mid forties. They were obviously life long friends. As I approached the two of them, the store owner said to his friend, "Here's Jimmy now. He's the one I was telling you about." He greeted me, "Hi Jimmy. This is my friend Ray. He and I have been friends all of our lives. We were classmates together when we were young and together in school."

"Hello, Sir," I responded politely and formally.

"Hi Jimmy," he responded in a very friendly manner.

"Jimmy, Ray lives here in Wisconsin, so I suppose you and I will be seeing quite a bit of him." said the store owner. He turned to Ray and continued, "Jimmy is the kid I was telling you about, Ray. He's smart as a whip. He reads a lot. He especially likes to read history and science books. He's the only grade school kid I have ever met who has read some of the Bible on his own, including most of the new testament. He and I were talking the other day about flying saucers and other great mysteries. He thinks all flying saucer reports should be studied on the site where they occurred, and keeping everything in the proper context. He has some insights you will find interesting."

"Really," responded Ray in an interested manner.

Jimmy there, thinks many alleged pictures of flying saucers are only pictures of aluminum cooking utensils being thrown in the air."

"Really," stated Ray, apparently unconvinced. "I'm not sure I buy that. If that were true, why would so many photographic experts declare the pictures to be authentic? And why wouldn't more Americans and more investigators have noticed that? Why aren't more investigators aware of America's history, and asking those kind of questions?"

"I don't know," replied the store owner. "But the next time you get a chance, you might check out Jimmy's ideas. They certainly make sense to me. Jimmy thinks if you get the chance, you should visit some of the people who took pictures of flying saucers, and try to get some pictures of their cooking stove and their cooking utensils."

"I'll do that if I can," replied Ray, sincerely. Then, turning to me, he continued, "Jimmy, have you heard of the Roswell crash in New Mexico, back in 1947?

"Yes," I replied. "The public libraries in Cambridge, and down in Deerfield, have many old and forgotten books which have long since been out of print. The libraries have been throwing them out because no one but me seems to read them anymore.

The books cover all sorts of topics, and unexplained mysteries. A few of the books are reports published by the U.S. Government. The government says the crash at Roswell was only a weather balloon carrying a radar reflector.

"What are your thoughts about it?" Ray asked, apparently wishing only to be polite to his lifelong friend, the store owner.

"Well," I replied, "In order to find out the truth, you personally would have to visit Roswell, New Mexico. You would have to talk with some of the people who have seen the place where the saucer is said to have crashed.

If you were to visit the Roswell area, talk with the local people, and visit the actual crash site, you might be able to obtain a piece of something unusual, such as a piece of the thin glass fibers, I read about in old magazines."

"Yes, Jimmy," Ray responded. "But the U.S. military has long since gone out and picked up all of the material and the other debris at the crash site and carted it off somewhere. What would I accomplish by going down there?"

"You could start by looking for very fine strands of flexible glass fiber." I answered. "It would have to be so fine that pieces of it would blow away in the wind.

One of the saucers is said to have crashed in a storm. So the crash would have thrown thousands of short pieces of flexible glass fiber up into the wind. Pieces of such fiber would have blown for miles across the New Mexican plains. Why don't you search a lot further out from the crash site than the other people did? All you have to find is just one short thin strand of glass fiber with unusual properties, such as bending light in a circle.

Ray stood looking at me for a minute or so, thinking. Then he said, "That's not a bad idea, Jimmy. Let me think about it."

Time passed. It was a cold, windy day in the fall. I was back in the little country store on main street in London. The owner and I were talking about flying saucers. Outside a car pulled up and parked out front.

"There's Ray, now," exclaimed the store owner happily.

The steps out front were a noticeable problem for him. His legs seemed to be giving him a great deal of trouble that day. After a few minutes, he was finally able to reach the front door, open it, and limp in. Ray probably never looked happier. "I want to show you a piece of thin, flexible glass fiber cable which I picked up down in Roswell, New Mexico." he exclaimed excitedly. "They call it Angel Hair. I want to show you and Jimmy how it bends the light from my flashlight."

"I have got to see that," responded the store owner emphatically. "Jimmy, step up here closer so you can see it too."

Ray finally reached the counter, and bent over, leaning on it to rest. He seemed to be having trouble standing up straight. He took a glass fiber cable approximately 3 feet long, out from one of his left pockets, and a flashlight from one of his right pockets. The cable had a very complex construction. It was constructed by bundling and winding a large number of individual glass fibers together. Each of the individual glass fibers was as fine as a single strand of human hair, and was itself coated with a thin protective coating of dark material.`

"You see," explained Ray excitedly.

When light from a flashlight was shown in one end of the Angel Hair, the light followed the bends of the fibers, making almost a full circle, and came out the other end. None of it came out of the sides of the thin glass fibers, or was absorbed.

Ray continued excitedly, "Of course, human scientists all say strands of glass like Angel Hair could never be made or could ever exist. Just as you said, Jimmy, this one piece of Angel Hair proves the craft was real and constructed by extra-terrestrials. It also proves Einstein is wrong about relativity."

I don't believe I've ever seen a happier man.

A week or so passed. It was another cold, windy Wisconsin day in the fall. Once again, I was back in the little country store in London. The owner and I were talking about Ray, and Roswell, and flying saucers. Outside Ray's car pulled up and parked out front. With great difficulty, he was able to get out from the car. I could see he was very dejected, and he was coming only to unload his sorrows.

The owner and I waited sympathetically at the counter. When Ray finally opened the door, the owner greeted his life-long friend, "Hi Ray. Gee it is good to see you. How have you been?"

In dejected fashion, Ray carefully limped his way across the store and up to the counter, before unloading his troubles and baring his soul.

"The Feds came and took the piece of Angel Hair cable from me." he began sadly. "I was so happy when I had it. I showed it to more than a dozen people.

But the Feds got wind of it. Three days ago, I went out to the grocery store down the street from where I live. When I got back to my apartment there were two government agents waiting for me inside. They were very polite, and they were very well armed. They were wearing three piece business suits, and seemed to be carrying identification cards from every Department in the U.S. Government, including The USDA. Laughing, one of them claimed the U.S. Department of Agriculture was his favorite department.

They made it clear they were not going to leave until I gave them the Angel Hair cable. I could hardly refuse them. I had it hidden behind my television set. They thanked me nicely as I was handing it to them.

Before they left, they told me I could go ahead and tell anyone I wanted to about the unusual cable, because without the actual cable, no-one would believe me anyhow."

After he finished, Ray seemed to want only to lay down and rest, and to remember happier times from his childhood. It didn't seem as if he would ever again care about Roswell, New Mexico—or about flying saucers. It was the last time he was ever willing to talk with me.

Lackland Rain Storm

"... And they waited for me
as the rain,
and they opened their mouths wide
as for the latter rain.
... Job 29:23

My enlistment in the USAF began in July, 1964, with boot camp at Lackland AFB, San Antonio, Texas. Lackland is situated on high ground on the southwest side of the city.

Boot Camp would last thirteen long brutal weeks. Marching, general military training, physical exercises, running the obstacle course, and extensive mental and classroom testing followed. One of my drill sergeants quickly convinced all of us that he was only part human.

The climate in Texas during the months of July and August is legendary. It has been said that not even Satan would be willing to run the obstacle course in August as I and my fellow recruits had to. One of the drill sergeants was certain that we would all succeed in doing it—or die trying.

Early on in boot camp, it appeared that two other men from other training units, and I, were singled out for additional classroom testing. Since this testing was ordered by very high ranking officers, it took priority over the otherwise daily routine. Our drill sergeants always appeared to approve completely of such testing sessions. So, for example, I was excused from the final running of the obstacle course. Someone in The Pentagon had asked I be given a special advanced test in logical reasoning—a test I passed in more than perfect fashion. Consequently, I made an extra effort to follow orders and to fit in with the other men in my training unit. I wanted to make certain none of the drill sergeants ever singled me out in front of the other men.

The heat of that brutal summer ended suddenly in early September when a group of huge fast moving thunderstorms entered the area late one afternoon. The storms lasted all through the afternoon and evening, as well as all through the night. The storms didn't let up until well into the following afternoon.

It happened that as part of my military training, I was scheduled to walk a post as one of the outside area guards from midnight until 4:.00 a.m. on that night. I was careful to put on my uniform and my rain gear early because I was afraid of reporting late. In boot camp, reporting even two minutes late for guard duty was an extremely serious offense. Consequently, I was prepared, alert, and ready to report for duty by 10:00 p.m. in the evening.

I spent most of the two hours from ten until midnight sitting on an empty bunk looking out a barracks window at the storm—and at the public highway which ran along the outside of the base. The highway connected Lackland AFB with far away downtown San Antonio—and freedom from the drill sergeants. The highway also connected the Lackland area with a large and very beautiful city park down in the valley on the way into town. The park was characterized by a set of old wooden buildings with an old wooden water wheel where children liked to play on summer days. Once in a while, during the hot summer afternoons of late July and August, I would see a young boy ride his bicycle on the highway past Lackland, and continue downhill towards the distant park.

On this stormy evening, there wasn't much to see out the window. There was the rain, the storm, and a handful of passing cars. One thing I did not see—I did not see any young boy passing by, riding his bicycle in the storm, heading downhill towards the distant park.

At five minutes to midnight, I reported for duty. I signed in as area guard and relieved the man before me who was still on duty. He had taken cover from the storm under one of the large trees in the barracks area. He seemed immensely happy to have been relieved.

Taking cover from the storm was not actually permitted under the training rules. Consequently, I buttoned down my rain gear, and proceeded to walk my post—up one sidewalk and down another in the barracks area, rain or no rain. The storm was terrible, and the rain was coming in heavy sheets. I was careful to remain alert, walk my post, and carefully observe everything in the surrounding area including the passing highway.

There were eight other area guards assigned to duty in the barracks areas next to mine. All of them sought cover under the large trees, and in the protected areas under the overhanging roofs of the WWII era buildings.

Along about 2:00 a.m., I was surprised to find one of my drill sergeants and one of the captains in our training wing, walking up the sidewalk to confront me. They didn't seem angry. I stopped and reported as per standing orders.

The Captain asked me nicely, ‘Airman Hall, Why are you still walking your post openly, out in this terrible storm?”

Taken aback, I responded by reciting one of my general orders, “I will walk my post until properly relieved, Sir!” I was quite nervous at the time, and so I accidentally left out part of the general order.

The Captain continued, “But Airman Hall, all of the other area guards have taken cover from this rain. See them hiding over there under the trees, and next to the buildings. Why haven’t you joined them?”

I was at a loss for words. Nervous, I responded with the only thing I could think of saying at the time, “Sir, Russian solders are not afraid of rain, Sir. I can’t be either, Sir.”

It was perhaps the only time I ever saw a Drill Sergeant laugh. The Drill Sergeant, and the Captain chuckled and laughed. Then the Capitan replied, “You are quite right, Airman Hall. Carry on.”

As I resumed walking my post, from a distance, I got to observe the Drill Sergeant and the Captain having the time of their lives. They were rounding up all of the other area guards—collecting them from under the trees and from the protected areas next to the buildings—and shipping them to the chicken wire brig for a week. They were charged with abandoning their posts during the rain. The Captain could be heard quoting me. The Drill sergeant never seemed happier.

For the rest of my duty shift, until 4:00 a.m., I was careful to remain alert, walk my post, and carefully observe everything in the surrounding area including the passing highway, a lonesome shift, with not a soul to be seen.

Out Of The Frying Pan

"... Then was Nebuchadnezzar full of fury,
and the form of his visage was changed
against Shadrach, Meshach, and Abednego:

therefore he spake,
and commanded that they should heat
the furnace ...
seven times more than it was wont to be
heated. ..."
... Daniel 3:19

The desert valleys and dry lake beds of the American Southwest, central Nevada, and the Death Valley area, are places of great antiquity. However, ancient as they are, they were never touched directly by the glaciers of long ago. None of the desert valleys contain glacial moraines or ice cut valley walls. The vast ice sheets which formed, retreated, and reformed so many times during the past 3 million years, never made it as far south as the now dry lake beds of Utah, Nevada, or Southern California.

The vast ice sheets affected the American Southwest only indirectly. The ice sheets brought on cooler, wetter, and rainier conditions. Such rainy conditions typically lasted for thousands of years. The melting ice, the run-off from the glaciers, and the long lasting heavy rains created fresh water rivers, streams, and large fresh water lakes. Long ago geologists, using what was then the international language of Latin, named such lakes "Pluvial" lakes from the Latin word for rain—pluvia.

The valleys and lake beds filled with fresh water for a time, leaving water lines on the surrounding rock layers. Wave action in the lakes formed beach strands and satellite hills in the high ground along their edges.

Eventually the glaciers retreated, the hot, dry climate returned, and the pluvial lakes dried up. The dry lake beds then sat empty and waiting while several thousand years passed—until once again the vast ice sheets returned—the rains began—and the pluvial lakes once again, filled with water.

Many of the now dry lakes and lake beds in the American Southwest may have filled, dried up, and then refilled, many times in the past 3 million years. Many valleys and lake beds may possibly have spent most of their geological existence filled with water. Many of the dry lakes and dry lake beds themselves, could easily have held fresh water, year around, as recently as 3,000 years ago—after having been filled with water for, perhaps, more than 20,000 years before that. The dry lake beds today, typically remain sitting on top of large, easily reached underground fresh water aquifers.

Now dry, and surrounded by a series of desolate stretches of ancient beach strands and underground rivers, the dry lake beds lay hidden, out in the mirages, out in the heat waves, baking in the summertime desert sun—looking like large mirage covered frying pans—still pretending to hold fresh water—still waiting for the rains to return.

It was a fall day in the mid 1960s. I was a weather observer in the U.S. Air Force. I was stationed at Nellis AFB, located just outside of Las Vegas, Nevada. I had spent the past many months on Temporary Duty at Indian Springs Auxillary Field, located at Indian Springs, Nevada. I was the duty weather observer for the Indian Springs Gunnery Ranges. The ranges were located out in the distant, desolate, desert valleys located north of Indian Springs, some 90 miles northwest of Las Vegas.

During the preceding months I had gotten over my fear of the Tall White extra-terrestrials I had encountered out in those valleys. They lived on a base at the north end of Indians Springs Valley. The base was provided for them by the U.S. Air Force.

I had been given a special set of orders. I could go anywhere I wanted, and do anything I wanted, when I was out on the Ranges. However, whatever I did, I had to be alone—always alone. It was solitary duty. However, I had grown to enjoy it.

I was just beginning a new two week long special "Climate Study". I had been ordered to drive from Indian Springs, up to Death Valley Center, to receive my special "Climate Study" orders.

It was late afternoon at Death Valley Center. The weather had cleared. The rains had stopped—cheating the dry lake beds of the water they stood ready to capture. The desert shadows were lengthening. The winds were calm. The disk of the sun was slowly approaching a gap in the mountains on the southwestern horizon. The moon was nearing its first quarter.

After receiving my new temporary duty orders, I got into my weather truck, and drove slowly down to the parking lot in front of the small public library. In addition to my equipment, I was carrying 30 extra gallons of gasoline in six jerry cans, all of which were riding in the back of my truck. Consequently, I was driving carefully for safety.

Reaching the library, I pulled the loaded truck off the highway for a few minutes.

Being Roman Catholic, and very religious, I sat quietly and said my evening prayers. I took the small notebook from the left front pocket of my military fatigues, and opened it up. Using a pen from the same pocket, I carefully wrote down the combination to the lock on the first gate that I was ordered to drive to. I did not want to risk forgetting it.

I waited patiently in my truck for a few minutes until it was just past 6:30 p.m.—as required by my orders. I placed my truck in low gear and, feeling very alone, headed out on my new climate study assignment.

The road I was following was paved, and well maintained. However, the directions which I had been given did not include any maps or distances. I had guessed that all of the distances were going to be very short, and the weather shack I was heading for, was going to be only three or four miles away. It was immediately obvious I was quite wrong. The distances were going to be much greater than I was expecting. I had already driven several times that distance, and night had fallen, when I arrived at the first road junction. I made the turn, as required, and continued along a narrower paved road for a very long time. I had expected the roads to be generally quite straight. However, both roads meandered a great deal, with many curves and sharp turns. I was certain I must have missed a turn. I had backtracked a couple of times to no avail, and it was now well into night-time. At last, I passed one of the referenced landmarks on the southern side of the road. Two miles, and several curves further on, I found the Range Gate which I had been searching for, located by the side of the road. I was already many, many miles out into a very desolate, and very restricted, stretch of desert.

I gratefully stopped my truck at the gate. As expected, there was no guard shack. The gate was bordered on both sides by a security fence which disappeared into the distance in both directions. It was obvious the gravel side road was hardly ever used.

Leaving my truck engine idling, with the help of my flashlight, I unlocked, and opened the gate. After pulling my truck through the gate onto the narrow, gravel road on the other side, I closed and locked the gate, and got back into my truck. I surveyed my new surroundings for a few minutes before proceeding. There was still some moonlight. However, I could see that generally, this was going to be a very dark night.

The gravel road ran smoothly uphill to a pass perhaps seven miles distant. The gravel road was fenced on both sides. Up ahead, roughly three miles on the right, sat a collection of weathered, wooden buildings, with a stainless steel water tower in the middle. The World War II era buildings were arranged in the form of an “L”. There was a larger building obviously designed as a meeting place. There were also seven large raised supply sheds, and several smaller supporting buildings in back of them.

The building area was fenced. The entire building area was set down at a lower elevation than the road. The area was in a desert valley, presumably because underground water was available at that location. A lamp on a desk in the larger of the buildings was turned on, as if waiting for me.

My truck proceeded slowly uphill towards the buildings in the distance. I noticed a large rectangular section of the desert on my right. It was heavily furrowed. It appeared to have been that way for a very long time. The section was roughly a mile wide, and more than two miles long. The furrowing followed the slope of the hill, and continued right up to the southern most fence of the building area. Water would obviously collect in the furrowed ground whenever it rained in the desert. From this I concluded, the furrowed area must be an ancient desert garden, and the buildings must be located at the site of an ancient desert oasis. I decided, considering the desert climate in the mid-1960s, whoever created the furrows, must have done so thousands of years before, when water was more plentiful in the desert.

One fact stuck in my mind as I drove past the furrows. They appeared to have been well maintained. It did not appear that any sand dunes, small or otherwise, had drifted into the furrowed area.

As I was approaching the buildings, in the distance, I could see through one of the windows in the larger building. The main room had a design similar to the ticket area at a small airport. The building sat parallel to the gravel road. A large counter ran across the northern end of the room. As I watched from afar, a person wearing a dark gray or black jump suit, came into the room from a door behind the counter, on the right hand side. The person was carrying only a single manila envelope and a ring of keys. Because of the viewing angle and the height of the counter, I could not see their head or face. I could only see part of their body—the part from waist to shoulders. The person seemed to be a little taller than I was. The person placed the envelope and the key ring in a wooden mail box on the left side of the room, and exited the same way they had entered.

I reached the metal gate to the fenced area, and stopped my truck next to the road. I turned off the engine. The gate was a sliding gate, on large metal wheels. It was roughly four and a half feet high, designed to be opened and closed by rolling it to the left hand side. It was closed and latched, but not actually locked.

It was already almost 9:00 p.m., and I was running much later than I had expected. My orders had requested the first weather balloon be released at midnight, just after the moon had set. I would have to hurry if I was going to make the release on schedule.

I still hadn't been told where my weather shack was actually located. However, I had been told I would be given the keys to one of the supply sheds in this compound, and that any weather supplies I requested, would be delivered to that weather supply shed. These supplies included the heavy helium cylinders which would be delivered to me as needed. The supply shed was also where I was supposed to deliver my completed weather reports and forms on a weekly basis, along with my empty helium cylinders. I naturally supposed my weather shack was going to be one of the buildings in this compound.

I got out of my truck. With difficulty I unlatched the gate, and tried to open it. To my surprise, the gate refused to open more than a foot or two. Sagebrush and other desert vegetation had grown up into the track area. In addition, the winds and the rains had rearranged the sand and the desert soils so that the track was completely blocked. The gate had obviously not been opened in awhile.

Looking over the fence, and down into the compound, the desert soil inside was still in its natural state. Directly inside the gate, there weren't any truck tracks, or vehicle ruts, or footprints to be seen. Yet, this was the only entrance to the fenced area. I was somewhat mystified, because the only other way to get into the fenced area was to fly. "So the person I just saw—how did they get in there?" I wondered to myself.

Supposing my weather shack was one of the sheds inside the compound, and since my equipment was in the back of my truck, I decided I was going to have to clear enough of the gate track, so I could drive my truck inside the fenced area. I put on my work gloves. Not having a shovel with me, I took my tire iron, and began the difficult job of clearing a ten foot section of the gate track. In a while I was finally able to force the gate open just wide enough so I could drive my truck into the fenced compound. I was quite proud of myself, really. It had been very hard work. I was glad I had brought plenty of water along, so I could wash the dust out of my throat.

I did not want to take my truck very far into the compound until I knew exactly where my weather shack was located. Something about this section of desert made me feel noticeably uneasy. As soon as my truck was just barely inside the open gate, I stopped and parked it. I turned off the engine, and set the hand brake. I got out of my truck, and began slowly walking down the hill towards the largest of the buildings. I began calling out in a loud voice, "Is anyone here? I'm Airman Hall. I've come to do the climate study. I'm looking for the weather shack."

There was no answer. However, the rustling leaves and quiet footsteps on gravel coming from the dark shadows on the far side of the larger building, convinced me I was not alone.

Running late, as I was, I decided not to go exploring. I walked over to the small front porch and the doorway on the near—southwest—side of the larger building. There were no front windows. The door was closed, but not locked. I knocked loudly a couple of times. There was no answer, so I slowly opened the door and went in.

Inside, as I had expected, was a large meeting room—or possibly a large classroom. As expected, it had a counter running the width of the room on the north end. A desk lamp was turned on and it sat on the counter on the left side. A telephone sat on the counter next to it. The lamp was not very bright. Consequently, most of the room remained in darkness, and shadows. The only windows to the outside were located on the left hand side of the building—the side which faced the gravel road on the hill outside. Behind the counter, on the right side was a doorway to a short hallway with apparently more rooms, and to an exit in the back. The bathrooms were apparently located outside in the back. I did not go very close to the open door on the right. Everything back in that section was shrouded in inky darkness. At the time, I wasn't feeling very brave—and I could hear someone moving back there.

The room also contained a number of chairs of different sizes. The smaller chairs appeared to be for children. A few of the smaller chairs were arranged in rows facing the counter. The larger, adult sized chairs were against the wall in the back, and along the wall on the right.

Shaky, and nervous, I picked up my manila envelope, and the ring of keys. I signed for them on the clipboard on the counter. My orders said I was to turn out the lights when I left—and to answer the phone if it ever rang. My orders were not classified—I was, after all, only the weather observer—and an enlisted man.

Nervously I turned off the lamp. Then I beat a hasty, and respectful retreat through the darkness, back to the front door. I closed the door behind me as I left the building.

I quickly retreated to my truck for safety, but I did not get in. Using my flashlight, I opened the envelope and began reading the contents in order to find out which of the sheds was my weather shack. The sheds and the water tower formed a line in front of me on the other side of the compound. None of the sheds had any windows. One of the sheets of paper clearly identified my weather supply shed as being the fourth shed from the left. However, My driving directions implied my weather shack was still further up the gravel road beyond a "Y" shaped intersection. "That can't be right." I said to myself. So, with my keys and flashlight in hand, I carefully walked across the compound to the front of my weather supply shed. There was no need to open it or look inside. The front doorway was the standard width. It was clearly too narrow for a fragile, helium filled weather balloon to pass through it.

As I stood there, I became aware that I was being carefully watched by something hidden in the dark shadows behind the larger building, which stood off to my left. I couldn't see clearly into the shadows. However, it appeared there were at least two people standing out there in the darkness. It also seemed there was a third person, come in off the desert to the southeast, hidden behind the supply sheds off to my right. I could hear the leaves rustling, and occasional footsteps. However, I could not actually see anything. Still, it was in fear that I hastily retreated to my pickup truck. I quickly got inside and started up the engine. I carefully turned the truck around, and drove it out through the gate, and back onto the gravel road. Once outside, I temporarily stopped the truck and set the brake. I put on my work gloves, got out and hurriedly closed and latched the sliding gate. As I did so, I got a glimpse of something out in the darkness. It happened too fast for me to be sure. However, I became convinced I had gotten a glimpse of the person who had been watching me from the dark shadows behind the larger building. I couldn't overcome the impression the person I had glimpsed, was a young girl. She always remained out of sight, as she hurried through the darkness, and through the open desert north of me, heading towards the gravel road.

In fear, I hurried back to my truck and quickly got in. I removed my work gloves, placed the truck in gear, and started heading up the road. I drove carefully. For a couple of miles or so, I also drove very quickly. I was afraid someone might appear in the darkness, and possibly block the road up ahead.

As I drove, I kept a careful lookout for anything that looked like a young girl standing alongside the road—or a weather shack hidden in the brush next to it. I didn't start to calm down until I had reached the pass. By the time I reached the pass, I was quite miffed because I hadn't yet found my weather shack.

By now it was well past 10:00 p.m. in the evening, and I was running very late. I momentarily stopped my truck in the pass, and reread my directions. They were unmistakable. I needed to keep driving until I found a "Y" shaped intersection. I was to take the right hand branch and just keep driving. After a while I would come to a mountain pass where there was a sharp right hand turn in the road. I would continue on, traveling downhill. I would find my weather shack and its supporting buildings lined up, sitting alongside the road, down on the valley floor.

"Some directions," I muttered to myself. "They look as if a kid has been writing them,—in addition to scaring me in the night-time".

I put my truck back in gear, and drove on. I was driving fairly slow, because by now, I was certain I had gone too far. However, I kept driving because there was nothing else I could do. The road was very narrow, and there were few, if any places to easily turn around.

At least by now, I had gotten over the tremendous fear that I had felt back at the desert oasis. I had gotten back to where I could laugh at myself—and my silly fear of the darkness.

It wasn't until 11:45 p.m. that I finally found the "Y" intersection, and realized to my surprise, I was actually on the proper road. The right hand branch looked even more unused than the road I had been on. The road had many twists and turns. I had never seen this section of the desert before, and there were still some clouds obscuring the stars. Consequently, I was no longer certain which direction I was headed. I had no choice but to drive on.

I didn't find the mountain pass with the sharp right hand turn until almost 1:00 a.m. in the morning. Completing the turn, I started the long downhill section of the drive. The narrow gravel road was now perfectly straight. The sky was now clear. Looking at the bright starry sky, I decided that I was heading south.

I was expecting the buildings to show up immediately after the turn to the south. I was expecting to find the buildings on the left hand side—the eastern side—of the road. My orders had clearly requested that I set up my portable theodolite, and perform all balloon releases out in the desert east of my weather shack. I began carefully studying the left hand side of the road. I, therefore felt a certain anxiety when I realized that next to the road on the eastern side, was a tall continuous, impenetrable security fence. The fence appeared to be in very good repair. I had no choice but to keep on following the road downhill towards the distant valley floor.

I drove on for another 15 miles, down onto the valley floor. Suddenly, the woven wires of the fence ended, and only the widely separated, bare metal fence posts continued on. To my surprise, I found the long sought after gray wooden buildings, hidden in the darkness along the right hand side of the road. “Lucky me,” I thought to myself as I stopped my truck on the gravel road. In the darkness, I had almost missed the buildings. By the time I saw them, I had already driven past the first building—the generator shack, and the next two supply sheds. I finally got my truck stopped in front of my weather shack.

“Lucky I brought 30 extra gallons of gas.” I muttered to myself, as I rested for a few minutes in my truck. “I’m going to need it to get out of this place.” By now it was almost 1:30 a.m. I had already missed my first scheduled balloon release, and was in the process of missing the second.

I was going to need to start one of the diesel generators and get some electricity in my weather shack before I could do much of anything. With my truck in reverse, I backed up the road past the supply sheds, and the generator shack. There was a surprisingly large graveled parking area in front of the generator shack. I parked my truck facing the doors of the generator shack, and back a ways. I placed my truck in neutral. I set the brake, left the headlights on, and the engine running.

I got out of the truck, and began walking over to the doors to the generator shack. Halfway there, I stopped for a minute to get my bearings. I was surprised to notice that another, still narrower and unused gravel road came across the desert from the west, and met up with the large parking lot.

I stood there, studying the collection of gray wooden buildings. Even though they had been painted and constructed to look fairly old, I found them all to be very impressively constructed—especially the generator shack.

I was feeling dumbfounded. I opened up the generator shack—the doors were closed and latched, but did not have a lock. I scanned the shack everywhere, inside and out. The entire generator shack and the two generators inside, were clean. They had hardly been used. Inside, there were no drifting piles of sand, no washed-in piles of mud. There wasn't even any dust to speak of. Outside, there weren't any dry tumble weeds within six feet of generator shack. The generator shack, as well as all of the buildings looked as though they had just been constructed a few days before.

As I further studied the area, I realized this entire set of buildings was intentionally constructed to be near perfect duplicates of my weather shack, supply sheds, and generator shack which I was used to, out at Range Three, back at Indian Springs, Nevada.

Alone in the night time desert as I was, the realization made me feel very ill at ease. It meant that somewhere, out there in the darkness, someone other than the Tall White extraterrestrials whom I had gotten used to working alongside, was watching me as intently and as carefully as a cat or dog would. I realized the security fence on the eastern side of the road must certainly form the boundary between two different security areas. The realization did little to settle my nerves. The buildings would naturally have been built in the safer of the two areas. Whoever or whatever was watching me, must certainly be watching from out in the desolate deserted valley—out in the darkness—on the other side of the road. I became more ill at ease when I remembered that no human other than I, was allowed beyond the first gate between 6:00 p.m., and 6:00 a.m. I decided that for tonight, orders or no orders, I would be happy to stay near the buildings, on this side of the road.

I quickly started up the diesel on my right. With a practiced hand, I adjusted the electrical generator. I turned the lights on, both inside and outside the generator shack. I returned to my truck, and turned off the engine and headlights. I left my truck parked where it was, and walked carefully down the road, past the supply shed, to my weather shack. I felt as though I were walking into a frying pan. Nervously, I unlocked my weather shack, turned on the inside lights, and went inside.

The inside of my weather shack looked almost exactly as I expected. The first difference I noticed between this weather shack, and my weather shack back on Range Three at Indian Springs, was that all of the linoleum on the floor was the same pattern. It had all been cut from the same large piece. The floor was smooth, and absolutely beautiful. The linoleum had even been washed and lightly waxed. "At least someone knows how to measure and lay linoleum, better than I do." I chuckled nervously to myself.

The desk, the tables, the equipment shelves were all the same as I was used to. On the desk sat a telephone, although there wasn't any dial tone. On the desk was a collection of IN/OUT boxes, and several new log books. Of course, none of the log books, as yet, had any entries. Mine would be the first. I began by logging myself in to my new weather shack.

There were two small filing cabinets on the floor—one next to the desk and one next to the ivory plotting table. There were several calendars hanging on the well painted walls. What I found surprising was that there weren't any maps hanging on the walls, or anywhere in the weather shack, for that matter. I had very little idea where I was. All I knew about the desert outside was whatever I could see on my own.

The weather shack was already fully supplied. It seemed to have more equipment, supplies, and manuals than I had back at Indian Springs. They were all in like-new condition. However, many of the items dated from the late 1940s. Some items, such as the immersible batteries, were manufactured at the end of World war II. On one of the shelves, for example, I found several packages of RAWIN radar reflectors for weather balloons, even though I never stocked or used any such reflectors back at Indian Springs. The only equipment which the weather shack seemed to lack, was the portable theodolite which I had brought with me in my truck.

This shack had lights outside as well as inside. Outside the double wide side door was a small picnic or park like area probably 70 feet square. A metal post with a platform for a theodolite stood in the center of the area. The entire area looked so natural, it could have been designed by the National Park Service. There were several wooden and stone benches, which could be used for sitting and relaxing. They were arranged at the edges of the surrounding area. Considering how late I was running, I decided to set up my equipment, and make one and only one balloon release from the park-like area.

I wanted to conserve my gasoline supply, so I decided to leave my truck parked where it was, and just carry the equipment over to my weather shack on foot. Singing loudly in the dark—I was never very good at whistling—I walked back down the road, got my equipment, and carried it to my weather shack. It took several trips. I was especially careful to bring my canteens, radio, and lots of water. I was quite tired by the time I finished. I set my radio on the shelf. However, I did not plug it in or turn it on. I had too much work to do.

By now, I was very hungry. Evening chow was little more than a memory. I had carefully brought the two box lunches in from the truck. I placed one of them on my desk in the weather shack. The other, I took outside to the park-like area and sat down to rest and enjoy it. The meal wasn't very large. However, the sandwiches and carton of milk never tasted better.

I was sitting on one of the benches on the western edge of the park area, studying the beauty of the evening, when I noticed two lights several miles down the road to the south. I had the outdoor light by the side door turned on at the time. Consequently, my eyes were not fully adjusted to the darkness.

The lights were down on the southern side of the valley by a bend in the road. Down there, where the road approached the east-west mountain range which formed the valley's southern wall, the road made a right hand turn to the west. East of the bend, a short stretch of low mountains jutted out from the wall. A fairly high desert pass connected the jutted out mountain with the wall. To the west, the desolate desert valley stretched slightly downhill for miles, disappearing finally into the darkness and into the distance. To the east, an equally desolate desert valley stretched slightly uphill for a ways, then leveled out, and also disappeared into the distance and into the darkness. In both directions, the valleys contained nothing but sagebrush, desert bushes, rocks, and sand. In its own way, it was an extremely beautiful location. In happier times, I might have come out here alone, just to enjoy myself.

The two lights down by the bend in the road were stationary, sitting side by side, roughly ten feet above the road. The lights were not particularly bright. They had a distinctly yellow-orange tinge, and appeared to be the headlights to a large truck. There wasn't any gray-white fluorescence associated with the lights, and the lights did not hurt my eyes when I looked at them. I reasoned the lights could not be the Tall Whites from Indian Springs. I decided the lights must be the area guards coming to check on me, so I decided to just carry on with my balloon release.

Setting up and aligning my theodolite on the portable tripod stand was much simpler and faster than setting it up on the permanent metal stand. Short on time, I brought my equipment out from the weather shack, and quickly set up my portable tripod and my theodolite in the park area a few feet south of the metal stand. It was set up near one of the benches. I continued to feel ill at ease because I remained convinced that something hidden out in the darkness across the road was watching me as I worked.

I went inside my weather shack and prepared the weather forms. I also prepared one of the helium cylinders. Attaching the gauges and valves was easy enough. I set out a white balloon and a suitable battery and bulb. There were some plastic and paper cups. I chose one to hold the water that I would soak the battery in, just before attaching it to the balloon, and releasing it into the night-time sky.

While I was preparing my equipment, I was not paying any attention to the lights down the road. Both the front door and the side door of my weather shack were wide open, and latched into position. However, the viewing angle wasn't very good. There was an east-west ridge perhaps a mile south of my weather shack, where the desert changed elevations. It obscured a large section of the road.

I kept expecting a large truck carrying area guards to drive by. However, so far, none had showed up. Before I began filling the balloon, I stepped out through the side door to see where they were. They weren't anywhere. All I could see were the same two lights down by the bend in the road. It was a quiet night and the lights made no sound.

While I watched, the two lights were joined by a third, which came slowly up the road from the west. As it did so, the second light—the one on the eastern side, drifted slowly across the open desert to the east for 50 feet or so, stopping at the bottom of the mountain pass. It was now quite obvious that the lights could not possibly be truck headlights—even though they had generally been following the road and hugging the desert. What was worse, it felt like the lights were watching me.

I began feeling very alone, and very exposed. It was now going on 4:00 a.m. and my last balloon release was scheduled for 4:30 a.m. I had missed all of the others, and having come so far, I felt I had to take this one. Not wasting any time, I filled my balloon, prepared and attached a battery, and proceeded with the balloon release. I was releasing the balloon several minutes early. I turned off the outside lights to make tracking the balloon easier.

My orders had requested 20 to 30 readings if possible. I decided to take only the minimum of 20 readings. I thought I would wait until tomorrow night, to perform the calculations, when I felt I would have more time. I was not required to notify anyone, or phone the weather reports anywhere. I was only required to perform the calculations and record the weather reports for posterity. At the end of each week, I was ordered to leave the completed reports and any supply requests in the weather supply shed at the Desert Oasis. I could pick up supplies from there, anytime I wanted. Consequently, I hurried the run. As soon as I finished, I could pack up and return to Indian Springs.

The winds were very light and from the northwest. As soon as the balloon was released, it began drifting towards the southeast. It rose slowly into the sky. As usual, I had measured and adjusted the helium level in the balloon so the balloon, with its attached light, rose at 1000 feet per minute—which is just over 11 miles per hour. As it rose, it drifted directly over the peak of the jutted out mountain. While I watched in between readings, the second light slowly followed up into the high pass, and passed out of sight on the other side. The first and third lights remained on station, down by the bend in the road.

Tracking a weather balloon with its attached light, on a night with no moon, requires a great deal of skill, and also requires careful attention to details. It is very easy to lose the balloon in the many star fields which are found in the Milky Way. Through a theodolite, the stars in the heavens, especially in The Milky Way, can take on many different appearances. After 17 minutes, as the balloon was reaching an altitude of 17, 000 feet, I became convinced that, although I was highly skilled at tracking balloons at night, I had lost the balloon in the Milky Way. I found myself tracking two objects which seemed to be moving together. I supposed that I was tracking a double star—even though one of the objects still appeared to be my weather balloon.

I broke off the balloon run at 17 minutes, and began closing down. I took my theodolite off its tripod, and carefully stored all the equipment back in the weather shack. I laid my forms and clipboard on the ivory table for later plotting.

I decided I better finish my second box lunch before beginning the long drive back to Indian Springs. With my box lunch in hand, I returned to the park area, picked a nice place on a bench, and enjoyed my second meal of the evening. As I was eating, I noticed the second light return from the other side of the high pass. It rejoined the other two. Once together, the three distant lights first spread wide. Then together while remaining spread wide, the three distant lights returned back around the bend, and continued down the road to the west until they were out of sight in the distance—vanishing at last into the large, distant, frying pan shaped valley from which they had come. All of the time, they remained roughly eight or ten feet off the gravel road. Sitting on the bench as I ate, I did the math. The lights seemed to be retreating at something over 120 miles per hour. "Pretty good," I nervously thought to myself. "All in perfect silence, on an old gravel road, and they didn't raise any dust."

At least now, I was feeling comfortable that I was totally alone, and not being watched. In a very relaxed manner, I turned out the lights, and locked up my weather shack. With my water, canteens, and radio in hand, and singing a little tune, I walked back to my truck. I loaded my belongings into the passenger side of the cab of my truck. Using three of the jerry cans of gasoline, and the funnel which I had brought, I refilled my truck's gas tank. I shut down the diesel and closed everything up.

I started my truck, and said a prayer of 'Thanks". Then, placing my truck in gear, I began the drive back to the Desert Oasis.

I was driving much faster now because I knew the road, and I knew where I was going. I was still surprised by the distance. The "Y" intersection was much further away than I was expecting.

It was well past 6:00 a.m. and already the light of dawn was filling the skies by the time I returned to the Desert Oasis. I parked my truck across the road from the sliding gate, and decided to just walk the keys back to the sign-in place in the deserted meeting room. The Desert Oasis was now obviously deserted.

Down in the main valley, parked along the side of the main road, a quarter mile or so, up from the range gate, I could see two nondescript gray cars. They seemed to be waiting for someone.

I was in a hurry to get back to Death Valley Center chow hall for a warm breakfast. I quickly opened the sliding gate just wide enough for me to go though. I hurried down hill to the meeting hall and returned the keys, signing the clipboard as I did so. I hurried back to my parked truck, closing the front door and the sliding gate behind me. Placing my truck in gear, I proceeded down the road to the main range gate, opened it, pulled my truck through, and closed the gate behind me.

As I was openly walking to my truck, I noticed that each one of the two cars had two men in them. As I got into my truck, one of the two cars started its engine, turned around, and disappeared down the road in the distance. As I pulled my truck out onto the main road, the second car likewise started its engine, turned around, and disappeared down the road behind me.

As I drove back to Death Valley Center, I thought about what had just happened. In my mind, the entire previous evening had been a complete waste. I had come so far, and spent so much time, just to take a single weather report and a single set of wind measurements. All my weather report, paraphrased, had said was "The weather on this evening in the desert, is whatever it has always been, and whatever you thought it was going to be".

As I drove back into Death Valley Center for breakfast, I questioned what, if anything, I had accomplished.

The Southern Border

Then your south quarter shall be
from the wilderness of Zin
along by the coast of Edom,

and your southern border shall be
the outmost coast of the salt sea eastward.

And as for the western border,
you shall even have
the great sea for a border.
This shall be your west border.
. . . Numbers 34 verse 3,6

Mizar is a Double, Double star system in the northern hemisphere. It is easily found. It appears as the second star from the end of the Big Dipper.

Mizar is not just one star. Rather it appears to be a system of possibly, at least six stars, located roughly 83 light years from the Earth. The Mizar system appears to be possibly more than 1 Light Year wide. It includes two sets of binary stars, each binary system orbits Mizar's common center of gravity.

The individual stars within the Mizar Star system vary greatly in their brightness. In ancient times, people tested their eyesight on clear desert nights, by checking to see how many of Mizar's many stars they could actually see. In the mid 1960s, a number of amateur astronomers—and at least one young, USAF weather observer with a set of high quality theodolites—used to verify the quality of their equipment by counting the number of stars they could see within the Mizar Double, Double system. With decent viewing conditions, I had no trouble finding three of the four Double, Double stars. I used to wonder to myself as I adjusted my theodolite, "If the Mizar system contains that many stars moving together, how many planets does it also contain, hidden in the surrounding darkness?"

I was late getting off the ranges that first night, even though I left my new weather shack ahead of schedule. The gravel roads were still new to me. I felt uneasy about being alone out in these unfamiliar desolate stretches of desert. I was extra cautious, and drove slower than necessary. I made it into breakfast at the Death Valley Center chow hall while it was still open, and it was with great satisfaction that I devoured the chipped beef on toast, along with bacon and eggs.

I hurried back to Indian Springs. Exhausted, I spent the remainder of the day sleeping in my barracks. At four in the afternoon, the only other person on base—Smokey, the cook, brought supper over to my barracks. He woke me laughing, and only half in jest said, "I just wanted to make sure you were still alive. Here, eat this and show me that nothing has happened to you."

The two of us laughed ourselves silly. Smokey and I were like brothers. I thanked him profusely. I might otherwise have slept until midnight.

Time was passing quickly. I showered, shaved, and rushed to get dressed in my work uniform. I put some pieces of wood, and lengths of rope in the back of my pickup truck. This allowed me to do a better job of securing my six jerry cans. Consequently I made much better time on the drive to Death Valley Center. The drive was uneventful, though the full metal jerry cans in the back banged a little.

Running late, I didn't have any time to spend exploring the local public library/museum at Death Valley Center. I rushed another quick evening meal. I picked up my two box lunches, a thermos of coffee, several jars of drinking water, and filled my canteens with drinking water as well. After filling my truck's gas tank, and topping off six jerry cans with gasoline, I began the long drive out to Desert Oasis. On the paved road, there was no particular speed limit, and I made very good time.

I was noticeably tired as I drove, and wished I had gotten more sleep. It was well after dark when I arrived at the sliding gate. In the large meeting room, the lamp was turned on—apparently waiting for me. It was a calm, clear night. The first quarter moon lit up the desert beautifully. Opening the sliding gate more than two or three feet was still very difficult. It seemed as if someone had again, intentionally placed dirt and sand in the tracks to limit the opening. I was determined to open the gate wide, and drive my truck right up to the front door of the meeting room. That would save me some time, and make it easy to get supplies from the weather supply shed, if I ever needed them.

Wearing my work gloves, and using my tire iron as before, I cleared the track, and opened the gate perhaps eight feet. As I worked, I kept getting quick glimpses of someone standing out in the darkness beyond the water tower—watching me. They were fairly tall—perhaps 6 1/2 feet—and wearing dark clothes. It made me feel very nervous, so I ignored them, and just worked faster. In any event, there didn't seem to be anything I could do about it.

I was quite proud of myself. I pulled my truck through the opening—leaving the gate open as I did so—and parked my truck nicely next to the meeting room. As I got out of my truck, I resolved to bring a shovel next time.

I wasn't wasting any time when I entered the large meeting room. I was, however, cautious and deliberate—as well as very nervous. I was certain there was someone out in the darkness in back. I greatly preferred to confront the unknown person face-to-face. I certainly did not want them coming up behind me—whoever they were.

I slowly approached the counter by the lamp, and went to reach for my directions for the evening. Before I could actually reach my directions, and the key ring, the phone on the counter rang. It startled me to say the least. My orders were to answer any phone that might ring. I carefully picked up the phone. Speaking slowly and deliberately, I said, "Airman Hall speaking. I'm out here on the ranges to perform the nightly climate study. May I help you?"

The voice on the other end sounded pleasant, and very happy. It sounded like my close friend Dwight, back at the Nellis weather station—but I knew that couldn't be right. I knew better than to ask who it actually was.

The voice began, “Yes, Airman Hall. I know who you are. You’re doing a tremendous job. Your commanders are very pleased with you.

There is one thing I would ask of you. When you come out to this building, do not bring your truck through the gate. Leave it parked on the road, and walk in. Just open the gate far enough so you can get through it, and close it behind you.”

I was totally taken aback, shaken and off guard. I continued defensively, “But there isn’t any place to park it up there, without blocking the road. I’m afraid if I leave it parked up there blocking the road, another car might come along and hit my truck. Other drivers might be upset.”

The voice chuckled at me, apparently because I was so naive, “The road is almost never used. No one but you is allowed out here past the gate at the bottom of the hill, after six in the evening. No one else could ever come past that gate until 6:00 in the morning. If you haven’t made it back to the gate by 6:00 in the morning, then anyone who wanted to come out here would have to wait until you arrived at the gate, and finished passing through it.”

“I understand,” I answered humbly. In the future, I will park up on the road.”

The voice continued, still in a happy, pleasant tone, “Before you take your envelope and keys, I would like you to move your truck and park it up on the road right away. Then walk back in, closing the gate behind you.

Please, turn out the light as soon as you hang up the telephone, and do not turn on the light when you come back in. In the future, whenever you come to this building, do not ever turn on the light. You may use your flashlight, but please always leave all of the lights turned off."

"Yes," I answered slowly. "If I do that, how will people know I have picked up my keys? I'm supposed to turn off the light so everyone knows I have picked up my envelope and my keys"

Chuckling some more, the voice answered, "Don't worry. We can always check the key ring.

Now be careful when you back up your truck. Back it up as though there might be children behind you in the compound."

With that, I could hear the phone being hung up, and the phone line went dead.

I was at my wits ends. Nothing seemed to be making any sense. However, that was what military duty had always been—Hurry up and wait. I did as was requested. I began by turning out the only light in the room—the lamp. Then I stumbled through the darkness out through the front door. I carefully checked around my parked truck to make certain there weren't any children hiding around—or in it. I got in quickly, and carefully turned the truck around. Still very nervous, I pulled my truck uphill, back through the open gate, and parked it on the gravel road, facing the direction I had been traveling.

I got out of my truck. On foot, feeling foolish, I walked back through the gate into the compound. I closed the gate behind me. I felt as though I had offended someone, since it was necessary to instruct me to leave my truck parked on the road in the first place.

Using my flashlight to light the way, I re-entered the meeting room, picked up my envelope and keys, signed for them, and returned to my parked truck. I carefully opened the gate a couple of feet to get through, then closed and latched it behind me.

Sitting in my truck, I carefully opened the envelope which had my name on it. There was nothing in it. I became very ill at ease when I realized the envelope had been placed in my wooden mail box, only to make me stop my truck on the gravel road, and walk in to get it. The stretch of desert where I was headed, was so distant and so desolate, my weather shack didn't need to be locked. At any rate, nothing in my weather shack was precious—or classified.

I started my truck, placed it in gear, and, immersed in thought, covered the many miles out through the desert—the mountains—the night-time moonlit darkness—to my new weather shack. It was a very long and provocative drive.

In the fullness of time, I reached the right hand turn in the distant mountain pass, and began the long downgrade to my weather shack. There were the usual drainage ditches along both sides of the road. The first quarter moon was still out and it lit up the desert valley, and mountains, in truly memorable fashion. As I continued down hill, I could see in the distance the widely spaced poles of the security fence on the left hand side of the road. They continued for only two miles or so past my weather shack. After the poles stopped, another small ditch continued on, in a straight north-south line, down past the distant bend in the road. It continued on and over the east—west range of mountains that formed the far southern end of the valley. The ditch obviously marked the boundary between the two areas. Although it appeared to be well maintained, there were many small sagebrush plants growing in the trench, suggesting the maintenance crews hadn't cleared the trench for at least two or three years.

Up ahead, the drainage ditch along the eastern side of the road continued unbroken for the entire length of the road. It continued all the way to and around the distant bend to the east down by the distant mountains.

Along the western side of the road, the drainage ditch ended before the buildings, the narrow side road, and the graveled parking area. The western drainage ditch did not start up again until perhaps a mile or so beyond my weather shack. Then it too, continued south along the road, down and around the distant bend to the west.

When I reached the buildings, I parked my truck in front of the generator shack, as before. Since there was still some moonlight, I turned off the engine, and the headlights, and set the hand brake. As I got out of my truck, I certainly felt totally alone.

I started the diesel on the right, adjusted the generator, and turned on the lights. I took my box lunches, canteens, and a jar of water from the truck. I always wore two canteens of water. I was carrying two more on straps, and I had brought several jars of water with me in the truck. The range area did not have a source of running water.

My hands were full, so I walked slowly down the gravel road, past the two supply sheds, over to the weather shack. I was singing one of my favorite 1960's Rock and Roll songs as I did so. It was going on 11:00 p.m., and the first scheduled balloon release wasn't until midnight. It seemed as if I had this two week assignment under control.

I opened up the weather shack, turned on the lights, and positioned my box lunches and canteens on the desk. I signed in. I had to go back to the truck to get the thermos and my radio, which took a few minutes. Back at my weather shack, I plugged in my radio, and adjusted it to a nice 1960's rock station broadcasting from somewhere in California. I turned it up fairly loud so I could hear it outside when I was working. So far, this was shaping up to be a pleasant evening.

Sitting down at the ivory plotting table, I quickly completed the computations from the previous morning's balloon release, recorded and filed the report. Without giving it much thought, I took my portable theodolite and its tripod stand, out through the side door to the park area. It seemed natural for me to set it up out there, as I had done the night before.

The work went quickly, and I was ready to prepare the balloon for the midnight run, which was now due in only a few minutes. I was still outside, looking around at the weather when, once again, in the distance to the southwest, I saw two yellow-orange lights coming up the road from the west. They seemed to be hurrying as they reached the bend in the road several miles to the south.

As before, the two lights stopped and remained on station down at the bend in the road. As before, at first I was certain they must be the headlights to the guard's truck. However, that didn't make any sense. The lights were roughly eight or ten feet above the gravel road, and the second light—the one on the eastern side—slowly split off towards the high pass connecting the jutted out mountain with the south side wall of mountains. The grade up into the high pass was too steep for a wheeled vehicle.

My vision was not fully adjusted to the darkness at the time, and the moonlight wasn't very bright. However, I could just barely make out the outlines of two black ellipsoidal objects behind the lights. The objects were not particularly large. The first was noticeably larger than the second. Still, the first object did not appear to be larger than a semi truck with a trailer attached.

While I watched, a third object with lights, came slowly up the distant road from the west. I estimated it was traveling only 30 to 35 Miles per hour at the time. This third object was somewhat smaller than the second object, and therefore also smaller than the first object. I certainly seemed to be drawing a crowd, I thought nervously to myself.

Running late, I broke off watching the objects in the distance. I turned off the outside lights in the park area. I returned inside the weather shack and prepared my balloon, along with the weather forms. I took my balloon outside and released it at ten minutes after midnight. I checked the lights down the road just before I did so. The second object was crossing up and over the high pass at the time.

Tracking the balloon was routine enough. As the balloon rose up into the clear night-time sky, it drifted slowly towards the south-southeast, passing at last between the gravel road in the distance, and the jutted out mountain peak. Once again, I lost the balloon among the star fields. This time, after only 12 minutes, I found myself tracking what appeared to be a double star—although the two stars did not appear to be moving exactly together.

Frustrated with myself, I broke off the run. I thought I had been very careful when I was tracking the balloon. I was experienced—and it wasn't that difficult a job. I considered my working conditions to be near perfect—and wherever I was, there weren't any officers or sergeants that could come out and bother me. I was kicking the dirt slightly when I went back inside.

After completing the run, and finishing the computations, I turned the outside lights back on. I brought out one of my box lunches, the thermos of coffee, and an extra canteen of water, from inside the weather shack. I set them down on one of the stone benches outside. I chose a bench on the western side of the park area. It had been a long time since the evening meal. While I ate, I watched the second set of lights apparently playing games up and around the distant jutted out peaks. I noticed how the second set of lights, if they were far enough away, took on the appearance of stars.

I was feeling refreshed after finishing my box lunch. I cleaned up the trash. I was starting to take some pride in my nice new weather station and I wanted to keep it looking good. There were some new empty garbage cans out front. I chose one for my use. I decided I needed to locate a suitable garbage dump for future use. Nothing could actually be taken off the range, so I wondered if perhaps there was a garbage dump located around back or out in the desert—or perhaps back at Desert Oasis.

Then there was the simple fact that my new weather station area did not have an outhouse. I decided I should probably get to know the surrounding desert areas somewhat better. I had an hour or so until my next scheduled balloon run. I decided to begin the discovery process now. My climate study was only scheduled to last two weeks—so why wait.

I began by casually inspecting the western edge of the park area. Down to the south, I noticed the third object began drifting slowly back down the road to the west. It seemed to be looking for an opening in the widely scattered fields of sagebrush down in that direction. As it did so, the first larger object remained on station, obviously blocking the road at the bend.

The third object found an open lane to the north through the sagebrush roughly a mile back down the road. It crossed the drainage ditch in a very hesitant fashion. In the same hesitant fashion, it followed the lane generally north for perhaps two miles, until it found the lane to the north blocked by sagebrush.

I stood out in the open, on the western edge of the park area, easily silhouetted against the outside lights. I was very obviously watching the third object. Its lights were on. It didn't seem to care that I was watching it. The third object was floating roughly six feet off the desert, as it was carefully maneuvering above the sagebrush—all in perfect silence. The sagebrush down in that area was only three or four feet high. I couldn't help but wonder why the third object was not willing to fly over the sagebrush itself. There was, after all, nothing physical actually blocking its forward progress. Perhaps it's a helicopter, trying to locate a landing site. I thought to myself.

The third object was now only a few miles southwest of where I was standing. Curious, I decided to walk down a ways in that direction to get a closer look. The moon had set, so I would be walking down through a darkness lit only by my flashlight—and the stars.

In the darkness, it was hard to find a suitable path though the sagebrush. At first the lanes were open and it was easy going. I hadn't intended to walk very far. However I soon found, I had walked much further than I had at first wanted to.

I was about half way down to where the object floated in silence above the sagebrush—although it was still probably more than a mile away—when the object began retreating from me. It began retreating back down along the lanes through the sagebrush. It obviously knew, exactly where I was out in the sagebrush. It was retreating slowly in a very hesitant, and confused manner. It rotated slowly as it retreated, so that the light was always between me and the object in the distance. The manner in which it retreated reminded me of the way young children on a Wisconsin farm typically retreat from cows and horses.

Seeing the object distance itself, reminded me that I was much further out in the sagebrush than I wanted to be. I stopped, turned around, and began finding my way back to the weather shack. The lights of my weather shack were very far away. Mid-level clouds were moving in, obscuring the stars, and the night was becoming even darker. Then a light fog started to form. The lanes through the sagebrush were very confusing. Soon, I was no longer following back along the path I had originally used to come out from the park area. In darkness and fog then, I was forced to pick my way through the sagebrush, breaking it down as necessary in order to get back to my park area. The trip was difficult, tiring, and, took a long time. With tremendous relief, I finally broke through the last row of desert brush and stepped back into my park area. I was already very late with the scheduled balloon run. My walk out into the desert had taken almost two full hours.

I rushed preparations for the next balloon release, turned off the outer lights, and released the balloon with its attached light. Down to the south, the lights of the first object remained on station. The lights of the second object could be seen sitting up behind the jutted out peak. The lights of the third object could be seen moving north through the lanes in the sagebrush, slowly returning to their previous position. I decided to ignore all the lights, and just concentrate on my work.

Tracking the balloon with its attached light against the backdrop of the dark mid-level clouds, was child's play. I felt I needed to get in at least one decent set of wind measurements this evening, so I continued to track the balloon until it disappeared into the base of the clouds at 25,000 feet.

By the time I completed my computations, taken the temperature and dew point, tidied up the interior of my weather shack, and made my log entries, it was time to prepare for another balloon run. The sky was now overcast. The lights outside in the distance, remained on station. What else do the guards have to do? I mused.

I turned off the outside lights, as before, and released the last balloon of the evening right on schedule at 4:00 a.m. As before, the balloon was easy enough to track. The base of the clouds had lowered somewhat to 20,000 feet, where I could no longer see the balloon. As I was closing up my theodolite, I could see the second set of lights come off the jutted out peak, and carefully join up with the first object. Then the two lighted objects, in formation, slowly retreated down the road to the west. When they were a short distance past the lane through the sagebrush, which led north to where the third object sat stationary, the first two objects stopped on the road and waited. The third object rose up perhaps ten feet above the desert, making it perhaps six feet above the sagebrush. Then, at perhaps 50 miles per hour, it traveled in a straight line directly back to the road, ignoring the lanes in the sagebrush beneath it. Once it reached the road, it came to a complete stop. It carefully formed up with the first two objects. Then all three objects spread wide, and proceeded back down the road to the west. Instinctively, I timed them. They were traveling at more than 120 miles per hour as they disappeared into the distance.

I wondered if there was anything special about the bend in the road to the south. I wondered if, perhaps, there was a guard shack down there which I couldn't see from my viewing angle.

Curious then, I completed my computations and made my log entries. I quickly ate my second box lunch and collected the trash. I collected my canteens, the thermos, water jar, radio, and my gloves. I closed up the weather shack, and returned to my parked truck. I shut down the generator and closed everything up for the night.

Getting into the truck, I decided I would drive down to the bend in the road before heading to Desert Oasis, and on to Death Valley Center. With my headlights on bright, I drove carefully the several miles south, down to the bend in the road. I stopped the truck. I did not get out. There was no reason to. There was absolutely nothing out of the ordinary to be seen. There was not so much as a tire track or a footprint on the gravel road. Off to the west, the desert stretched for as far as could be seen in the darkness. There was nothing out to the west except a sea of darkness, desert plants, and sagebrush. On a bright moonlit night in the summertime, it was obviously a place of enchanting beauty.

I carefully turned my truck around on the narrow road, and headed back north towards my weather shack. Reaching the buildings, I continued north without stopping, and headed on in to Desert Oasis. I parked my truck out in the open on the gravel road. The entire Desert Oasis compound and the buildings were obviously deserted. Even so, I didn't waste any time returning my keys. I left all of the lights turned off as requested.

Returning to my truck, I started the engine, and continued downhill to the main gate. Once through, I was relieved to see both of the waiting gray cars disappear down the paved road. I was certainly going to have a lot to think about over breakfast at the Death Valley center chow hall.

One, Two, Three

But if he will not hear,
take with you one or two more,

that by the mouth of two or three witnesses
every word may be established
. . . Matthew 18 verse 16

Breakfast at Death Valley Center chow hall was very good, one of the meals I would remember fondly, a year and half later when I was serving in the Mekong Delta. The box lunches I enjoyed the night before, were good, too—though on the small side.

After breakfast, I hurried back to my barracks at Indian Springs. I was very tired. I slept until once again, Smokey woke me in the late afternoon.

Soon, I was driving back to Death Valley Center for the evening meal, two box lunches, a thermos of coffee, and plenty of drinking water. On schedule, with my truck and jerry cans full of gasoline, I headed back towards the combination lock gate and the Desert Oasis. I was getting to know the roads better now. Consequently, I was driving much faster and making better time, than the night before.

It was only 15 minutes to eight in the evening when I pulled up by the sliding gate at the Desert Oasis. Darkness had fallen. The sky was clear, and the moon was out. There was very little wind—only the occasional light desert breezes. It was a quiet night.

All the lights in the buildings were turned off. I parked my truck on the open road just past the sliding gate, and walked in to the Oasis. Again, the gate would open just enough for me to slip through, close and latch the gate behind me.

As I walked towards the large building, I sang a happy tune, so anyone hiding in the darkness would know I was there. I sang loud, and probably off-key. I was not otherwise armed.

The front door to the meeting room opened easily. I made enough noise as I entered. However, I did not turn on any lights—not even my flashlight. I could hear someone in the darkness beyond the open doorway on the right behind the counter. They were moving around slowly.

Still singing loudly, I gingerly approached the counter on the left, picked up the key ring and my obviously empty envelope. I momentarily turned on my flashlight. As I turned on the flashlight, I suddenly heard two of the full jerry cans in the back of my truck, clang lightly together. I quickly signed for the keys and turned off my flashlight. The quiet sounds coming from the vicinity of my truck, parked out on the gravel road continued.

This left me in quite a quandary. I had no desire to go outside and confront whatever was out there in the darkness. I couldn't see anything out of the ordinary through the meeting room windows. On the other hand, I certainly had no desire to remain inside in the meeting room, either. Having no real choice, I quietly and fervently recited a few of my staple prayers. I started with the "Our Father" and, ended with the sign of the cross. Pretending bravery I wasn't sure I felt, I carefully made my way through the darkness to the front door, and returned outside, singing loudly as I did so.

In a careful and deliberate manner, with my flashlight off, I made my way back up the hill, through the moonlight. I opened the gate a couple of feet, and squeezed through, closed and latched the gate behind me.

I approached my truck with extreme caution. Everything appeared to be in order. However, I was certain someone was watching me from out in the darkness in the bushes beyond the fence on the other side of the road. Still singing, and trying to act normal, I got into my truck, started the engine, placed it in low gear, and headed out towards my weather shack.

After I was up the road a ways, I started breathing easier. I thought about the events so far this evening. I hadn't actually seen anyone outside at the Desert Oasis. Neither had I seen any lights—fluorescent white or otherwise. The fences were roughly four feet high. There was only one gate, and I was the only one who had used it. I decided I was either becoming afraid of my own shadow, or I was missing something.

I mulled these events over some more as I drove on through the night. There was adequate moonlight to see the road and the desert, clear to the distant mountains. I decided if there had been anyone out there, tall enough to just step over the fences, I would have seen them in the moonlight when I looked out of the meeting room window. Only a child, or a small animal could have disturbed the jerry cans in the back of my truck, without my being able to see them from the window.

The conclusion was inescapable. Logically, there must be a hole in the fence, or a loose panel of woven wire, on the northern side of the road. The opening must be large enough for a child to slip through. I decided that in the coming days, I would inspect the fence for openings on the north side of the road, in the area of the Desert Oasis. If there was an opening, I wanted to see how large it was. The conclusion caused me a great deal of concern. In this dark, desolate, stretch of desert there couldn't be any human children—and there didn't seem to be any Tall White children—their night-time play suits generated a zone of white fluorescent light. They could be seen from miles away. Any child out there tonight, had to be able to naturally stay hidden in the darkness. I put my truck into high gear, with sudden imperative, to reach the emotional safety of my weather shack.

It was only 10:00 p.m., when I arrived at the weather site buildings which sat hidden in the moonlit brush along the side of the road. I had made good time. It took only a few minutes to start the generator and carry my food, water, and radio over to my weather shack. This time I brought some trash bags with me.

As I walked past the supply sheds, I took note of the two large diesel fuel tanks sitting behind the generator shack. The gauges on the tanks showed they were both still completely full. The diesel could run continuously for several months before either one of them would need to be refilled. It seemed odd the U.S. Government had chosen to put two such large diesels so far out here in the desert. The only electrical connections to the generator shack came from my simple weather shack. I was only turning on a handful of lights and my radio. I was not even starting up the kerosene heater with its fan. Oh well, I shrugged, I suppose the electricity is there if they should ever find another use for it.

As I walked on, I noticed the second supply shed, which sat next to my weather shack. It had an elevated hundred gallon gasoline tank out in back of it. It also had electrical wires connecting my weather shack with the supply shed—as had my weather shack out on Range Three at Indian Springs. I made a mental note to check the second supply shed to see if it had a small gasoline driven electrical generator, as was the case at Indian Springs. I also made a mental note—while I was at it, I suppose, I should open up the other supply shed and see what was inside—as well as the weather supply shed back at the Desert Oasis. I asked myself—What else was there to do, this far out in such a desolate stretch of desert?

Starting up the large diesel generator in the generator shack was so much fun—even if the second supply shed had a small gasoline generator, I had no intention of using it. Whoever designed the buildings in this area certainly knows me, I laughed to myself.

I opened up the weather shack, positioned my food, water, plugged in and turned on my radio. I turned on the lights, and opened the side door.

I had just begun setting up my portable theodolite in the park area, when the telephone on my desk rang. The ringing telephone made me break out in a cold sweat. This was the earliest I had ever arrived for duty at this weather shack. The only way, whomever was calling, would know that I was here to answer the phone was, if they'd been watching me from the darkness out in the desert. Additionally strange, was the fact that, the line had been dead the last time I checked.

Stepping back into the weather shack, and walking slowly over to the desk, I carefully picked up the receiver, and answered the telephone. "Desert Range weather shack. Airman Hall, speaking." I said slowly and distinctly.

The voice on the line sounded like my friend Dwight, down at the Nellis AFB Weather station. However, I knew it couldn't be him—and I had no intention of asking who it actually was. I decided they could wait to tell me when they got good and ready—and when I was ready to be told. If I wanted to continue to enjoy the bliss of the desert—well, everything in life comes at a price.

The voice on the line began in happy, polite, and pleasant fashion. "Hello, Airman Hall. You are doing such an impressive job. You can be very proud.

Tonight, you should not set up your theodolite next to your weather shack. Tonight, you should set up your equipment out in the desert across the road from your weather shack. Don't release your balloons from next to your weather shack. Release them from out in the desert, where you set up your theodolite. ", the voice requested.

"Yes", I answered simply. "I'll release the balloons from the desert area across the road."

"Thank you." giggled the voice. With that, I could hear the telephone being hung up. Then the line went dead.

I was beside myself with confusion. I didn't see the difference between releasing the balloons from the park area next to the weather shack, or from across the road, 50 feet out in the desert to the east. However, orders were orders—and that was what my orders had originally requested.

Checking my two canteens, and putting on my work gloves, I set out across the road to locate a suitable spot. I could see immediately finding a spot was going to be difficult. Crossing the drainage ditch on the eastern side of the road was the first problem. The drainage ditch was roughly three feet deep with generally steep sides. Beyond it to the east was a steep embankment which added another four or five feet to the barrier. In the darkness, I wasn't able to cross it on my first two attempts.

Not having a shovel, I walked to my truck and returned with my tire iron. I chose a sturdy piece of wood from the surrounding brush. I picked what appeared to be the easiest place to force the ditch crossing. I located a point just opposite the southern side of the second supply shed. My tools weren't very good, the roots of the desert bushes protected the hard packed desert. The work was difficult. After perhaps 30 minutes, I had constructed a makeshift crossing point. I returned the tire iron to the truck, and refilled my canteens, before continuing.

I gathered up my tripod stand from the park area, and brought it with me. I carefully crossed the drainage ditch to the high desert on the other side. Picking a suitable place to set up was going to be difficult, as there wasn't much available space to pick from. I had no intention of crossing into the next security area to the east. The boundary was very close to the drainage ditch, and well marked by a small ditch of its own. One of the widely spaced security fence poles stood just a few feet north and east of my makeshift drainage ditch crossing point.

I finally chose a place on the eastern edge of the drainage ditch, and perhaps 100 feet south of my crossing point. The area I had to work with could hardly have been much more than 5 feet wide.

Bringing out the heavy theodolite and setting it up correctly at the location I had chosen, without damaging it, was next to impossible. This was especially true since the theodolite had to be sitting level and aligned to the north star in order to function correctly.

Midnight was rapidly approaching, and I was finally ready to try the first scheduled balloon release of the evening. Bringing out the balloon to the release point without breaking it took some doing. However, eventually I had carried it and its attached light across the drainage ditch and down to the theodolite.

I was able to release the balloon on schedule. Tracking it was another matter. The light night wind immediately began carrying the balloon towards the south, straight down towards the next security fence pole. Clearing the pole, the balloon continued drifting south towards the distant bend in the road. Tonight there weren't any lights to be seen down there—or anywhere. In order to track the balloon, I had to stand on the western side of the theodolite tripod stand, which meant I had to stand right on the edge of the drainage ditch. I nearly fell in. I accidentally jiggled and moved the theodolite stand. The theodolite with its stand almost fell into the ditch—such a fall would have broken it. Limping a little, and smarting badly from bumps and bruises, I abandoned the balloon, and carefully moved my still undamaged theodolite and its stand to a safe and secure location a few feet away in the brush. I couldn't use it from there. However, it could at least sit there safely for a while.

I had taken only 5 readings, none of which were of any use. I spent the next several minutes trying to explain to myself why the last balloon release had not been a complete failure—I had learned so much—I said to myself. At least, I concluded, tonight I have learned the night wind is blowing slowly from the north.

I returned back across the drainage ditch to my weather shack to finish licking my wounds—I had some rubbing alcohol in a first aid kit. I make my log entries, filed the near empty wind and weather report. I sat down outside to eat my first box lunch. As I was eating, I noted—still no lights to be seen anywhere.

I thought about that carefully. I supposed the lights were somehow connected with the security guards—even though I had never actually seen any security guards out in this desolate stretch of desert. If I couldn't see any lights, then perhaps there weren't any security guards in the area, either. I remembered having been told by the Park Ranger when I took this assignment that between six at night and six in the morning, not even security guards were allowed east of the range gate, back at the main highway. The Ranger had been very explicit—No other human except me.

I was going to need to locate a safe level area to set up my theodolite for the next balloon run. There weren't any on this side of the security fence. I had noticed a suitable spot just inside the next security area. It was located directly opposite the bench on which I was sitting, and was roughly 30 feet on the other side of the eastern security fence. If I did it carefully, maybe I could set up there and the guards wouldn't notice. It was, after all, a very big desert.

I finished my box lunch. I picked up the trash and placed it in a bag inside the weather shack. After preparing the balloon, I attached a long second piece of cord, so I could tie the balloon to a piece of sagebrush for a short while.

Carrying the balloon and my other gear, I set out for the next balloon release. After crossing the drainage ditch, I walked over to where my theodolite was standing in the bushes. I temporarily tethered the weather balloon to one of the sturdy pieces of sagebrush. I checked the surrounding area—still no lights—or security guards. I carefully retrieved my theodolite and its stand from the brush. Cautiously, I carried it some 30 feet into the next security area and set it up in the open level area. The theodolite leveled and aligned up perfectly. I retrieved my tethered balloon, brought it to the theodolite stand, and released it on schedule. I was so proud of myself. At last, I was going to take my first perfect and acceptable set of balloon wind measurements.

I was resting my eyes after taking reading number 15. I was looking around at the beautiful surrounding moonlit desert as it stretched far into the distance, when I suddenly noticed the lights had returned. Down by the bend in the road to the south sat the large black object and to its left the smaller object, apparently the same ones I'd seen the previous day. As before, the lights were yellow-orange, and closely resembled in appearance the distant headlights of a truck. The first object was clearly blocking the gravel road at the bend.

Turning back to the northwest, I could see the middle sized object coming slowly down the road from the north, heading towards the gravel parking lot. It was still roughly two miles from the graveled area. It too, was completely blocking the road as it progressed. Like the others, it was roughly eight feet off the gravel road.

I became immediately concerned for my safety. It seemed for a minute or so, as if the security guards may have come to ask questions. The last thing I wanted was to have to conduct business with two armed security guards out in this desolate stretch of desert at 2:30 in the morning. I was going to break off the run, pick up my equipment, and immediately move back west of the security fence line. That way, I reasoned, I could play dumb. I would be able to tell the guards I hadn't realized where I was until they showed up—as though any decent set of security guards would believe that story. Then I saw the middle sized object to the northwest stop its forward progress and remain stationary. Breathing easier, I decided maybe if I completed the readings up to 20, I wouldn't look so guilty—or so stupid—to the guards when they finally came to talk to me.

The next five minutes seemed like an eternity, although nothing actually happened. I took the remaining five balloon measurements, and broke off the run at 20,000 feet. All the while, the middle sized object stayed in place over the road some two miles to the north.

I quickly picked up my belongings, and moved my theodolite and stand back west of the fence line. It took me three trips. I breathed a big sigh of relief when it appeared the guards weren't coming any closer to ask me questions.

Now I had a real problem: Where do I set up my theodolite for the 4:00 a.m. balloon release? My choices were very limited. I chose a truly miserable spot, with my theodolite almost touching the security pole opposite my pathway across the drainage ditch. From this questionable position, I performed the 4:00 a.m. balloon release. I pretended I was able to get seven usable minutes of data. Then I broke off the run, packed up my equipment, ate my second box lunch, and closed up the weather shack for the evening. The lights had left and cleared the roads by 4:30 a.m. It was past 5:00 a.m. By the time I recovered my equipment, and locked up my weather shack. I shut down the diesel, packed up my truck, and left for Desert Oasis. All in all, I saw it as another lost evening.

I didn't waste any time driving back to the Desert Oasis. However, when I was within a mile or so of the sliding gate, I slowed to second gear, and made certain my headlights were on bright. As I drove, I carefully inspected the fence which bordered the northern side of the gravel road. I was looking for a loose panel of wire, or maybe a hole in the fence. At first I didn't see anything. Then, roughly 500 feet before the sliding gate I began to spot a series of panels that appeared to be suspiciously loose as I drove past them. I took special note of three of them. I did not stop the truck in the pre-dawn darkness to inspect the panels more carefully. Knowing they were there was enough for me.

The desert oasis was completely deserted. I turned in the keys without incident, and quickly left the Ranges by way of the main gate with the combination lock. I put my thoughts about the evening on the back burner, and proceeded to again enjoy breakfast at the Death Valley Center chow hall.

The Watchers

And he bearing his cross
went forth into a place
called the place of a skull,
which is called in the Hebrew,
Golgotha:
. . . John 19 verse 17

The next day, 8:00 p.m., Wednesday, the fourth evening of my first week, found me again parking my truck, next to the sliding gate at The Desert Oasis. Picking up the keys and my empty envelope in the meeting room, was still spooky. The usual someone, once again, was watching me from the darkness beyond the doorway on the right. I signed for the keys, and quickly exited the meeting room, always keeping a few chairs between me and the darkened doorway. Based on the sounds they were making, whoever was back there was obviously an adult. Tonight for a minute or so, it seemed as if they intended to show themselves. I for one, was very glad they chose not to. They were clearly becoming braver.

I was in a quandary, driving out to my weather station. So far, there wasn't a suitable location, where I could set up the theodolite and release the weather balloons. Tonight I had brought with me, a long handled shovel from Indian springs. It rattled around in the back of the truck, and made a lot of noise as I drove.

Arriving at the large gravel parking lot, a decision had to be made. The only reasonable plan was to walk south, down the gravel road, searching for a suitable spot east of the drainage ditch. The shovel would make it easy to create a crossing point, clear the brush, and level the ground on the other side. What could be simpler?

I opened my weather shack and positioned my belongings. I was putting on my work gloves and checking my canteens when once again, the telephone rang. My nightly visitor—I said to myself. Cautiously I answered the phone, "Desert Range weather shack. Airman Hall speaking."

The voice on the other end sounded very happy, almost excited—and—just like the night before, the voice sounded like my friend Dwight—as though I were willing to believe that ruse any more.

The voice began, "Good evening, Airman Hall. You're doing such a wonderful job. You need to be careful. Last night you almost hurt yourself. Tonight, please go further out into the desert in front of your weather station. Don't be afraid. Just go right past the metal poles."

"Do you mean its alright if I set up my theodolite at the spot east of the line of poles, where I had set up last night? The spot is quite a ways into the next security area. The line of poles appears to be the boundary. It's at least 30 feet past the poles. I don't want to get into any trouble." I responded.

The voice laughed a little, sounding as if they were enjoying this. "Of course its a separate security area. Just go right in. But don't stop where you did last night. Just pick up your equipment, and just keep walking east. There's a large wooden pole set up over there. You can set up anywhere you want to, but we would like you to go at least as far as the pole. Walk in a line straight out from the front door of your weather shack and keep walking. Its a long way. Don't worry. There are no humans out there to stop you. You will be totally alone. That's why you were chosen. You'll be the first human that has ever been allowed out there."

"Yes," I answered, noticeably in shock. The voice on the telephone hung up and once again, the line went dead.

I sat down in the chair at my desk, stunned. I collected my thoughts, and realized the ditch crossing, needed to be improved before anything else. The next 20 minutes were spent putting the shovel to good use. Hard manual labor is always good to get a man's blood flowing again.

After returning the shovel to the weather shack, I positioned the tripod on my shoulder, and set out walking east. The voice on the phone had said there was some walking to be done.

I finally located the large wooden pole standing more than a mile out in the desert. It was surprisingly hard to find. It stood at the top of a small rise on high ground, in the middle of a wide shallow pass. The pass joined the valley where my weather shack was located, and another huge, desolate valley to the east. I decided to name the desolate valley to the east "The Valley of Forgotten Lake Beds".

It had been quite a hike. Finding a path through the sagebrush, without becoming lost, was no easy matter. Patches of heavy sagebrush frequently blocked the direct route. At one place, the only available path circled to the north, in and out of a small hollow in the desert.

Setting up my tripod stand was easy enough. The sagebrush was thinner in the vicinity of the pole, so there were several obvious spots available.

I made the long walk back to my weather shack, and ate my first box lunch. Now the awkward, heavy box containing my theodolite, had to be carried back to the release site. It wasn't any shorter the second time. I had little time to rest. The first scheduled release had already been missed. Two more releases were still scheduled for this evening, so two filled weather balloons had to be retrieved from my weather shack. When I got back to the release site, I tethered the first balloon to a sturdy piece of sagebrush, set up my theodolite, and released the second balloon.

The balloon run was near perfect. The balloon could be tracked all the way to 30,000 feet. My first successful balloon run left me feeling very elated.

After breaking off the run at 31,000 feet, the alignment of the theodolite needed to be verified. I also wanted to record the direction to some important landmarks and buildings, such as my weather shack. The information would help me turn my ivory plotting table into a makeshift map of the area—thereby increasing my level of safety, in this desolate stretch of desert. A decent map would improve the quality of my weather reports, as well. I began by pointing my theodolite towards the northwest. All of the lights on the buildings back at the range area were on.

The theodolite easily focused in on my distant truck, which was parked in the gravel parking lot, in front of the generator shack. Looking through the theodolite, I recoiled in shock. Several black ellipsoidal craft could be seen parked in the gravel area. They were northwest of the well lit generator shack. They were sitting where the light met the darkness, partially hidden in the shadows. There were two large craft, both roughly the size of a house trailer. In between them, could be seen a smaller, medium size craft. Beside, and somewhat behind the western-most large craft, rested a still smaller size craft. The smallest craft was almost completely engulfed in darkness. To me, this suggested, the smaller craft had trailed the formation, and, had arrived last.

Each of the craft had two large windows in front, and several smaller windows along the sides. It was obvious none of the craft had been built by the U.S. Air Force. It was also obvious, none of the craft were large enough to have made the deep space crossing. The conclusion was obvious. Either each of the craft were carried across deep space to the inner solar system on board a much larger craft—or else each of the craft had been assembled here on this earth or on the moon.

Thanks to my theodolite, I could see an adult, next to my truck on the driver's side, wearing a dark gray, or black jump suit. The person's eyes were larger than those of a human. They appeared to be wearing something that looked similar to a surgical mask or a small breathing device, along with light headgear. The person was slightly bent over looking through the open window of my truck, inspecting the inside.

I estimated that when he stood up, he was roughly 6 and a half feet tall. The skin on his face appeared to be approximately the same color as the light on the generator shack—namely yellow-orange. Some distance beyond him, on the other side of my truck stood two other adults similar to the first. The adults were not very active. However, based on their movements, at least one of them appeared to be a woman roughly six feet tall.

In between the craft and the generator shack, I could see two teen-aged versions of the taller adults. They were shorter, roughly five or five and a half feet tall. However, they were not wearing the surgical mask type breathing device. One was wearing a small device which fit over his nose, and gave him the appearance of having a normal, albeit fairly large nose. The other wasn't wearing any surgical mask or breathing device. While I was watching, the first took off his Big Nose breathing device, and didn't put it back on. The teenagers walked around quite a bit more than the adults did.

In the doorway to the generator shack, out in front of the supply sheds, and down by my weather shack, I could see five younger children. Two were playing around and inside my weather shack, obviously having the time of their lives. The others stayed much closer to the adults. All of them were wearing dark gray or black jump suits. None of them were wearing any breathing devices. Like children everywhere, they were each playing in a very excited manner.

I especially took note of the two children playing around my weather shack. One appeared to be a young girl about the same age as a young teenager. She seemed to be baby-sitting a younger child, perhaps a younger brother.

The theodolite had only one eyepiece. I was forced to pull away from the theodolite to rest my eyes for several minutes. A light fog was slowly forming out in the valleys.

The fall evenings were slowly becoming cooler. The lights of the buildings in the distance were beginning to show the effect of the fog. I carefully readjusted my theodolite, and returned to studying the objects in the distance. The gray creatures in the distance were in the process of re-boarding their various craft. The five children were boarding the smallest of the craft. The two teenagers were boarding the medium sized craft. The adults waited until last to board the large craft. They were obviously checking to see that no child was left behind.

Once boarding was complete, the large craft on the eastern end of the line lifted three or four feet off the graveled area, and slowly backed away into the darkness to the north. After a couple of minutes, it could be seen in the distance with its forward lights on, traveling slowly up the narrow gravel road to the west.

In like fashion, the medium sized craft lifted off, backed away into the darkness, and could later be seen following up the road to the west.

Then, it was the turn of the smallest craft to lift off, back away into the darkness, and proceed up the road to the west.

Finally, the last of the large craft lifted off, backed away, and followed the others up the road to the west. I watched them until the lights had completely disappeared into the gathering patches of fog.

As I pulled away from the theodolite, I was emotionally exhausted, physically tired, with fatigue sapping my bravery. After what I had seen, I had no desire to be alone at night, in this desolate stretch of desert. This assignment wasn't anything like what I had expected. I was used to dealing with the Tall Whites, and I was used to dealing with "The Norwegians With 24 Teeth". However, the people wearing the dark gray suits whom I had observed through the theodolite, appeared to be an extraterrestrial race I had not met before. With the thin night time fog slowly moving in, I decided to release my last weather balloon early, return my equipment to the weather shack, and head in to Death Valley Center to rest.

The final run of the evening went quickly enough. I broke off the readings at 20,000 feet. I packed my theodolite into its sturdy case. The case had room for both the theodolite and its heavy rubberized protective plastic bag. The bag was of excellent military quality weather protective covering. I left my tripod standing in place. It was totally weatherized. With the thin fog moving in, I wouldn't have time to return for the tripod tonight.

After returning the theodolite to the weather shack, I hurried through the calculations. I refilled my gas tank, shut everything down, and ate my second box lunch in the truck. As I was leaving the building area, I checked my watch. The time was only 4:00 a.m. I returned the keys to Desert Oasis, and drove into Death Valley Center. There was still time for me to sleep in my truck before breakfast, and the long drive back to Indian Springs.

The Wind Coming Up The Road

"... And when thou prayest,
thou shalt not be as the hypocrites are:
for they love to pray standing in the synagogues
and in the corners of the streets,
that they may be seen of men.
Verily I say unto you, They have their reward.

But thou, when thou prayest,
enter into thy closet,
and when thou hast shut thy door,
pray to thy Father which is in secret;
and thy Father which seeth in secret
shall reward thee openly. . . ."
. . . Matthew 6:5-6

I left Indian Springs early the next afternoon. I noted it was Thursday afternoon, the beginning of the last shift of my first work week. I was looking forward to spending the coming Friday night, and all day Saturday, resting and recuperating, down in the Las Vegas casinos. I was singing happily to myself as I headed towards Death Valley Center. I planned on spending a few minutes in the Death Valley Center Public library / museum. I was interested in learning more about the Native American legends from the American Southwest. One legend I remembered having come across when I was still in grade school back in Wisconsin. The legend told of a young man from the Navajo tribe probably back about the year 600 A.D., who visited a mountain in the desert where tall white spirits lived in tunnels. I wondered if there were any similar legends from that long ago time describing other kinds of spirits wearing gray clothing.

As expected, the library was open and unmanned. It operated on the honor system. There were many interesting books to choose from. I quickly picked two. One was on the history of the American West. The other was on its geology. Both of the books had a nice set of maps of the American West. I checked out the books and left for the evening meal.

At 8:00 p.m. , once again I brought my truck slowly up the gravel road from the gate with the combination lock. I stopped on the road next to the sliding gate at the Desert Oasis. After turning off the engine and also turning off the headlights, I sat in the truck for few minutes. I wanted to adjust to my night vision.

When I felt my eyes were ready for night, I got out of my truck. Quietly I opened the sliding gate a couple of feet, and stepped inside, closing the gate behind me. I was listening carefully for sounds in the moonlit compound. There were plenty to be heard, coming from the dark shadows behind the buildings. I recited my favorite prayers in silence as I walked to the front door of the meeting room.

I left my flashlight off, for my own safety. I wanted to keep my night vision. I slowly opened the front door to the meeting room. Faint beautiful desert starlight streamed in through the windows on the northern side, faintly illuminating the darkened room inside. The usual someone once again, was watching me from the darkness beyond the doorway on the right. Only tonight, I could catch glimpses of two children bent over, as they scampered out from the darkness beyond the doorway, and hid behind the counter at the front of the room. I could hear them as they ran. They both remained hidden down behind the counter. The taller, older one, was hiding directly opposite the telephone and the clipboard I needed to sign for the keys. The shorter, younger one, was hiding down behind the counter at the other end. The usual someone continued to watch me from the darkness beyond the doorway on the right.

There are hardly words for the fear I felt. I began speaking softly and slowly towards the darkness, and towards the counter, much as if I were speaking to a horse or a dog. "Good evening. I'm Airman Hall. I've only come for my envelope and my keys." I began slowly walking towards the left side of the counter where I could reach my keys and my envelope. I continued talking as I walked. "I will not turn on any lights. As soon as I sign for the keys, I will immediately leave the building and go back to my truck. I am sorry if I am stuttering, but you frighten me greatly."

I was still perhaps 5 feet from the counter, when the first of the two children decided to make a break for it. The younger child, still bent over slightly and facing the open doorway, stood up in the darkness and ran back through it into the safety of the darkness beyond. A screen door in the back could be heard opening and slamming shut as the child escaped into the night.

I carefully took another two steps forward. The taller child then decided to make a break for the safety of the darkness. I saw immediately it was a young girl. The girl was so close, had I reached out my hand, I could almost have touched her on the shoulder. However, as soon as she reached the safety of the darkness beyond the door, she stopped. It sounded as if she was turning around so she too, could watch me from the darkness.

I stood frozen in fear. There was no place for me to run to—no place to hide. I had no choice but to use my shaking left hand to pick up my envelope and the keys. I used my shaking right hand to sign for them, and began backing away from the counter. As I did so, it sounded as though the young girl was planning to reenter the room behind the counter on the right, and show herself. I certainly had no intention of waiting around to find out. I quickly exited the meeting room, always keeping a few chairs between me and the darkened doorway. I guessed that I had gotten the front door closed behind me as I left. I was in too much of a hurry to be sure.

I wasted no time getting back to my truck and heading out towards my desert range weather shack. The envelope, as before, was empty.

As I drove, I decided I needed time to think. My truck was practically the only safe place I had left anymore, so I slowed to a normal rate of speed. I decided for my own safety, I needed to start putting things together. After all, a climate study consisting of only 3 or 4 wind measurements a night lasting only two weeks was hardly worth the paper the results were written on.

I wondered if the phone at Desert Oasis and the phone in my desert range weather shack, both connected to the same switch board. This being the mid 1960s, and the phones being located so far out in this desolate stretch of desert, any such switchboard would have to be manually operated. Young human girls knew how to operate such switch boards by the time they had completed the sixth grade. Any young alien girl could be expected to do just as well. If the two phones were in fact using the same switchboard, the obvious place for the switchboard to be located would be somewhere in a rear hallway located in the building with the meeting room / classroom, back at Desert Oasis. When I returned in the morning, the Desert Oasis would be deserted, as it always had been in the mornings. I decided this trip, I would intentionally stay late out at the range weather shack. I would wait for dawn before leaving the ranges. That way, when I returned in the morning to the deserted Desert Oasis, the sun would have already risen. In bright sunlight, I would be able to carefully inspect the buildings and the areas behind them. There would be no one out at Desert Oasis to bother me, no matter what I did. With my truck parked in plain sight out on the gravel road, the guards would be forced to remain parked out on the main road, beyond the combination lock gate at the bottom of the hill, and wait for me—no matter how long I took. So what if I take an extra hour, I said to myself. The guards are not allowed, under any circumstances, to come out here when I am here.

As I drove on, I thought some more. The young gray alien girl hiding behind the counter was crouched down directly behind the telephone. She must certainly be well acquainted with the area where she was hiding. I wondered if she was the person who had previously spoken to me on the telephone. I also wondered if she was the same young girl I had seen the previous night babysitting her younger brother. If she was, I decided, it would mean this entire two week climate study was just a charade designed to make it easy for the young gray alien girl to get used to meeting and talking with me. She was, after all, at an age where she would normally stop seeing the world through the eyes of a child, and start seeing the world through the eyes of an adult.

I thought some more. Human children at that age frequently take part in cultural exchange programs. The young gray alien girl was old enough to begin training for the gray alien lead position in a joint USAF technology transfer program. I decided to start looking at this entire Climate Study program in a different way. I decided to start looking at this entire two week climate study, the way the young gray alien girl and her parents must certainly be looking at it. After all, The Tall Whites back at Indian Springs had shown humans that technology transfer—and shared industrial bases—could help both ways. However, the Tall White Teacher had shown The USAF Generals that for such programs to be successful, the program had to start with at least one alien and one human who have overcome their natural fears of each other, and had learned to trust each other. Those two then, could teach others. What better place to start such a program than with a well protected young alien girl—and an enlisted USAF weatherman who is already used to being around extra-terrestrials, and who was, for all intents and purposes—otherwise expendable. I wasn't sure if I was more afraid of the gray extraterrestrials—or of the American Generals.

A light evening fog was already starting to form when I arrived at the Desert Range buildings. I proceeded as before. After opening up my weather shack, I was just turning on my radio, when the telephone rang. Only tonight I was expecting it. Picking up the telephone, I said, "Desert Range Weather Station. Airman Hall speaking." I was careful to sound happy and pleasant, since I suspected I was speaking to the young gray alien girl.

It was the usual voice on the other end of the telephone line, still trying to sound like my friend from down at Nellis. "Good Evening, Airman Hall. I noticed you brought your theodolite back to the weather station this morning when you came back from the desert".

"Yes." I responded pleasantly.

"You really don't have to do that." the voice responded. "I see your equipment is very heavy, and it's a lot of work for you to carry it out into the desert and set it up. Your equipment is very safe out by the pole. I promise you, no one will touch it. Just leave your equipment set up out in the desert, when you finish the last run, tonight. It comes with a protective bag. Just put the bag over it. Tie the bag securely, and leave it there until you come again."

"Yes," I responded. "I'll be happy to do so."

The voice continued, "You can do anything you want when you are out at your weather shack, or out in the desert. You can relax, write letters, read books, or paint pictures. We are hoping you will stay out at your weather shack, or out in the desert, until at least 5:00 in the morning. That way, if someone wants to come out and talk with you, they can."

"Yes," I answered. "I'll be happy to stay out here until at least 5:00 a.m. Usually, I suppose, I can be found at my weather shack."

I could hear the phone being hung up. Then the line went dead. Yes, I thought to myself. I must certainly be talking to the young alien girl. Lucky me, I said to myself—I figured out a few things before she phoned.

I expected to have a busy night ahead of me. Already a light fog was drifting in from the mountains and the valleys to the east and northeast. Silently it filled the pass into the valley to the east. With considerable difficulty, I carried my theodolite back out to the tripod which was still standing by the distant pole.

While I was traversing the shallow hollow which arced towards the north, I had the strangest feeling my guardian angels were walking behind and beside me. About half way through the shallow depression, I began to feel as though my angels wanted me to set down my heavy load for a few minutes, and follow them up out of the hollow a short distance to the south. After only 40 feet or so, the way south was blocked by a large, oddly shaped sagebrush plant. I wondered to myself why my angels had brought me here. I was going to try to circle counter-clockwise around the plant and bypass it. However, I felt certain my guardian angels did not want me to do that. So I returned to my original stopping point on the north side of the plant. I stood there facing the plant. It felt as though one of my angels was calmly pointing out the appearance of one of the longer branches on the left hand—the eastern side—of the bush. After I had taken careful note of the appearance of the large bush, my angels seemed to be satisfied. It seemed as if I should now just return to my equipment, and carry on with my work. As I was returning to my equipment, I wondered about the significance of what had happened. I had, after all, seen a great many sagebrush plants before.

I returned to my equipment, and continued on to the pole, setting everything up as soon as I arrived. I returned to my weather shack, and finished my first box lunch. With three filled balloons in hand, I headed back out to the pole and my theodolite. I chose a sturdy sagebrush bush and tethered two of the balloons to it. On a whim, I specifically chose a very sturdy bush to the east of the pole. To get to the bush, it was necessary for me to walk some 50 or 70 yards through the pass and into my "Valley of The Forgotten Lake Beds". The desert valley, surrounded by distant mountains, was huge. It stretched for many miles in all directions. The valley was rapidly filling with very cool, very dense, and very thick fog.

The first balloon run went easy enough. However, because the fog was continually becoming thicker and denser, I had to break off the run at only 15,000 feet.

I decided to just wait out in the desert by the pole, and enjoy myself until the second scheduled balloon release. I had many extra forms, and two canteens full of water. My two spare balloons remained securely tethered to the sage brush bush east of me, so there wasn't any reason to return to my weather shack. Although I had been somewhat late with the first release, I still had roughly an hour and a half until the next scheduled release.

I didn't have a decent place to sit down, other than the ground itself. Sitting on the theodolite storage box was very uncomfortable. It had a large metal handle on top. I tried leaning against the wooden pole to no avail. The pole was quite strong—and also quite uncomfortable to lean against. I began assembling a few of the larger slabs of flat rocks from the surrounding area, to form a bench and a table. It worked pretty well, but it was hard work. I set them up near the pole, and decided it was time to test them out.

As I was sitting on my newly made rock bench, something about the wooden pole struck me as odd. The desert soil in the area was very rocky, and extremely well packed. I estimated the pole to be at least six and a half, maybe seven feet tall. It was too tall for me to reach up and feel the top. The actual wood from which the pole had been constructed did not appear to be more than a few years old. Yet, the soil around the base of the pole did not show any evidence that it had ever been disturbed. The hole was either very old, or had been clean cut in the rocky soil. Since the voice on the phone had said I was the first human ever to be allowed east of the distant security fence, it meant the pole had to have been erected by the gray aliens. They did such a good job erecting the pole, I said to myself, they must be incredibly good at tunneling.

I wondered if the pole was actually all solid wood as it appeared. Considering its strategic location between two huge desolate valleys—and the open sky with the moon up above—I wondered if perhaps, the top of the pole had been hollowed out and capped. If so, it could now be concealing an electronic homing beacon, or perhaps a transponder to relay electronic communications. I noticed it was positioned to line up with the gravel road which connected the large gravel parking lot next to the faraway generator shack, and the distant mountain pass to the west. Suddenly these desolate valleys didn't seem so uninhabited any more. I wondered what other gravel roads it lined up with. Such roads must surely be hidden out in the desolate valley to the east.

The fog in both valleys was now becoming very thick, and it was beginning to concern me greatly. I decided to release the second balloon, and return to my weather shack for the remainder of the evening. I got lost in the fog for several minutes going to retrieve my second balloon. I was just barely able to find my way back to the pole and to my theodolite. I had to pay careful attention to the slope of the land to do it.

The fog made tracking the balloon hopeless. I just released the balloon, secured my theodolite, picked up my clipboard, and began walking back towards my weather shack. I was in for one very long ordeal. I could seldom see even five feet in front of me. I was unable to find any of the footprints which I had made earlier in the evening when I walked out from my weather shack. For at least twenty minutes I was hopelessly lost in the slowly thickening fog.

Remembering my previous encounter with my angels, I decided to start carefully inspecting each sagebrush plant I encountered, to see if by chance it looked familiar. I also prayed, asking my guardian angels to help me out of the desperate mess I found myself in. It felt as if, once again, my two guardian angels came to join me in the fog. They seemed to be leading me to a special place next to a special large bush. I stood there for a few minutes. Then it felt as if one of my angels began by pointing out the branches on the left hand side of the large bush which I was facing. It felt as if the second of my two guardian angels was standing behind me, reminding me that the shallow hollow which I knew so well, was located a short distance behind me. I now knew exactly where I was in the fog.

I thanked God and my angels profusely for saving me. Feeling a tremendous amount of relief, I found my way through the heavy fog, back to the shallow hollow. Once there I easily located the footprints I had made on my previous trips through the hollow, and carefully followed them back to the security boundary and the drainage ditch on the eastern side of the gravel road. When I got close, there were several such footpaths, so I wandered around a small amount. I was not singing or making any noise as I walked, because I was listening to the sound my feet were making in the darkness as they struck the ground—or the sagebrush—as a way of judging where I was on the trail.

The fog had become so thick, I almost physically bumped into the metal security pole which stood just north of my makeshift crossing point. I was actually quite relieved I had bumped into the pole, and not fallen into the ditch by accident.

I was afraid to attempt crossing the ditch using my makeshift crossing point in this heavy fog. I was unable to see the lights of my weather shack, even though I knew it sat only a hundred feet directly across the ditch and the gravel road from me. Even in the best of times, crossing there was difficult. The soil was quite rocky, and if I fell into the ditch and hurt myself, I would be in very serious trouble. I decided to play it safe. I knew of a much easier crossing point which lay a half mile or so further south where the ditch became quite shallow. There the soil was quite soft with very few rocks, so even if I fell, I wouldn't hurt myself. I decided to follow the eastern side of the ditch down hill until I reached this southern crossing point.

It took a while to locate the southern crossing point, but it was a pleasant walk. The fog was rising and thinning out. After a while I could occasionally see the lights of my weather shack in the distance behind me, to the north. Because of the patches of drifting fog, I paid no attention to the dark shadows I could also see moving next to those same buildings.

When I finally arrived at the southern crossing point, I could hardly believe how easy it was to cross the ditch and finally gain the gravel road.

The base of the fog was now roughly 30 or 40 feet above the ground. The ditch and the road itself in that area, except for a few patches, was essentially clear of fog.

In careful but relaxed fashion, I began the easy walk north up the western side of the gravel road, towards the range buildings. I was walking in darkness. My flashlight had been turned off to conserve batteries. Most of the time, I was walking with my attention focused on the gravel road itself. Consequently I was quite surprised when I finally broke out of the fog completely, and could very clearly see the range buildings—and the dark shadows moving next to them. The buildings were less than 200 yards up the road. I stopped where I was, and struggled to contain my fears, as I surveyed the scene ahead. Three of the gray adults were spread wide up and down the road in front the range buildings. They were carefully watching the still fog shrouded desert to the east of the road, obviously expecting me to break out of the fog from that direction. Based on their movements, the most distant adult Gray appeared to be a woman. Each of the adults was wearing a surgical mask type breathing device.

The young alien girl was standing in the park area next to my weather station, very carefully watching my makeshift ditch crossing. The doors to my weather shack had been opened, and her younger brother was playing inside. One of the teenagers seemed to be babysitting him. Another teenager could be seen disappearing around the corner of the generator shack. He was wearing a large nose type breathing device. He was apparently heading back towards their craft which sat parked in the large gravel parking lot. I was further surprised when I realized that none of the Gray Aliens were aware I was standing down the road to the south watching them. Had they been the Tall Whites, they would have certainly seen me by now.

As I watched the Grey Aliens from the distance, it all made sense to me.

The smallest of their craft are too small for an adult to use, so the small craft must be carrying only young children. The largest of the craft are too awkward to steer, to be trusted to a teenager or to a child, so the large craft must be piloted only by adults. Likewise, the medium craft must be piloted only be teenagers.

The children can easily breathe the earth's thin air—the adults cannot breathe the air without the help of a breathing device. The breathing device must filter out most of the nitrogen in the earth's thin air, and allow the adults to breathe only air with a much higher percentage of oxygen. The teenagers can still breathe the earth's thin air—but as they grow, their breathing organs do not grow in the same proportion as the rest of their body—so they have had to start using the simpler breathing devices. Now I understood why the Generals wanted the young alien girl to be a part of a joint technology transfer team—she's the oldest person in the group who can talk and breathe at the same time, in the Earth's thin air, for any extended length of time.

I mulled things over in my mind some more. If the Gray Aliens have come in this close, I nervously thought to myself, sooner or later, they are going to come to within a few feet of me. I worried the adult men would approach me from behind, while the children approached me from the front. Since I was forced to resume walking up the gravel road towards the safety of my weather shack and my truck, I decided to stay as close as possible to the western side of the gravel road. That way, if the Grey Aliens came near, I could retreat into the thick sage, and force them all to remain in front of me when they approached.

Having no other choice, I said my favorite prayers. In silence, I resumed my slow and careful walk up the gravel road towards the weather shack. Still they didn't notice me. For my own safety, I began to hum a song. As I continued walking, I begin to sing a quiet love song which was popular at the time. I was singing in a normal—albeit greatly off-key—manner. The three adults and the young girl suddenly took note of me. Almost in unison, they turned toward me, and began studying me intently. I stopped walking as they did so. However, I did continue singing.

As I stood waiting, the three adults assembled in front of the nearest supply shed, forming a line spread across the road and took several steps in my direction. They stopped there. The young girl moved out to the western edge of the road, turned towards me, and took up a position several feet in front of the adults. All of them stood waiting, apparently for me to approach them.

I was filled with a great deal of fear, and I certainly had no desire to approach them. However, I very obviously did not have any choice. Not all of the range buildings lights had been turned on. The gravel road itself, out in front of the supply shed, was dark and had many shadows. However, the park area was quite well lit up. I decided to force them to come out of the shadows, and meet me face to face in the well lit park area. I carefully followed along the western side of the gravel road, and took a diagonal path through the edge of the sagebrush, until I had reached the southern side of the park area. Then I found a well lit place along the southern edge. I stood with my back to the sagebrush, facing the Gray Aliens, and waited for them to make the next move. I said my prayers, and continued singing my songs. However, I did not actually speak to the aliens.

The young girl slowly approached the eastern side of the park area and stopped 30 feet or so from me. Still, she hadn't said anything. She was obviously afraid to come very close to me. She stood there in the light in much the way any other Alien child might have, and I concluded she was alien. However, except for the gray clothing she was wearing, and the fact that the adults she had come with were obviously older adult Grey Aliens. there was little else to suggest she wasn't human. For my own safety, I decided to try to talk to her.

"Who are you?' I carefully asked. There was no response.

"Where do you and your parents come from?" I continued slowly.

There was still no response. I paused for a moment to carefully consider my next question. The young girl was obviously ill at ease, and unprepared to carry on an extensive conversation. I guessed the young girl had probably expected our first face to face conversation would begin through the open side door of my weather shack.

"Don't be frightened," I said. "I am going to go into my weather shack and begin the wind computations. I will sit down at my ivory table. You can stay out here and watch if you want to."

There was still no response.

Slowly I began taking steps toward the open side door of the weather shack. As soon as I did so, the young girl, without warning, suddenly retreated back onto the gravel road, and returned to join the adults. While I stood waiting, all of the Gray Aliens retreated in military fashion back up the gravel road to the parking area. One by one they loaded their craft, and departed. The lights of their craft could be seen following up the western road towards the distant pass. I was left to spend the remainder of the evening in splendid total solitude.

As they were leaving, I was feeling quite disappointed with myself. It had not been my intention to make any enemies among the Gray adults by frightening their children. Out here in this desolate stretch of desert, a man could use all the friends he could get—human or otherwise.

Returning to my weather shack, I quickly completed my wind computations. I decided, for my own good, I needed to rest the remainder of the evening. I adjusted my radio to a nice soft music station broadcasting from someplace in faraway Los Angeles. I proceeded to enjoy my second box lunch relaxing out in the park area. There was a lot I had to think about.

I waited until well past 5:00 a.m. The desert was bathed in dawn sunlight, when I shut down the weather shack and the other range buildings. As I did so, I was careful to open and inspect each of the supply sheds. I also inspected the many supplies stored within them. The supplies included copper wiring and other electrical parts, as well as roofing and fencing supplies. As expected, the shed next to my weather shack contained a small gasoline driven electrical generator.

Once I had the range area shut down and secured, I returned to my truck and began the long drive back to Desert Oasis. As expected, the Oasis was deserted when I arrived. The sun was well above the horizon, and the entire Oasis area was bathed in bright morning sunlight. I was running very late. Down on the main paved road, I could see three parked cars, waiting for me to clear the ranges. I didn't care. "Let them wait and eat cake." I laughed to myself. They had their problems—I had mine.

I left my truck parked in plain sight out on the gravel road, and walked in to the large building with the meeting room. I carefully returned my keys. Then, with a grim determination, I began a careful systematic inspection of the buildings and the entire Desert Oasis area. I began by carefully and cautiously inspecting everything behind the counter at the front of the meeting room. Aside from empty boxes and shelves, there was nothing there. However, I could easily see that this building, as well as the other buildings in the compound, were quite old. I guessed the wood shelving to have been constructed before 1920.

I continued with my inspection. I turned my attention to the remainder of the building. I approached the doorway on the right behind the counter. Calling out loudly, I cautiously went through the doorway into the short hallway beyond. As expected, the back of the building was deserted. The hallway led to an ordinary wooden door with a screen door, which opened out to the desert beyond. Just before the exit door, the hallway intersected with a double wide cross hallway. The cross hallway connected to two more rooms.

The room on the left was an ordinary sized room with a few ordinary adult sized chairs—obviously a waiting room for adults.

Down the hallway on the right was a larger sparsely furnished room which was obviously a little used day care center for young children.

However, in between the hallway intersection and the day care room sat a 1940s style manually operated telephone switch board, with a medium sized chair in front of it. I was stunned by my discovery. The phone switch board was sitting right where I had expected it to be. The switch board had obviously been installed many years after the building had first been constructed.

I was too cautious to actually touch the equipment, so I just stood at the hallway intersection and visually inspected it. It had phone jacks for approximately 30 phones. However, only 5 or 7 of the phone jacks were shiny from regular use. Looking around, up and down the hallways, it was now obvious to me that at one time, this building might have functioned as a school house, and the surrounding compound as its playgrounds.

I continued my inspection. The entire building was very clean and had almost no dust anywhere. I left the building by way of the back door. Out back I found a relatively modern and clean restroom. Some distance away sat an old and unused outhouse.

To the east and south of the building was a very large, lightly graveled area. The area was inside the Oasis perimeter fence. The area had been intentionally leveled, and cleared of all sagebrush and other obstacles. It was very well maintained. I judged it was the landing ground and parking area for alien craft. I noted that because of the various hills, valleys, ridges, and changes in elevation out here in the desert, alien craft using the area would not be visible from the main paved road—down where the guards still sat waiting for me to clear the ranges. This would be especially true at night.

I circled around out back and began inspecting the storage sheds—only a few of them were locked, and several sat empty. I noticed that none of the buildings at the Oasis had been intentionally winterized. All of the buildings were well maintained. Each of them would be a safe and secure haven during a rainy day or winter storm. However, the entire Oasis seemed to have been designed and built to function during warm summer nights only. I thought about that. The early warm fall evenings would last only another week, maybe two, at the most. After that, the evenings would become too cold for the Gray alien children to use the facilities at Desert Oasis. Everything would have to wait until spring.

However, my experience as an enlisted man had been that Generals by nature, both human and alien, tend to be impatient. Both the human generals and the Gray Generals must want the young alien girl to join the Joint Technology Transfer Team as soon as possible. The fictitious climate study was only scheduled to last one more week. From the point of view of the Generals, the young alien girl was very close to being able to communicate with me face to face—of course, no-one cared how close I was to anything. If my reasoning was correct it meant that this coming week, the generals on both sides would want to press the issue. They would reason that tonight I had spoken to the young girl—now it was her turn to respond.

I completed my inspection of the Desert Oasis compound, returned to my truck, and cleared the ranges. I returned to the main road, and finished closing the combination locked gate behind me. As I did so, the first two cars carrying two guards each, started their engines and pulled away. The driver of the third car had his front window rolled down. He and his partner pulled up alongside me, as I stood preparing to get back into my truck. He said nothing. I said nothing. The look in his eyes said it all. It was a look of tremendous respect. He spent a moment carefully studying my face to see if I was still all right. Then he too, drove off.

Hungry for breakfast, I got into my truck, and headed into the Death Valley Center chow hall.

In The Desert

. . . If I have told you earthly things,
and ye believe not,
how shall ye believe,
if I tell you of heavenly things?
. . . John 3 verse 12

Butterflies have always been associated with flowering plants. Mental pictures of a tranquil field of beautiful flowers sitting openly in the afternoon summer sun, usually include butterflies.

However, for perhaps the first 50 million years to 100 million years that flowering plants existed here on this earth, there were no butterflies. The oldest known fossil of a butterfly dates only from 40 million to 50 million years ago. By comparison, the oldest fossils of a flowering plant date from, perhaps 140 million years ago. The earliest ancestors to modern day horses appeared on this earth before butterflies appeared.

In ancient Egypt, the marshes of the Nile river delta contained many types of butterflies. Yet surprisingly, ancient Egyptian Hieroglyphs do not contain an icon based on a butterfly. If the ancient Egyptians developed their hieroglyphic characters by carefully observing the types of things living in the Nile river valley and river delta, it is surprising that butterflies were not included. One wonders who it was in ancient Egypt that decided not to include butterflies but to include the horned viper and vultures instead.

Butterflies might be a type of flying insect unique to this Earth. If the planet Earth were somewhat larger, the force of gravity on the Earth would be somewhat stronger. In that case it would not be physically possible for butterflies to exist on the Earth. Extraterrestrials, such as the Tall Whites and the Grey Aliens, who come to the Earth from planets larger than the Earth, must not have butterflies living on their home planets either. So it follows; the written inscriptions of those extra-terrestrials must not include any symbols based on the shape of a butterfly. This must be true, even though the writing of the Tall Whites does bear a marked resemblance to ancient Egyptian hieroglyphs. The Tall White inscriptions which I personally observed in their scout craft hangers in the mountains north of Indian Springs, Nevada, were pink lettering set against a white background. They did not include any butterfly shaped characters.

It was Sunday evening of the second week of my climate study—the beginning of my second work week. The weather was cool and clear, but otherwise fine. Evenings were coming earlier as the season progressed. I parked my truck as usual, opposite the sliding gate at the Desert Oasis. It sat out in plain sight on the gravel road while I walked in to the moonlit compound. I left my flashlight turned off as I walked in. There was no point to turning it on. The Gray Aliens seemed to prefer darkness. I wanted them to feel as relaxed as possible—since I figured they must be well armed—and they would be waiting.

I had a fun time down in the Las Vegas casinos over the weekend. I was also able to get a lot of rest, and do some reading in my library books. According to the book on geology, for several thousand years after the last ice age ended, some 12,000 years ago, my Valley of The Forgotten Lake Beds to the east, had remained partially filled with water. I noted back then, to extra-terrestrials coming from a larger desert planet, this entire area would have looked something like a Garden of Eden. This would be especially true if the aliens ate only plants. I wondered if all the plants growing down in the furrowed area were native to this earth. I decided to check when morning came.

In a normal, but cautious manner, I approached the front door of the meeting room. I opened it, and entered the moonlit room inside. I closed the door behind me. I stood for a minute or so by the door, surveying the moonlight and the meeting room. The young girl emerged from the darkness beyond the open doorway on the right. She took up a standing position behind the counter on the right and stood with a pleasant expression on her face, just looking at me.

I was feeling a great deal of fear at the time. The young girl was certainly not alone. Since I considered it to be her turn to initiate any conversation, I remained standing at the front doorway, waiting for her to speak.

After a minute or so, without saying anything, the young girl stepped back into the darkness beyond the doorway. I was a bit confused and wasn't sure what to do next. I was hoping I hadn't offended anyone.

To my surprise, a man emerged from the darkness beyond the doorway and walked quickly down behind the counter to the sign out board on the left. The man was not quite as tall as I was. He was wearing a white shirt, no tie, a short wig, and dark trousers. If I hadn't known better, I might have thought he was a middle age human man, slightly overweight, with a large nose. He was too light on his feet for the bulge around his waist to actually be the 30 pounds of fat his disguise made it out to be.

"Only a teenager is that light on his feet." I thought to myself. "And if no humans but me are allowed east of the main gate . . ."

Turning toward me, the man said politely, "Don't worry. When you come in here, don't turn on any lights. Just walk over here, pick up your envelope and your keys, sign for them, and leave. Be sure to close the front door behind you."

Then the man turned around, and returned back into the darkness beyond the doorway. As he spoke, I noted his voice sounded just like the voice of my friend down at Nellis.

I was now too nervous and taken off guard to wait for any further instructions. I quickly picked up my empty envelope and my keys, signed for them, and left the building. I double checked the front door to make sure it was closed, as I left.

It took the entire trip out to my Desert Range weather shack for me to settle down and unscramble my thoughts. I was wishing the distance was greater so I would have had more time to settle down. When I finally arrived at the parking lot in front of the generator shack, I was still so frazzled I didn't do a very good job of parking my truck. I left it parked away from the generator shack, in the far northwest corner of the graveled area. My truck sat directly next to the terminus of the narrow graveled western road.

It sat almost hidden in the darkness. I was stepping out into some stunted sagebrush when I got out of my truck. "Who cares," I shrugged. "It's a big desert. The extra walking will do me good."

The walk, starting the diesel, and carrying my box lunches down to my weather shack allowed me to finally settle down. After opening up my weather shack, and setting up shop, I noticed the telephone had not yet rung. Its silence seemed odd, since I had been expecting it to ring. It suggested to me that something had gone wrong, or was out of place. I decided to take my time preparing for the night's balloon runs, so I could spend as much time as possible near the telephone.

After filling three balloons, and eating my first box lunch, the phone still hadn't rung. I had another half hour to kill before I would be forced to carry the balloons out to the distant pole, and begin the first scheduled run.

In order to pass the time, I decided to study the equipment in my weather shack. I began by opening one of the boxes of radar reflectors. I, myself, did not use radar reflectors with my weather balloons, since I did not have any corresponding radar equipment to track them with. I always tracked the balloon visually using my theodolite.

On each balloon released on my night runs, I tied only a single light with an attached battery. The battery was a dry cell made especially for use by the military. The battery had to be soaked in clean water before its use. Each balloon, along with its light and battery could be used only once.

The zinc coated battery itself, reflected radar signals so there was never any reason for me to use an additional radar reflector. I had, however, been trained to use radar reflectors during weather training school. With a certain curiosity and nostalgia, I began inspecting the contents of the open box.

The radar reflector was very fragile, and it was not particularly large. It was constructed out of tin foil and thin I-beams. Some of the I-beams were aluminum, others were balsa wood. Each reflector could be used only once. The reflectors in my weather shack were quite old. They appeared to be army surplus, manufactured towards the end of World War II, or maybe afterwards, in the late 1940s.

The reflectors came disassembled. Because they were so fragile, they had to be assembled just before releasing the balloon to which they would be attached.

The reflectors had been initially designed for specialized research use by Ph.D. level physicists and engineers during the 1940s. Back then radar was still in its infancy. For example, the reflectors could be used to test the design and operation of new radar stations and equipment. They could also be used to measure the electrical properties of a storm cloud—or a cloud of radioactive particles—if a physicist chose to. The reflectors were not intended for everyday use with ordinary weather balloons, or to be used by ordinary radar technicians. Consequently, I was quite surprised to discover them among the supplies in my Desert Range weather shack. I did not have any use for them. To me, they were little more than shiny toys that children might play with.

Each reflector could be assembled in a number of different ways. Each reflector did not reflect the radar signal equally in all directions. The manner in which the reflector was assembled, determined the pattern of the reflected radar signal. The most common reflection pattern looked like the silhouette of a butterfly. However, many other reflection patterns were possible. Sometimes a large number of these different "butterfly" patterns were stamped on each of the I-beams so the technician could easily decide how he wished to assemble a particular reflector before releasing it.

To make it easy for Ph.D. level physicists to work with the radar reflectors in my desert weather shack, a set of Ph.D. level mathematical equations describing the reflective properties of the assembled reflectors, had also been stamped into the I-beams themselves. Some I-beams contained the equations, others contained the stamped "butterfly" patterns.

The equations were full of letters from the Greek alphabet, and also from the field of advanced vector calculus. One symbol I remember was the Greek letter rho. It referred to the cross-section of the assembled reflector—i.e. to the percentage of the incoming radar signal which would be reflected by a particular arrangement of the reflector parts. I noted that if a person was unfamiliar with the appearance of the equations from advanced vector calculus, a person might mistakenly think both the equations and the stamped "butterfly" patterns were alien writing. For example, they could easily go astray by trying to read the Greek mathematical symbols within the equations as though they were intended to form Greek words.

As I was returning the box to the shelf, the telephone rang. Stepping across my weather shack, back to my desk, I answered it, "Desert Range weather shack. Airman Hall speaking."

As before, the voice on the phone sounded like my friend from Nellis. "Good evening, Airman Hall," he began pleasantly. "We would like you to not park your truck in the parking lot. We would like you to only park your truck on the gravel road right in front of your weather shack."

I was quite taken aback. In surprise, I calmly responded, "Yes, if you want. But there is very little extra space out there. If I park out in front of my weather shack, I'm afraid my truck will be blocking the road for the entire evening. If I park the truck up in the gravel parking lot, it makes it easy for me to start up and shut down the diesels."

Once again the voice chuckled, "Don't worry about blocking the road. You're the only human out there.

We were also hoping you would not start up the diesel generators when you are on the ranges. I know you are very good at assembling the balloons in the dark, just using your flashlight. You will be spending most of the evening out in the desert anyway, so leaving the building lights off for the entire evening shouldn't be a problem."

Now I was really starting to feel pressured. Spending the entire evening out here in the moonlit darkness was not without its risks. Stammering somewhat, I responded, "But having the lights on, does make it much easier to perform the wind computations, and keep my weather shack clean."

There was a short pause, then the voice continued, "Well, there is a small gasoline generator in the supply shed next to you. It was put there for your use. You can start it if you ever have an emergency. But, never leave it running when you go out into the desert. Just before you leave in the morning, you can start it up for a few minutes if you have to. But please don't start it up until at least 5:00 in the morning."

"Yes," I responded.

The voice on the telephone continued politely, "Remember, Please move your truck, shut down the diesel generator, and turn off all the lights before going out into the desert this evening."

"Yes," I answered politely. "I will do so right away."

With that, the phone was hung up and once again, the line went dead.

I did as the voice had requested, but I wasn't very happy. I remember complaining a great deal to myself as I was shutting down the diesel, and moving my truck. Up the narrow gravel road to the west, the lights sat waiting at the pass.

I settled down and enjoyed the hike in the moonlight out to my theodolite. It was a clear cool night. I tethered my balloons to the same sagebrush plant down to the east in The Valley of The Forgotten Lake Beds. The balloon runs came off easily enough and I put my rock bench to good use. I spent some time remembering the fun I had over the weekend, in Las Vegas—and remembering how homesick I was for Madison, Wisconsin. I kept my flashlight off for the entire time. I wanted to conserve my batteries, and keep my night vision. After completing the 2:00 a.m. run, I kept hearing sounds of something quietly moving around out in the sagebrush. The quiet sounds were coming from several different places, most of them north of me. I guessed—or wished—the sounds were coming from range cattle—even though that explanation was clearly impossible.

I was sitting on my rock bench facing west when I became alarmed because I could hear someone walking heavily, slowly coming up the hill from the east—meaning I was being approached from behind. I stood up, turned around, and called out into the moonlit darkness. After a few minutes, I could hear the sounds slowly retreating back down hill to the east.

Soon it was time for my second scheduled balloon release. To do so, I first had to get control of my nerves, recite my favorite prayers, and carefully walk down the hill to the east to retrieve the tethered balloons. Doing so in the moonlit desert darkness, was not a task for the faint hearted. I brought both balloons with their attached batteries with me. There wasn't a suitable sagebrush plant close by to tether them to. So, without thinking I carefully tethered both of them to the wooden pole. I had plenty of extra string. However, the balloons were fragile, so I had to be very careful when I did so. For this reason, I used extra string, and tied the balloons with their batteries, as high up on the pole as I could.

I always had several paper cups with me. As usual, I filled one with water and inserted the dry battery into the water for a couple of minutes to activate it. Once the attached light was shining brightly, I untethered the second balloon from the pole and released it. The entire process seemed pretty ordinary at the time.

The second release went smoothly. The third release at 4:00a.m. also went well. I untethered the third balloon from the pole, and released it along with its battery and light, on schedule.

The quiet sounds out in the night-time desert had now fallen silent. I closed down the theodolite and walked back to the weather shack. It would have been a pleasant enough walk. However, I was quite nervous at the time since I was expecting to have company once I arrived—and I would have to meet them in the dark with all the lights off.

When I reached the eastern side of the drainage ditch, I stopped. By now the moon had set. For my own safety, I called several times into the darkness across the road, "Is anyone there?" There was no answer. Everywhere, the desert remained silent.

Carefully I crossed the drainage ditch and took up a defensive position next to my truck. Once again I called out into the darkness, "Is anyone there?" Still there was no response. As before, the desert was silent.

I decided I was probably alone. I opened up my weather shack, both the front and side doors. I placed my balloon tracking forms on the ivory table. The lights and my radio were all turned off. The generator remained shut down.

Taking my second box lunch, I found a comfortable position sitting on one of the benches in the park area, and began enjoying the lunch. Like all of the box lunches, it contained a nice sandwich, a container with salad or coleslaw, some sealed packets of dressing, mustard, a small candy bar or a container with dessert, a container of milk, and plastic utensils. I was always careful to eat everything. I never threw food away—even chow hall food. I had grown up poor and probably wasn't as fussy as some others. In addition, I always took one or two vitamin pills in the morning. I spent so much of my time alone out in the desert, I felt I needed to do everything possible to keep myself well-fed, physically safe, and healthy. In any event, the food in the box lunches always tasted good, and I always enjoyed eating them—so why not?

I was sitting in starlit darkness, facing my truck, which sat parked out on the gravel road. As I sat there, I began hearing sounds off to my left. They were coming from something moving through the sagebrush behind my weather shack. For my own safety, I did not respond to the sounds. I continued slowly eating my sandwich. After a few minutes, the young girl stepped out from the shadows beyond the southwestern corner of my weather shack, and stood watching me.

I decided to try again to communicate with her. Without otherwise reacting to her presence, once again I began speaking to her. "Good evening." I said slowly. "Who are you?" She did not answer.

"Where do you and your parents come from?" I asked. There was no response.

"Do you and your parents live out here in this desert?" I asked.

Still there was no response. The young girl stepped back behind the weather shack and disappeared into the darkness. For my own safety, I remained sitting on the bench, until I had finished my second box lunch. After awhile, off to the west, I could see the lights moving up hill towards the distant pass on the narrow western gravel road.

I decided I must now be truly alone, and it was well past 5:00a.m. I unlocked the supply shed, and started the small gasoline engine. I felt a certain humiliation as I did so. The gasoline engine was so much smaller and simpler to start than the large diesels in the shed down the road, that I much enjoyed starting up. I said my morning prayers. I decided being humbled was good for my soul. I remember reciting to myself, "Remember man; thou art dust, and unto dust thou shall return. When that day comes, you will be the dust that is outside, blowing in the wind."

Once back in my weather shack, I turned on the electricity and the lights. I relaxed, calmed down and took my time. I listened to my radio and completed my wind calculations. The desert was actually a quiet restful place of enormous starlit nighttime beauty—when a person was alone. The moments when I was certain I was alone, when I could relax and enjoy the stars above and the starlit nighttime desert—to me—were so precious—and so few.

I waited, and enjoyed myself until the disk of the sun had just started to rise above the eastern horizon. Then I closed down my weather shack, shut down the small gasoline generator, and headed back to Desert Oasis.

The Oasis was deserted as I had expected. After returning the keys to their proper place, I decided to visually inspect the plants in the furrowed area.

The furrowed area extended all the way up the hill to the western fence of the Desert Oasis. Another fence separated the furrowed area from the gravel road and its southern drainage ditch. Still a third fence separated the furrowed area from the main paved road at the bottom of the hill. There weren't any gates or breaks in the fences—although curiously the southern boundary of the furrowed area was open to the desert beyond. It was not fenced. Consequently, I was not able to actually walk out into the furrowed area. I had to content myself with looking across the fences, both at the Desert Oasis, and by the ditch along the road. Further downhill there was a culvert under the fence so water in the drainage ditch could feed into the simple set of water channels which were formed by the furrows.

I couldn't see much of anything across the fence at Desert Oasis. So I stopped my truck on the gravel road opposite the culvert, and got out to take a look. It didn't bother me that I was keeping the guards in the three cars parked down on the main road waiting.

Looking across the fence near the culvert, there wasn't much to see this time of year, even though the desert was just completing its natural "second spring". There were still a few scattered plants growing in the furrows. I was never much of a botanist. However, all of the plants appeared to be ordinary terrestrial desert plants. Many of them were flowering plants with seeds. I supposed the seeds were edible. Not surprisingly, a few of the plants were in bloom, since many types of desert plants naturally bloom at night in the fall.

Further downhill it appeared wheat or oats had been raised during the previous summer. I decided my suspicions must be correct. Someone must be using the furrows as a garden area.

One very small patch stood out from the others. It was growing downhill directly across the fence which I was looking over. That area was especially well watered by the flow from the culvert and the water channel in the furrow. Those plants too, appeared to be perfectly ordinary desert plants. However, one of them was strikingly beautiful. It appeared to be remarkably similar to a drawing of a plant I had seen in a book on botany, in a section relating to desert regions. Several months had passed since I had looked through the book. However, the plant I remembered seeing in the book was native to the deserts and mountains of northwestern Africa. The plant was said to be quite rare, even in the mountains and deserts of northwest Africa.

A plant with such large beautiful flowers, on a warm day in the spring, summer or early fall, growing out in the open on the side of a large desert hill, would naturally attract all types of "Painted Lady" butterflies. "Painted Lady" butterflies are migratory, and come in many different types, sizes, markings, and colors. Some types even change their colors as they age, as the heat of the desert afternoon increases, and as the summer progresses. Such butterflies can be found all over the inhabitable parts of the Earth—including the deserts of the American Southwest—and Australia

I made a mental note and decided to check further on the beautiful plant. As I was getting back into my truck, I let my mind wander. Families with children frequently keep gardens for their enjoyment and for that of their children. Frequently they let their children chose seeds from special plants, from unusual plants—or from beautiful plants living very far away. Typically, the children then plant the seeds in a special section of their home garden, just for the fun of it. The plant with the beautiful flowers was a natural choice to include in that special section of the garden. Its large beautiful flowers naturally attract beautiful Painted Lady butterflies—making such a summertime garden an enchanting place for a young girl. It seemed natural that young alien girls would appreciate flowering butterfly filled gardens just as young human girls do.

If I was right then, this wasn't just an ordinary garden area—it was a family garden area next to an old school house. If I was right, this garden area must be maintained by one or more families whose members were very intelligent, and very widely traveled—for finding and growing the plant with the beautiful flowers in this harsh desert climate must have been quite a challenge.

If I was right, it would mean some of the classes taught to the children at the school house would be advanced farming and agricultural techniques. I made a mental note to check the storage sheds back at the Desert Oasis, to see if they were being used to store sacks of seeds for use in the garden area. I decided to start Friday morning, by checking the storage shed used to store my weather supplies.

I wondered if some of the joint technology transfer programs involving the USAF and the Gray Aliens were designed to develop better desert farming methods for use here on Earth, and also on similar nearby earth-like planets elsewhere in the galaxy.

I wondered. There was a logic to it. I did after all, grow up, and work extensively on dairy farms in Wisconsin. I already had several years of experience growing and raising every plant on the farm from corn to dandelions and Canadian thistle.

"Yes. It makes perfect sense." I said to myself. "The Tall Whites have the best technology. So the USAF sets up its high tech Joint Technology Transfer programs with the Tall Whites.

On the other hand, the Tall Whites have little interest in agriculture and farming techniques here on Earth, because they consider the Earth to be a cold desolate wilderness. Such projects are not worth their time.

In addition, The Tall Whites did not appear to be willing to share the design of the propulsion systems used on their Deep Space craft, or their scout craft.

The Gray Aliens have the greatest experience with agriculture and farming techniques both here on the Earth and on nearby earth-like planets. Every topic in Agriculture and Botany is of great natural interest to the plant eating Gray Aliens. So the USAF would naturally set up the Joint Technology Transfer programs which pertain to agriculture, farming, and food production with the Grey Aliens.

In addition, the large Grey craft were obviously capable of making the Deep Space crossing. The Grey Craft were designed using the same physically real force fields which The Tall Whites used in design and construction of the Tall White Craft. The Grey Aliens might well have used those same force fields, and pieces of that same technology when they were designing and constructing their farm equipment.

Yes, as I thought about it—It all made perfect sense. Now I understood exactly what the Generals meant when they said I was performing a “climate study”.

I started up my truck, and headed in for breakfast.

Superstition

"... And king Herod heard [of him];
(for his name was spread abroad:)
and he said,
That John the Baptist was risen from the dead,
and therefore mighty works
do shew forth themselves in him. ..."
... Mark 6:14

Superstition is a belief that is not based on reason or knowledge. Gambling in the casinos of Las Vegas, Nevada, in the mid 1960s, would probably—and very quickly—have made any man superstitious. Teaching every gambler in Las Vegas how to be superstitious was one of Las Vegas' harmless—and lesser known—vices. For one thing, a gambler could be superstitious in a completely silent manner. For another, being superstitious made playing the games and the slot machines in every casino in Las Vegas more fun.

Of course one of the problems with superstitions is that they are hard to leave behind once a person has left the city of Las Vegas.

For example, during late 1965, before I would play any slot machine in any casino in Las Vegas, I would first lay both my hands on the machine and get the feel of the machine. If it didn't "feel right", I wouldn't play it. One night in late 1965, I walked into a casino in North Las Vegas and got $2.00 worth of dimes from the change girl. I proceeded to a row of dime slot machines, and laid my hands on two or three of them in turn to decide which one it felt like I should play. Oh, I knew I was being silly and superstitious, but I was having fun doing it, so what the devil? I laughed. As I did so, I carefully avoided the machine on the end of the row. After looking at it from a short distance, I laughed that it didn't feel "up to my high standards".

I chose one of the other machines. I had just started playing when a nice little old lady walked up to me, and in a very pleasant and unusually forceful manner asked if she could play my machine. She said it felt to her is if I should be playing the machine on the end.

Laughing, I refused. I said I trusted my feelings more than I trusted hers.

Laughing back, she exclaimed, "All right then. Just remember that I'm your friend. I'll just have to show you what you're missing." She proceeded to play 5 dimes in turn in the slot machine on the end of the row, and won two $10 dollar jackpots.

Once again, she turned to me and pleasantly and forcefully stated, "I'm sick of playing this machine. You play it for a while. I want to play with yours."

"Are you nuts?" I politely exclaimed. "I just saw you win back to back jackpots on that machine. It's probably not going to pay anything for the next three months."

"All right." She responded, "But remember, I'm your friend. I gave you your chance."

Using just five more dimes, she proceeded to win three more $10 dollar jackpots off the same machine on the end of the row. After paying her for her fifth jackpot, two slot machine technicians came out, declared the machine to be broken, and removed the machine from the casino floor.

I thought my pain and agony was over. However, I was quite young—and quite wrong. While the little old lady stood and watched me, the machine I was playing took all of my dimes. I had to surrender the machine to her while I went to get change for another dollar. From the change booth, I watched as the little old lady proceeded to begin playing "my" machine. She proceeded to win two more $10 dollar jackpots.

As I left the casino, I was laughing at myself, and laughing at how blind I'd been, and laughing at my own silly superstitions. I was catching on to the fact, that in late 1965, in the city of Las Vegas, Nevada, employees of secret government agencies came in all shapes and sizes. I never knew when a group of them might unexpectedly arrange to come play with me in some out of the way Las Vegas Casino, just to see if I was still OK.

. . . .

It was Monday evening of the second week of my climate study. I was running almost an hour late. I was very tired and unaccountably, had overslept in my barracks down at Indian Springs.

It was a very cool evening, and the skies were darkening rapidly. A thin fog already enveloped the mountains and filled the valleys of the entire Desert Oasis area by the time I arrived at the main gate with the combination lock. I fumbled with the lock and I seemed to be having trouble remembering the combination, but eventually got it open.

Finally I got my truck parked on the gravel road next to the sliding gate which protected the entrance to the Desert

Oasis compound. I sat in my truck praying for a few minutes, before going to get the keys. I really didn't want to leave the safety of the truck. I wasn't feeling well, and I was certain that tonight the Grey Aliens would be waiting for me—out there in the darkness where they could see me and I couldn't see them. As always, the adults must certainly have come well armed—and able to close on me.

I asked God for help. I decided that on these last four nights of my scheduled climate study assignment, things would go easier for me if I could find a better technique for communicating with the young girl—or, more properly, for letting her communicate with me. That was, after all, what the Grey Alien Generals and the Blue Uniformed USAF Generals seemed to want. To accomplish that goal, I decided I needed to identify more topics to discuss with her, and things to do which she might find interesting.

It did not seem possible to talk with the young girl about women's fashions and children's colorful play clothes, the way I did with the Tall White women I encountered at Indian Springs. The clothes I had seen the young girl wear were all the same color—namely gray.

Exotic flowering plants and Painted Lady butterflies were a different topic. I decided, the next time I saw the young girl, to ask if the beautiful flowering plant growing out in the furrows, was hers—and if it attracted Painted Lady butterflies.

I collected my courage, and got out of my truck. Carefully I opened the sliding gate, and entered the darkened and thinly fog veiled compound of the Desert Oasis. For my own safety, I decided to sing songs as I walked. I wanted everyone out in the darkness to know I was coming—and that I was happy. I sang a song about flowers since my intention was to make it easy for the young girl to communicate with me.

Reaching the door, I paused to change songs. Then I carefully opened the door and entered the darkened room. I paused again as I sang another verse in my flower song. I was very ill at ease and struggling to control my fears, so I left the door open behind me.

Almost immediately, the young girl stepped out from the darkened doorway on the right, behind the counter. Except for her gray clothing, most of her features were hidden by the darkness. However, her sudden appearance took me off guard, because in the darkness, she appeared to be almost completely human. Judging by her motions, she seemed happy, although very defensive, as she carefully stepped to the space behind the counter—facing me all of the time as she did so. She stopped at last almost opposite the sign in sheet, which she obviously knew I was going to have to use after I picked up my keys. She did not say anything as she did so.

"So far. So good." I thought, as I struggled to calm myself. I noted she did not seem to know what I was thinking, the way a young Tall White girl in the same situation would have. "Well, I did not expect their technology to be as good as that of the Tall Whites." I thought to myself.

For my own safety, I did not want to break the current mood. The young girl was obviously not alone—or unprotected. I decided to just keep singing my flower song, go on about my business, and let her be the first to speak. So, singing and keeping a steady gaze on the young girl as I did so, I carefully approached the counter. I picked up my empty envelope, and my keys. While the young girl stood watching me, I carefully signed the sheet on the clipboard.

Still singing, I backed away from the counter, turned slowly, and carefully left the building—closing the door behind me. As I walked—and sang—my way back to my truck parked up on the gravel road, inside myself I felt terrible. I felt I had failed because I did not have the courage to just stand at the counter, singing softly, waiting for her to speak.

The fog was still thin, although it was slowly getting thicker when I arrived at my Desert Range weather station. I was still tired, and not feeling very well. I left the truck parked on the gravel road out front and unlocked the door. I was unloading my box lunches from the truck when, as expected, the phone rang.

I was quite worried as I picked up the telephone. I was afraid the voice on the other end would be angry with me because of my failures back at the Desert Oasis. Alone, out here in the desert, I hardly needed to make any enemies. "Desert Range weather shack," I answered politely. "Airman Hall speaking."

The voice on the other end, still mimicking my friend from down at far-away Nellis, sounded quite happy, and surprisingly respectful as he spoke. "Airman Hall. The Generals are as happy as I have ever seen them. Your work is so impressive. None of them expected you to accomplish so much, or for you to survive alone out in the desert for so long."

I was surprised by his words, and did not respond.

He continued, "We are worried about your safety because your theodolite is set up so close to the pole out in the desert to the east of your weather shack. We would like you to move your theodolite and disassemble the rock bench which you use to sit on. We would like you to stay at least 1000 feet away from the pole. We would like you to disassemble your rock bench and put those particular rocks back the way you found them, if you can."

Surprised and off balance, I stammered a response, "Yes. However, the pole is my best reference point so I don't get lost out in the desert on a foggy night like this. The pole is the best place for me to tie my balloons before I release them. I feel much safer being close to the pole, especially when I am close enough to touch it. I use the rocks to sit on. They're just ordinary rocks. They're nothing special."

The voice on the phone seemed to find my response to be thought provoking. After a short pause, he continued, "That's quite interesting. However, it really isn't safe for you to be tying your balloons to the pole with their batteries attached, or to be touching the pole, or to be anywhere close to it. It is also not safe for you to be sitting on those particular rocks.

We want very much for you to move your theodolite, equipment, and balloons at least 1000 feet away from the pole. There are nice places southeast of the pole where there are breaks in the sagebrush. You can build a new rock bench when you are over there. You can use any rocks over there that you want. You can go anywhere you want. You can go as far as you want. However, you need to move your equipment far away from the pole, and disassemble your rock bench, as quickly as you can. Whatever you do, never touch the pole, or sit on those particular rocks. Put the rocks back the way you found them if you can remember how they were arranged."

"Yes, I understand. I am happy to do it. I only went out to the pole because a few days ago I thought that was what you wanted me to do." I argued politely.

"You are so much braver than anyone, including the generals ever expected. They thought you would be too afraid to walk all the way to the pole." He explained. "No one else before you has ever been willing to even sign in and pick up their orders. They were all too afraid to even open the gate and enter the compound. The few who made it that far just turned their trucks around in fear, and returned back to the main gate and back to the highway."

There was obviously no reason to argue any further, so I responded politely, "Yes, I understand. I'll go immediately and move my equipment." With that the voice on the other end hung up the phone, and the line went dead.

I thought over the words he had spoken. It was unusual for any extra-terrestrial to repeat themselves. I decided it must be extremely important for me to immediately move my theodolite and to disassemble my rock bench—and to never touch the pole.

I put on my work gloves, gathered up my canteen belt, water, and shovel from the back of the weather shack. I still hadn't eaten my first box lunch, so I brought it with me.

I crossed the gravel road in front of my parked truck, crossed the drainage ditch, and set out into the night-time, on the well worn path into the desert to the east.

First I located an acceptable open space in the sagebrush probably a half mile southeast of the pole. I was still in the pass which connected to my Valley of the Forgotten Dry Lake Beds located off to the east. I was much closer to the northern extension of the desert covered mountains which jutted out from the Desert Range's southern boundary.

I was careful to trample down lots of sagebrush, and mark a wide path to the new location using upright sticks set in the ground. I needed to be able to always find both my new location, and my way back to the weather shack, no matter how foggy or rainy the nights might become. I had also taken to carrying a box of kitchen matches, several books of cigarette matches, a cigarette lighter, and a folding pen knife, with me so I could always start a fire for both heat and light if I ever needed to when I was alone out in the desert.

It took me several trips to move my theodolite, the stand, the equipment box, and various other items, from the old location to the new location. That was the easy part. Next came disassembling the bench. The rock bench was sitting just a few feet from the pole. So I felt the need to hurry as I was disassembling it.

The work was brutal. The rocks were very heavy. The rocks I had chosen were in three different sizes. I used my shovel as a crowbar to help me. The rocks had originally been sitting on top of a relatively small and apparently insignificant rock outcropping. The outcropping connected to the northern extension of the desert mountain which jutted out from the Desert Range's southern boundary.

One of the rocks had originally been sitting uphill from my rock bench. Returning the large rock to its original uphill position sitting on the rock out-cropping, was just barely possible. I did the best I could. When I was finished, the rocks were roughly in their original arrangement. However there were some small differences. I was so tired when I finished, I was forced to declare the work completed—such as it was—and head out to the new, safer location.

I could understand how the wooden pole could be concealing navigational equipment—transmitting beacons and the like out into the open air and out into space. The rocks, however, were a mystery to me. Except for their somewhat unusual weight, they appeared to be perfectly ordinary rocks. In the darkness, I could not make out any markings or petroglyphs on them. They were not particularly large as desert rocks go. In the darkness, they did not appear to have been artificially altered, or manufactured. Likewise, they did not appear to be radioactive. Of course, the Grey Aliens, may have had eye sight, similar to the Tall Whites, at least as good as that of a cat; the rocks could easily have contained markings which only the Aliens were capable of seeing.

I thought for a while. I wondered suspiciously if the rocks marked some sort of tribal boundary between two or more different groups of Grey Aliens.

The Grey adult aliens certainly were not territorial here on the surface of the Earth. The adults could not even breathe our air without a breathing device. They had no reason to become emotionally attached to the land itself, and therefore to form tribal boundaries. However, The Grey Alien teenagers might be another matter. They were growing up here.

Human teenagers are typically territorial and emotional regarding the land where they grow up. For example, it is not uncommon for them to refer to such places as “the old stomping grounds”.

Human teenagers growing up together on such lands, naturally form into groups and tribes, to which they always identify using special names. For example, when I was a teenager, I was part of the Cambridge High School Class of 1962. It was as well defined as any human tribe. It had well defined tribal boundaries. The high school districts of Cambridge, Deerfield, Fort Atkinson, and Jefferson, Wisconsin were all very well marked.

I, and the other members of my tribe, supported and defended our Cambridge honor, pride, and sports teams from other such tribes. We defended our proms, dances,—and yes, our “stomping grounds”. I wondered suspiciously if The young Grey teen-age Aliens naturally formed the same types of tribes, and proudly defended their special places from similar tribes. If so, it would mean the reason humans had not been allowed into the Valley of The Forgotten Lake Beds for many years, might have nothing to do with how Adult Greys viewed adult humans. I wondered suspiciously if instead the reason involved the manner in which the teen-age Greys naturally formed tribes, and the manner in which those tribes reacted to humans entering their tribal territories.

I thought about the rocks some more. If I was wrong—if the rocks did not mark a type of tribal boundary, perhaps the rocks might be part of an underground communication or navigation system. Of course, I suspiciously wondered, the rocks could be serving both purposes.

The pole, all by itself, could certainly conceal any above ground communication system—including any necessary supporting power sources. I wondered if there was an underground communication system. The voice on the phone wanted the rocks returned to their positions sitting on the out-cropping leading to the jutted-out mountain. I wondered if the Grey aliens had an underground scout craft base, formed by tunneling into the jutted out mountain. However, there were no tunnel entrances on this side of the mountain. If any of my suspicions were correct, then tunnel entrances would have to be found on the other side of the jutted out mountain. Such entrances would overlook the Valley of the Forgotten Dry Lake Beds.

It might have seemed silly to others, but, my conclusion made perfect sense to me. If the Grey Aliens had come to earth several thousand years ago, they would have arrived at a time when the dry lake beds were still filled with fresh water. The entire valley would have looked like a giant Garden of Eden to them. At that time, the other side of the jutted out mountain would have been a perfect choice for a scout craft base. Over the thousands of years which have passed since then, many Grey teen-age aliens would have grown up here in these desolate valleys—making the desert pass a natural location for a teen-Age tribal boundary. I wondered if one of the Joint Projects under consideration was to turn portions of the Valley of The Forgotten Dry Lake Beds back into agricultural food producing regions. Such a joint project, and the technological knowledge derived from it, would benefit both humans the world over, as well as the Grey Aliens. Yet, because of the desert's geography, such a project would have to cross a number of tribal boundaries. My "climate study" was starting to make sense.

Of course, the craft which I saw leaving the Desert Range on many mornings, did not head towards the jutted out mountain. Instead, those craft very carefully followed the narrow gravel road over the desert pass to the west. So their base had to be dug into some mountain many miles west of the Desert Ranges. Such a base, presumably overlooked another dry lake bed—possibly being protected by a tribe of teen-age Grey Aliens of its own.

After thinking about it, I decided I had to know if my logic was actually making sense. I had to know the truth. I had to know if I was just being superstitious, or if there really were tunnel entrances dug into the other side of the jutted out mountain.

I was already too tired, and it was too late tonight to go exploring. I would have to wait for a clear night with better weather before I could risk taking a long hike into the valley to the east.

I quickly built a new rock bench at my new theodolite location. I ate my box lunch, and returned to my weather shack for the balloons. I ignored the midnight run which I had missed, and proceeded with the two remaining runs, and the remainder of my nightly duties. After a while, the weather cleared, the fog blew away, and the beauty of the moonlit night-time desert returned.

When I got back to my weather shack in the morning, the entire Desert Range area was obviously deserted. I had thought a lot on the walk. Armed with my new insights, I decided to go looking for them. I decided I could better handle the fears and emotions of meeting the Grays face-to-face out here in moonlight in the open desert, over being forced to meet them face-to-face in darkness and the confines of the meeting room back at Desert Oasis.

Consequently, I carefully inspected all of the buildings, including the graveled parking lot. I was certainly alone. I had no idea why.

As I sat on one of the benches in the park like area, eating my second box lunch, I carefully considered whether or not it would be possible for me to set up my own flower garden somewhere in the Desert Range area. Such a garden would make it easier for the young girl to practice communicating with me. That was what the Generals seemed to want. It wouldn't have to be large. For a water source, I could use the run-off from the drainage ditches.

After thinking about it for a while, I discarded the idea. For one thing, there wasn't enough time. The climate study was scheduled to end in just three more nights, and it was already very late in the growing season. For another, the water source was too undependable.

Of course, I thought to myself, I don't actually need a separate flower garden area. The surrounding desert already has so many beautiful flowering plants, why don't I just adopt a section of the desert located on the edge of the park-like area, check out a book on desert plants, and enjoy being a part-time horticulturist for awhile. As I sat there, enjoying the beauty of the moonlit desert which surrounded me, it didn't seem like an idea that anyone but me would ever care about.

Suspicion

It was Tuesday evening of the second week of my climate study. The weather was clear. However, the nights were steadily becoming much cooler. As I slowed my truck to a stop out in front of my Desert Range weather shack, I could see it was going to be another beautiful night in the desert. I was arriving somewhat ahead of schedule. So far, it had been a near perfect night. For one thing, the Desert Oasis was deserted when I arrived to pick up my empty orders envelope and the keys. Naturally, I hurried through the process. I saw no reason to hang around the compound any longer than necessary.

I opened up my weather shack and enjoyed my first box lunch in the park-like area. I collected the paper trash, and filled two balloons only. Then I made ready to head out to my new theodolite location.

Except for me, the Desert Range area was obviously deserted. The phone still hadn't rung—not that I cared—or wondered why. Every time they had phoned in the past, it had been one pain in the neck after another. Tonight I was quite happy being left alone.

I decided this would be a perfect night to make a long hike into the Valley of The Forgotten Dry Lake Beds. I decided to skip the scheduled midnight balloon release, and make the 2:00a.m. release late. I could then make the 4:00a.m. release on time, and call it a night. That would give me time to hike at least six miles into the valley to the east, and take a good look around.

Singing as I walked, I set out for my new theodolite location. Once there, I secured my two balloons to a large sagebrush. Carefully giving the wood pole wide berth, I headed east into the Valley Of The Forgotten Dry Lake Beds. It was an exhilarating hike. There wasn't an actual trail or path to follow. However, once I was far enough into the valley, the sagebrush and the other desert plants, though of normal size, were spread very thinly across the desert. Thus, with clear starlit skies, I made good time and I could easily keep my bearings. Soon I was more than five miles into the valley.

I stopped a few times along the way and inspected the sagebrush and other desert plants—especially those that might produce flowers. I wondered if all of the plants were native to this Earth, and if any of them were edible.

I didn't discover much of anything. All the plants appeared to be perfectly ordinary plants found in the deserts of the American Southwest. I wasn't good enough as a part time botanist—or a Native American—to know if any of them had edible parts. I did, however, have lots of fun amusing myself. I imagined I was both a part time botanist—and a Native American—I imagined that I would know an edible plant if I ever saw one growing in the wild. Desert hikes could be a great deal of fun—if a person happened to be making then alone.

My chosen path led downhill and arced first to the southeast and then to the south. I easily kept the jutted out mountain range on my right, and the vast dry lake beds in the distance on my left. In the far distance, on the horizon, several other large valleys connected to this valley, and to surrounding mountains. The valley and surrounding mountains were stunningly beautiful. If a small group of humans not familiar with the deserts of the southwest, had been blindfolded and brought out to where I was; released, provided with food, water, clothing, and shelter, and told to live there for a while, they might never figure out they were still on this earth.

As I hiked, I carefully inspected the eastern slopes of the jutted out mountain range—especially high up above the old water line. Because of the dark overhangs and purple mountain shadows, it was soon obvious that even if tunnel entrances existed, I would not be able to see them under these night-time lighting conditions.

One thing I could be certain of, though, was that these mountains did not contain any old mine entrances. Old mine entrances are usually quite obvious because back in the days of the old west, miners usually just dumped the waste rock in a pile outside the mine entrance. These piles of waste are usually easy to spot, even in moonlight. The fact that the miners of the old west had not mined these mountains was itself a suspicious sign.

The lighting at night in the valley wasn't very good. However, I also did not see any large furrowed areas, buildings or water towers. Whatever was in the valley or dug into the jutted out mountain range was very well hidden.

After hiking in some five or six miles, I decided to stop and turn around. I had seen all I was going to be able to see.

The place on the trail where I chose to stop, was a wide open area on the side of the jutted out mountain range, well below the old water line. At my stopping point, the alluvial fan was composed of the usual desert gravel, and was sloping downhill to the south and the southeast. The beauty of the night-time moonlit desert, and the stars overhead in the night-time sky was beyond description. I remember wishing I were an artist, good enough to have painted the captivating scene overhead, and in front of me.

I had been standing still, enjoying the view, for only a few minutes when I heard something out in the sagebrush off to my right. I turned my head, and spent a minute or so, studying the night-time sagebrush and the moonlit jutted out mountain. I couldn't see or hear anything, so I turned my head back to the left to study the evening sky one last time. To my surprise, it seemed as if the stars had moved when I wasn't watching them. Alone, as I was, in the night, the apparent sudden movement of the stars, made me feel quite nervous. Based on the new position of the stars, it seemed as if roughly a half hour had passed.

I decided it was time for me to return to my new theodolite location. I had just taken a few steps back up the trail when I realized that someone else felt the same way. Off on my left, between me and the jutted out mountain range, I heard someone out in the sagebrush obviously paralleling me. Remembering that no other human except me, was allowed in this valley, didn't alleviate my nerves any. Because of the Grey shadows and my mounting level of fear, I hurried to return along the path I had hiked in on. I couldn't make out much of anything when I looked to my left, or behind me on the trail. Soon I could hear three more large Grey shadows paralleling me out in the sagebrush. There were two on each side of me. On each side of me, one was even with me, and the other trailed slightly behind me. They obviously intended to protect something in the jutted out mountain range, as they patiently herded me back in the direction from which I had come.

I decided this was no time to let fear get the best of me—or to upset the apple cart by looking directly at them. I considered their presence to be proof that a Grey Alien scout craft hanger must be somewhere fairly close, dug into the eastern slopes of the jutted out mountain range. I gladly noted they did not show any desire to close on me, even when I paused to re-inspect my adopted flowering plants which were located on the steady upgrades, which I had to traverse as I climbed my way back out of the valley. The large Grey shadows appeared content to just parallel me.

The well lit weather balloons, which I had been releasing nightly from the mountain pass, typically drifted towards the south and southeast. I noted that any small child watching the sky from a tunnel entrance, playground, or skylight located on the eastern slopes of the jutted out mountain range, would have a perfect, enchanting view of the balloons and their attached lights, as each one in turn drifted, and rose slowly into the night-time sky.

Yes, my little corner of the world was now starting to make perfect sense. To get out of the mess I found myself in, all I had to do was hurry back to my waiting theodolite stand, and release another lighted balloon. I began carefully singing to comfort me as I hiked. Occasionally I would stop to rest—studying the plants and flowers along the way.

The Grey figures in the shadows, didn't break off the pursuit and stop paralleling me until almost 4:45a.m., when

I finally reached the drainage ditch along the eastern side of the gravel road in front of my weather shack. I stopped for a while at my new theodolite location to release and track the two balloons, on my way back. I was quite nervous and fearful at the time. However, no one had actually gotten in my way on the way back, so I felt it necessary for me to release the balloons the way they wanted. I was quite happy to see each balloon in turn, drift southeast over the eastern slopes of the jutted out mountain range after it was released. I hoped every young child watching, enjoyed the enchanting night-time scene the two balloons, in turn, created.

Embers

“ . . . Out of whose womb came the ice?
and the hoary frost of heaven,
who hath gendered it? . . .”
. . . Job 38:29

An Ember is a hot glowing coal that remains in a fire pit or a fireplace, after the fire has finished burning openly. Although embers are quite hot, they do not burn openly. Some embers are capable of glowing for hours.

It is hard to imagine an outdoor romantic evening without also imagining embers glowing in an outdoor fire pit, after the fire has subsided. The fire pit can be dug anywhere—on the beach, in the mountainous highlands, or outside the entrance to a well protected cave. The fascination with glowing embers is simply part and parcel of being a romantic, emotional human.

The ice age hunters of the American Southwest must have been romantic, emotional humans. Archaeologists have found more of their ancient fire pits and the remains of the last embers to glow in them, than they have found of the ancient humans themselves.

Since no animal other than man, builds fires, the discovery of an ancient fire pit and its last embers is always considered to be proof that some ancient human was present, sitting and watching the fire until the last of the embers finally burned out. Archaeologists photograph the fire pit and its last embers. They record, catalog and classify everything about it which they can see and touch.

However, it never seems possible to see or to recapture the romance and the emotions and the pride in the fire and the fascination with its embers that ancient humans must have felt when they last sat around their ancient fire pit—watching silently until the last of the glowing embers had finally burned out. For while we today, in the American Southwest, can study the ancient past and the ancient ice age hunters who lived there, ancient ice age hunters themselves, were never able to know what the future held. For the ancient ice age hunters of the American Southwest of 15,000 years ago, hunting the ancient mammoths and cooking meat around a fire pit at night, was all humans had ever done—and all they would ever do. For them, building the fire and studying the embers, would be their greatest technological accomplishment.

It was Wednesday evening of the second week of my climate study. Only two nights remained. The evening was starting normally enough. However, the flu or sickness which I felt earlier in the week had returned, and it was starting to interfere with my plans. I had gotten a large bag of marshmallows from the chow hall back at Indian Springs. I was planning on building a small fire pit in the park-like area. That way, in the morning I could build a small fire and roast a few marshmallows, while eating my second box lunch. It seemed like an appropriate way of celebrating the completion of my climate study, and my having survived two dangerous weeks alone in the desert.

However, the weather had turned much cooler. A significant fog had already formed by the time I arrived at the sliding gate. I was feeling very sick, and that included an intense headache. No one had come out to greet me in the meeting room of the Desert Oasis. I was coughing quite badly. Perhaps they didn't want to get the sickness I had. The meeting room was noticeably cold when I entered. It did not appear to have a visible heater, or fireplace. I guessed it was because The Gray Aliens had no interest in sitting around an open fire—or dreaming while watching its decaying embers. Their vision is better than ours—but perhaps not attuned to seeing romance and emotion. I picked up my empty envelope and keys, signed for them, and headed out for the Desert Ranges without wasting time.

Arriving at the weather shack, I began by inspecting the park-like area to decide where it would be safe to build a small fire pit for roasting marshmallows. I was interrupted in this happy pursuit when the telephone rang.

Reaching the telephone, I answered, "Desert Range Weather shack. Airman Hall speaking."

"Hello, Airman Hall," the voice began happily, and audibly respectful. As with the Tall Whites, it was extremely unusual for the Gray Aliens, to explicitly greet a human. The voice continued, "Your work is extremely impressive. The work you are doing is extremely important. The Generals would like to extend your climate study for several more weeks."

The words made me break out in a cold sweat. Spending several more weeks out in this dangerous, uncomfortable stretch of desert was the last thing I was willing to agree to. I had to think fast, as I struggled for words. "Well, thank you for your kind words, and for the offer. However, I am quite sick this morning, and having trouble thinking clearly. The last orders I received from my commanders down at Nellis said that on this Friday morning I am ordered to load up my portable theodolite and other equipment, turn in my final report, and return permanently back down to Nellis. I am only a low ranking enlisted airman. Unless I receive different orders from my Nellis commanders, I will have to return to Nellis on Friday morning."

Thankfully, he didn't seem offended.

"I understand." He responded nicely.

"Winter is coming on." I continued. "The nights are becoming a lot colder. It is possible it might even snow next week. The elevation of the desert in this area is quite high. Once it snows, in order to keep myself healthy and have a place to warm up, I would probably have to start the electrical generator and the fuel oil heater here in my weather shack. I would probably have to move my theodolite back to the park-like area outside, and take my readings from there."

"I understand." He responded pleasantly. "Do as your commanders at Nellis have ordered. The Generals will have to talk among themselves."

The phone was hung up and the line went dead. I returned to inspecting the park-like area to find a safe place for my fire pit. The desert was so dry, there didn't seem to be a safe spot to start an open fire. I decided to just eat my marshmallows without roasting. The bag I had brought, was so large, I had several days supply.

The night progressed routinely enough. As before, the Desert Range area seemed to remain completely deserted, except for me. The fog steadily thickened. However, I had previously marked the trail out to my new theodolite location so carefully I had no trouble making the trip both ways, even in the extremely thick fog. I released all the balloons on schedule. They could not actually be tracked in this heavy fog, but would be visible to children who might happen to be watching from the scout craft base over on the eastern slope of the jutted out mountain range.

Since I couldn't actually track the balloons, and therefore had no data on which to perform the computations, there wasn't much for me to do. I was running a great deal ahead of schedule. I finished my second box lunch, locked up the weather shack, and started up my truck sharply at 5:00a.m. I turned my truck around, and headed back through the darkness towards Desert Oasis. The fog was still extremely thick. I had gotten to know the road very well, so it didn't slow me down much. After all, I didn't have to worry about meeting other vehicles on the road.

Finding the Desert Oasis and returning the keys was more difficult. The fog was extremely thick in the area. The sun had not yet risen. I had to pick my way carefully along the road to locate the sliding gate. Walking into and out of the compound was normal.

Finding my way back to my truck, I now had to carefully pick my way downhill into the increasingly dense fog to reach the main gate—without running into it. Opening the combination lock in the darkness and fog was just barely possible. Opening the combination lock took more time than it ever had. I still remember my intense frustration. I had no choice but to keep trying until I had opened the lock by myself. The human guards waiting for me out on the paved road did not have the combination, and were not allowed to help.

Eventually, I found myself back in my barracks at Indian Springs, nursing my flu and intense headache. I was getting into my bunk when Smokey came in to see me. He had come to deliver a message from the Nellis Base Commander. He said that after completing my duties on Friday morning, I was ordered first to rest up here at Indian Springs, then to report back to the weather station at Nellis. I was ordered not to arrive on base at Nellis before fifteen minutes to midnight on Saturday night. I was not to arrive at the Nellis weather station before ten minutes to midnight. I was to wait outside in the parking lot until the observer before me left the station. Only then was I to enter the Nellis weather station. I was to work the Saturday night/Sunday morning midnight shift. I would be entirely by myself in the Nellis weather station and Base Ops building. I was to use the Indian Springs weather truck for transportation. I was to bring all of my personal belongings with me. However, I was to leave all of my belongings in the truck. I was not to check into any of the barracks at Nellis. I was to return directly to Indian Springs when my duty shift was over. Smokey was more serious than I had ever seen him.

"They seemed concerned about your safety, and awfully impressed with something you did with flowers when you were hiking out in the desert." he stated emphatically. "They wouldn't tell me any more than that."

"I haven't been doing anything out in the desert." I laughed. "All I have been doing is releasing a few balloons and not bothering to record any of the readings." Smokey and I laughed together about that.

Thursday evening began routinely enough. The weather continued to turn cooler. It was a clear night with very little in the way of winds.

I was still not fully recovered from the flu, so I was being unusually careful as I walked into the dark compound at the Desert Oasis. I was singing one of my flower songs as I walked. The moon was just starting to rise. It had not yet reached the third quarter.

I entered the meeting room, leaving the outside door open behind me. I paused just inside the doorway, in order to determine if I was alone in the building. Patiently I let my eyes survey the darkened room as I continued to quietly sing my song.

Off to my right, the young girl stepped out from the dark doorway behind the counter. She seemed to have overcome her fear of me. Tonight, she did not go behind the counter. Instead, she stepped through the opening between the counter and the wall on the right, and stepped completely into the meeting room itself. She stopped and took up a standing position next to the wall and the end of the counter. The room itself was quite dark, and the section along the far wall was part of the darkest section. I was not able to see much detail in either her face, or in the gray clothing she wore.

She hadn't spoken to me yet, and she did not seem to be interested in talking to me. So, I made no attempt to talk with her. Rather, it seemed her purpose was just to practice doing ordinary things while humans were present—and while I, being human, knew she was present. I understood. I was, after all, just the "test human". I wondered if I was the first human she had ever actually seen at short range.

I decided the safest thing for me to do was to just go on about my climate study activities, and let her join in whenever she got brave enough. Still singing, I walked up to the counter, retrieved my empty envelope and keys, and signed for them. I turned around in a clockwise manner. She continued standing normally in the dark shadows across the room while I turned, momentarily facing her. She had obviously gotten over her fear of me—at least as long as she could remain concealed in the darkness.

Still singing, I left the building, walked back to my truck, and headed out to my weather shack.

The evening was routine enough. Once again, it felt as if I was alone out at the Desert Range buildings. However, there was something going on in the dark shadows out behind the storage sheds. I heard some quiet noises coming from back there in the darkness. When I went to inspect, something ran away too fast for me to see what it was. I was happy to believe it was probably a rabbit.

After completing the 4:00 a.m. balloon release, I packed up my theodolite and all of my equipment. I carried it in from the desert, carefully packed all my equipment, my radio, and belongings into my truck. I assembled the wind forms, and records, and placed them in the truck as well. I picked my favorite spot on a bench out in the park-like area, and enjoyed my second box lunch.

It took quite awhile for me to pack my truck. Consequently, I was running late when I arrived back at the Desert Oasis. The sun was already well above the horizon.

Before I could return the keys, I had to deliver my completed reports and weather forms to the weather supply shed in the compound. It was a simple enough task. However, I could hardly contain my curiosity as I opened the front door. I didn't have to spend any time searching for old garden seeds such as oats or barley between the floor boards. There were several bags of them still sitting in the corners in the back.

After returning the key, and taking a late breakfast at the Death Valley Center chow hall, I made the long drive back to Indian Springs. Once there, I quickly returned the portable theodolite, the tripod, and the other UASF equipment to the safety of the weather shack at Range Three. The Ranges, of course, had remained closed to everyone during my absence. When I finished safely stowing my equipment, I was finally able to return to my barracks. I was exhausted by the time I got there. I climbed into my bunk, and slept for hours.

I rested all day Friday, and Saturday. When Saturday night arrived, I put on my uniform, packed my belongings in the Indian Springs weather truck. I made certain it was full of gas and oil. On schedule, I pulled the truck onto the highway, and headed in to Nellis.

I had to carefully time my arrival at the Nellis gate and the parking lot of the Nellis weather station. I was in uniform and driving a government truck. On Saturday night, I couldn't park and rest just anywhere. For example, parking the government truck in the parking lot of a casino or a tavern in order to kill time, didn't seem like a good idea—much as I would have enjoyed doing so. Surviving alone in the deserts of Nevada required that an enlisted man master several different types of self discipline.

At five minutes to midnight, I sat waiting in my truck, parked out under the lights in the parking lot of the Nellis weather station. I saw the duty weather observer open and close the front door of the weather station, assuring himself it wasn't locked. Then he used the inside corridors to walk down to the door to the Base Operations section of the building—proving the remainder of the building was deserted—and left the building permanently.

I waited until he disappeared down the road using his personal car, before I got out of my truck, and entered the weather station. I signed in and began the routine duties of the graveyard shift.

At 1:00 a.m., I saw two Air Policemen pull up across the parking lot, and park next to my truck. My commanding officer was with them. While the Air Policemen waited outside and across the parking lot, my commanding officer got out of the car, walked across the parking lot, and into the weather station. He was carrying an envelope which contained a few completed forms.

"Good Evening, Sir." I greeted him in nervous military fashion. The duty weather observer—an enlisted man—does not salute officers when indoors.

"Good Evening, Airman Hall." He responded much as a father might. "They cautioned me not to get too close to you for the next few days, until you have gotten over that cough of yours. The Nellis Base Commander and his high ranking friends required that I come in and talk with you alone tonight. I need to talk with you awhile and I need to make certain you are still OK.

We will talk here in this room. But first, I need to close the curtains, and make certain all the doors are locked."

After he had satisfied himself, he took up a standing position on the other side of the room—unusually far away for a personal discussion—and began the discussion in military fashion. "No one tells me anything. I'm not allowed to ask you any questions. I can listen if there is anything you wish to share with me, but that is all I am allowed to do. I am not even allowed to visit Indian Springs, which I guess, is where your bunk is at the minute."

"I understand, Sir." I responded.

He continued in a respectful and fatherly manner, "Your friends down at the Pentagon are ecstatic with the work you have been doing, and the success you have achieved. They say you have been further out there than any human in living memory. They can't believe how simple you make everything appear. I asked them if they could tell me anything about the work you are doing. All they would say was you had done something simple with plants and flowers. They said you have been acting the way a young girl would."

A wise man knows his friends—As a young man, I wasn't at first sure how to take his compliment. I decided since he was an officer and I was only a low ranking enlisted man, if he had wanted to offend me, he certainly knew how to. So I thanked him kindly for the compliment, "Thank you, Sir. Your kind words mean a lot to me."

"They want to make your climate study permanent, and send you back up there for the remainder of your first enlistment. I told them it wasn't a good idea. I told them not to ride a good horse to death. Every man gets tired after a while, and needs a rest, or a change of pace. I need to know how you are, and how you feel about extending your assignment."

I thought for a minute before answering. I chose my words carefully, knowing that whatever I said would find its way back to The Gray Aliens out in the desert, and probably back to the young girl as well. When dealing with the Gray Aliens, I was, after all, dealing with children and young teenagers.

"Well, Sir," I began carefully. "If it means that much to The Generals, I am willing to return to the desert and extend my climate study for one more week only. The weather will probably remain warm for only one more week. The weather is rapidly turning colder out in the deserts at those high elevations.

The current setup really isn't a suitable location from which to conduct a permanent climate study. It is really only suitable for short term use during the spring and fall months.

I can not run the electrical generators at night because either the electricity interferes with a communication system somewhere, or else because the exhaust of the engine interferes with an older person's oxygen breathing system somewhere. My weather shack is unheated at night because without electricity, I cannot run my fuel oil heater. This means I would be in extreme danger from the weather if I got caught out there in a bad winter storm. To survive a winter storm I would need a warm sheltered place where I could rest and dry off.

In addition, there isn't a source of fresh drinking water out at the site. It would be dangerous for me to be out there alone during hot summertime days and nights.

There isn't a source of agricultural water, garden seeds, or agricultural equipment. My part-time hobby of working with the beautiful flowering desert plants and food grains, is one of the ways I rest between balloon runs. I like to grow plants, and study them, and talk to others about them. Without a source of agricultural water or other agricultural supplies at the site, I am limited in ways to relax when I am out there.

Lastly, I am concerned about the effects on my health. I get sick very easily. I catch every germ. Cold wet weather causes me lots of health problems. I am not feeling well right at the minute. I much prefer to return to Indian Springs, or come back to Nellis."

My commander listened intently as I spoke. After a short pause, he replied with great respect, "The Generals tell me you are the bravest man they have ever met. They tell me if anything ever went wrong out there, you would never come back alive.

I will tell The Nellis Base Commander you will extend the climate study for only one more week. You orders will say two weeks, but only if the weather holds, and you should happen to change your mind. As soon as you finish up out where ever you are, you will return to Indian Springs to immediately resume your duties. The Pentagon was saying they wished they had two of you. For some reason, they're getting desperate to get you back to Indian Springs as well."

"Thank You, Sir." I answered gratefully. "Yes. At The Generals request, I will extend my climate study for one more week only."

My commander continued, "It's going on 2:00 a.m. now. File the 2:00 a.m. report as normal. At 2:50a.m., I want you to sign out and return immediately to Indian Springs, so you can rest, and be ready for your next week of duty out in the desert. Don't wait to be relieved, and don't talk or greet the next observer. Leave the front door unlocked as you leave. I have made arrangements for another observer to relieve you at 2:52a.m. and work the remainder of your shift.

Remember if that cough doesn't go away, or if you ever get in trouble, and want to cancel the remainder of the assignment, just tell Smokey. The Nellis Base Commander will cancel the assignment immediately."

"Thank you, Sir." I responded. "I will be sure to remember."

I signed the simple form which said only that I had met with my commander and he had reviewed the status of my training.

With that, my commander left the station, returned to the waiting Air Police car, and returned the completed forms to the Nellis Command Post. At 2:50a.m., I signed out, and began the long, lonely drive back to Indian Springs. As I was leaving, I could see the next weather observer in my rear view mirror. I could see him drive up to the Nellis Weather Station and park his car. It was the same car, and the same observer I had seen leave just before midnight.

Sunday afternoon came. I drove back out to the Range Three weather shack. I reloaded the portable theodolite, the tripod, the equipment, my radio, shovel, and other things back into my weather truck. Then I headed back in to Indian Springs, and once again pulled my truck back out onto the highway and headed towards Death Valley Center. I wasn't particularly happy about extending my "climate study". However, the military is the military. If that's what it took to make the Generals happy . . . well, I was only a low ranking enlisted man—and not a particularly military one at that. I wanted only to complete my term of enlistment honorably, and return to Wisconsin as a civilian again.

The weather was steadily turning cooler. The skies were dark and partly overcast. A slight mist filled the air as I parked my truck by the sliding gate at the Desert Oasis, and walked into the meeting room—again singing one of my flower songs. I was still sick and walking slowly. Because of the weather, I was expecting the Desert Oasis to be deserted, and when I arrived, it seemed to be. So, without stopping or pausing, I opened the front door, carefully entered the darkened room, and walked directly to the counter to retrieve my empty envelope and keys. The unheated room felt noticeably chilly. I estimated the temperature of the room to be not more than 55 degrees Fahrenheit at the time. Because of the darkness, and the cold, signing for the keys took an extra minute. For my own safety, I wanted to keep my night vision, and wasn't using my flashlight to assist me.

While I was at the counter signing for the keys, the young girl entered the room from the dark doorway on the right. Once again, she entered the room where I was, and continued following down the darkened far wall. She finally stopped in the darkness, and took a standing position facing me roughly three quarters of the way down.

Her appearance caused me to become very apprehensive. I was afraid at first that she might be going to block the front entrance I had used when I came in. The darkness and the mist obscured everything, including the details of the gray clothing she was wearing. However, she did appear to be wearing warmer clothing than the week before.

There were only a few chairs in the room. Consequently there was a great deal of open space between us. Not feeling well, I stopped and waited at the counter, for the situation to clear. I continued singing as I did so. More from fear than anything, I decided to just stand there singing, and wait to see what she would do next. I was afraid to return to the open front door for fear she would chose to further close the distance between us. She could easily do so—and in the darkened room, with my level of fear, it would be easy for me to accidentally bump into her. If that happened, disaster might quickly follow. As far as I knew, none of the Aliens ever wanted to be touched by a human—especially a sick one.

After a short time, the young girl very intentionally walked down to the row of chairs which sat along the back cross wall. A few of the chairs in that section were her size. Acting like she had all the time in the world, she walked down to one of the larger ones. Then she walked back to the opening in the counter on the far side of the room, and disappeared back through the dark doorway. I could hear her and perhaps two others, exit the building through the doorway out back.

I stood there, collecting my nerves and enjoying the solitude, before I left the building by way of the front door, and hurried back to the safety of my parked truck.

It was cold, and misty when I arrived at the Desert Ranges. I spent a brutal night setting up my theodolite in the desert pass to the east at my new theodolite location. My phone did not ring, and it seemed as if I was alone at the Desert Range building area.

I chose the same location I had used before. The Desert Range building area remained deserted all night. However, I seemed to be drawing a lot of company at my theodolite location. Several large dark Gray shadows seemed to be waiting in the darkness, out in the desert to the east, just over the pass. Every now and then, when I turned around, I would catch a quick glimpse of something watching me from out in the sagebrush. Based on the quiet sounds I would hear behind me to the east, I decided that one or two of them were always waiting along the path I had used the night I had gone hiking.

Shorter Gray shadows seemed to gather from time to time in the shallow hollow in the desert located to the north of me. Sometimes I would get quick glimpses of them watching me from behind the bushes, or down the darkened paths. When I checked the hollow for new footprints, there were several which did not seem to be mine. One set entered the hollow from the north, whereas I never entered the hollow from the north. They had come in from the desert, from someplace even further away, up along the mountains to the north. I wondered if perhaps a second Gray scout craft base was dug into the mountains on the north side of the pass. One night, for a few brief minutes through the rain, I could see some lights come in from the west, opposite the narrow gravel western road, and continue floating to the east and then north across the boundary line. They finally sat down in the desert to the north of me—turning out their lights after they did so. I never saw them leave. However, at the time, I was afraid to spend much time looking in that direction. They could easily have left without me seeing them.

The remainder of my third week now fell into a brutal routine. The weather continued to get colder, and the fall rains began in earnest. The gravel road out to the Desert Ranges became muddier, and more beautiful—and more impassable—as each night progressed. My cough, and flu continually got worse. The Desert Oasis was now always deserted when I arrived at night, and when I returned the keys in the morning—and the Gray shadows continued to wait for me out in the desert—paralleling my every move—always at a distance—always staying out of my way.

Tuesday morning came. I broke off the 4:00a.m. balloon run early. I was coughing too badly to track the balloon. I returned to the Desert Range weather shack. I started the electrical generator and the fuel oil heater. I was starting them earlier, I suppose, than I was expected to. However, I had no choice. I was very sick, and I needed the heat, and the electricity.

I waited for my weather shack to warm up, before I began eating my second box lunch. I sat huddled close to the heater, and thought some more about the rocks out by the wooden pole.

"What about the rocks?" I wondered. "What if the rocks do mark a tribal boundary for Gray Alien teenagers? That would mean when I walked east of the wooden pole, it would have been sort of like me walking across one high school's football field out onto another's, with teams present on both fields and games in session."

I now felt I understood why the Generals had been so worried about my safety. Still I wondered, "Why have I been allowed to just walk around unharmed out here, and out in the desert pass to the east, and into the Valley of The Forgotten Lake Beds, when other humans were not?"

I remembered a Friday night football game at Cambridge High School, back in the fall of 1959 when I was sophomore. I had signed up for the high school class in agriculture that year—rather than wasting my time sitting through a second Study Hall.

At the football game, I remembered watching a group of agriculture teachers from several different high schools in southern Wisconsin. The group walked around the football field, laughing with one another. The group of several men and one woman appeared to be the closest of friends. They appeared to care nothing about our social boundaries—or which team won or lost. Some of them also functioned as Wisconsin County Agricultural Agents.

I remembered the surprise I felt when I noticed that all of the teen-agers and all of the adults at the football game just naturally enjoyed coming up to them and talking with them—without regard to our rivalry.

The agricultural teachers obviously cared only about agricultural topics, about plants, farming, crop rotation, fertilizer, large gardens—and the weather—when to plant, when to harvest. Wisconsin society allowed the agricultural teachers and the Wisconsin County Agricultural Agents, to go anywhere they wanted, anytime they wanted. They were completely free to strike up a friendly conversation with anyone, anytime, anywhere they chose. I wondered if that was how the Gray Alien teenagers had learned to view me; the same way I had learned to view the agricultural teachers. I wondered—maybe the young girl wasn't coming to actually talk with me. Maybe she was coming so the other teenagers would get used to seeing the two of us together, as the nucleus of an agricultural group, working on agricultural pursuits in the same areas of the desert. Such a group would be a group without tribal boundaries. The young girl would never have to speak to me at all for that to happen. I wondered—maybe the young girl was one of the Gray shadows that kept paralleling my every move out in the desert pass. I wondered some more—teenagers form groups quickly. If I was right, the new agricultural group might well have already formed—literally behind my back.

If that was the case, then any pair of human weather observers could now replace me. They could now just walk right in and take over on the climate study. All the two human weather observers would have to do was to behave as high school agricultural instructors behaved. They would also be releasing weather balloons on schedule—to entertain the younger children.

They could study the plants, set up a desert garden area on the south side of the park-like area, and practice desert gardening, between balloon runs. The Generals could make provision for drilling a well, and providing for a source of electricity year round. Nobody needed me out here anymore. The climate study could now go permanent without me—and I could go back to Indian Springs.

The young girl had apparently gotten over her fear of humans, so now her technology transfer project could also proceed. The two human men could stay together at all times, and take things easy. In time, they could learn to control their fears when out here together in the desert at night. All they would need was time to adjust, rest, and something I never had—a briefing from the Pentagon Generals. The Gray Generals could ask all of the gray shadows to keep a respectful distance, while the climate and the agricultural potential of the Valley of The Forgotten Lake Beds was studied and analyzed. Musing as I ate my box lunch brought me satisfaction. Suddenly, I didn't feel like such a failure anymore.

Wednesday morning, I was still just as sick as the night before. I was running a noticeable fever. The night was very dark. Mist and a slight fog filled the air. However, to test my hypothesis, I decided to expand my Agricultural Instructor activities. After the midnight run, I intentionally selected a large patch of very healthy sagebrush which sat on the slightly higher ground to the south of my new theodolite location. Singing with difficulty between coughing spasms, and carefully using my flashlight, I spent 10 or 15 minutes, obviously and openly studying the plants, foliage, roots, and soil around the Sagebrush patch. I was talking and singing to myself as I did so. I turned off my flashlight when I finished. I doubt I was discovering much of anything scientific. However, I was wondering if any of the gray shadows would take notice of my activities—and how they as a group would respond.

As I returned to my theodolite for the 2:00a.m. balloon release, from a distance, I could see the gray shadows, as a group, collecting around the patch of sagebrush I had just studied. The group seemed to be studying the plants too.

I released both the 2:00a.m. balloon and the 4:00a.m. balloon together at 2:00a.m.—one after the other. I closed up my theodolite and returned to my weather shack. I simply had to rest and attend to my health.

When I returned to Indian Springs, I told Smokey to inform Nellis that I was ending my climate study at the end of the next duty shift. I was too sick to continue. I also asked Smokey to tell The Nellis Base Commander that a team of two weather observers who always stayed together, could be permanently assigned to replace me on the climate study. They would need to take several months to get used to the place, and to get used to releasing a few balloons at night on schedule. They should have a few gardening projects scattered around the desert—flower gardens, and so on. They should chose projects, and gardens they both naturally enjoyed. I told Smokey, it was my belief The Generals already knew the rest of the details.

Smokey thought I was delirious from the high fever I was running at the time. He was shaking his head and saying, "You're wrong there Charlie. There ain't nobody can replace you. I don't know where you have been going, or what you've been doing out there but that's what they been telling me on the telephone. That's why they got me here looking after you."

However, he promised to deliver any message I wanted, exactly as I stated it. Smokey was always as good as his word.

Later I heard from Smokey that the officer who answered the telephone at the Nellis Base Command Post reacted in shock as soon as Smokey began reciting my message. According to Smokey, the officer immediately stopped him and began shouting to some General in the next room, "General! You have to hear this directly!" Smokey was then asked to recite my complete message for the General, only, to hear. He said the General was laughing in amazement at the time, and exclaiming, "By Golly, he's done it! He's right!" Then the General thanked him for delivering the message.

When Thursday morning arrived, I was almost too sick to bring my theodolite in from the desert and back to my truck. It was with great difficulty, I recovered all of my equipment. However, for a while, I was seriously considering leaving the tripod out in the desert pass to the east. At least the walk between my Desert Range weather shack and my new theodolite location was on reasonably level ground. The rain made the muddy ground slippery, and I was able to drag my tripod and my equipment trunk for some of the distance.

I will always remember how the Desert Ranges looked that cold rainy morning as I packed the equipment; my radio, the theodolite and tripod, and personal belongings in my truck. I was very sick, feverish , and very happy, as I turned my truck around on the muddy gravel desert road, and began the long drive back to the Desert Oasis, and back to Indian Springs. My commander, as per his orders, never once mentioned anything about those three weeks—and never once asked me about my decision.

A few months later, I happened to be momentarily alone with the weather observer who had vacated the Nellis Weather Station the night I agreed to extend my climate study. Without thinking, I thanked him for completing my shift at Nellis that night. I said I had been feeling very sick, and I appreciated being able to rest. The weather observer immediately paled in fear, and quietly exclaimed, "They ordered me to forget that night ever happened. They'll transfer me immediately to a base in Hawaii if they even suspect you ever spoke to me about whatever you were doing." Then he hurried quickly away from me. I was left standing there, quite confused. Hawaii seemed to me, like a pretty good place for a weather observer to be stationed.

The observer would never again allow himself to be anywhere alone with me. A few months later, I was told he had asked to be transferred from Nellis to some other base. I never knew where—I guessed it to be Hawaii. All I was ever told was he put in his request one morning—and was shipped out by 4:00p.m. They said he was very happy at the time.

Every Form Of Refuge . . .

"... Come, behold the works of the LORD,
what desolations he hath made in the earth...."
... Psalms 46:8

A refuge can take many forms. A refuge can be a state of mind, or an actual place of physical safety. Either way, by the mid 1960s, my experiences in the deserts of Nevada, California, and the American Southwest, soon convinced me that every form of refuge came at a price.

For example, a mountain hut, usually thought of as being a building located in the mountains, surrounded by pine trees, can be a refuge for travelers in remote mountainous areas. It might provide food and shelter to any and all hikers, or mountain climbers, who may possibly need to take shelter in the area. Of course, such travelers do not all need to be human.

One such Mountain Refuge is an old forest cabin sitting roughly at 8,000 feet elevation, up a desolate canyon on the western slopes of Sheep Mountain, in the Desert National Wildlife Refuge, northwest of Las Vegas, Nevada. It was built next to a large spring filled with Wire Grass—imaginatively named Wire Grass Spring—possibly as long ago as the 1880s. No one knows who built it—or who named the fresh water spring. Considering that the mountain refuge, and the Sheep Mountains are located just a few miles from the old-time Corn Creek ranch house and buildings—and a short distance from Indian Springs—the old forest cabin of long ago, must certainly have provided safe refuge for Tall White hikers as well as human ones—for extra-terrestrials need to take refuge from the Earth's harsh elements, too.

I had come to enjoy my duties at Indian Springs. I had overcome my fear of the Tall Whites, and learned to enjoy the time I spent on the Indian Springs gunnery ranges. Quite some time had passed since I had completed my climate study out on the Desert Ranges at Death Valley Center. I used the time which had passed to good advantage. For one thing, I was now back in perfect health. For another, I had done my best to push all memory of those fearful evenings from my mind. I had no desire to ever return to the Desert Ranges at Death Valley Center.

Consequently, I was quietly very upset the Friday morning I was informed that my Commander at Nellis had ordered me to report to the Nellis Weather Station and work the coming Sunday graveyard shift—midnight to 8:00 a.m. Sunday. I was even more upset when I was informed the same rules applied as before. I was not to arrive at the station until 10 minutes to midnight. I was to wait outside until the station was empty, and so forth—just as had been the case before.

However, the military is the military. I reported as ordered. My commander arrived with the two Air Policemen at 1:00a.m. As before, they waited outside by their vehicle as my Commander came in to talk to me. I stood quietly, and received my new orders in military fashion.

He was not allowed to mention my previous climate study. He said only that everyone down at the Pentagon was extremely impressed and extremely satisfied with my work.

He said the Pentagon was requesting I perform a new "Mountain Climate Study". He said I would use the Indian Springs weather truck, since it had been my place of refuge so many times in the past. He said like the previous climate study, and my work at Indian Springs—nothing I did on this new mountain climate study would ever be classified. No-one, including himself, could ever ask me any questions. No-one could ever come visit me, or conduct an inspection of my facilities. I could tell anybody I chose, anything I wanted to about it—but everyone he knew was afraid to listen. I was strictly on my own.

I would keep my personal belongings with me at all times. He said the Nellis weather barracks would always have an empty private room reserved for me to use anytime I wanted—no questions asked. He said the same was true for Indian Springs.

He said the Pentagon insisted I be able to return to Indian Springs or back to Nellis, anytime I wanted—although I would probably only have time to do so on weekends. He said the Pentagon orders said I could sleep in the barracks, go into Las Vegas, or do anything I chose—no questions asked.

He said the first stage of the Mountain Climate Study would last six weeks. If I was successful, my assignment would be made permanent until the end of my enlistment. He said I could turn down the assignment if I chose. No one would ever question my decision. If I accepted the request from the Generals, my new assignment would begin Monday morning—the following day.

He handed me my sealed orders for me to read, before making my decision. I opened the envelope and read the request carefully. The orders said practically nothing. Based on the way the orders were written, I guessed the Generals had chosen two other weather observers who would carry on with the original climate study. I guessed the Generals only wanted me to train the new guys, show them the ropes, introduce them to the Desert Ranges, and help them move the climate study on to the next phase. It certainly seemed like a simple enough request, and a reasonable enough request at that. A cold winter was in progress. Three men together out on the Desert Ranges should work out just fine. I decided I could hardly refuse such an easy request from a set of high ranking Pentagon Generals. I was, after all, still just a low ranking enlisted man.

I informed my Commander I could surely complete the Mountain Climate Study within six weeks, so I was accepting the request for just six weeks, after which I would ask to return to Indian springs, or to come back in to Nellis. I told my Commander if I got sick again, or got in any trouble, I would ask to come back early. If I got sick, for sure I would ask to come back to Nellis to regroup. He replied indicating he understood. I signed and annotated my orders accordingly.

As before, I signed out at 2:50a.m. as ordered, and immediately returned to Indian Springs.

The next day, Monday morning, at 10:00a.m., with my truck packed and loaded, as per my new orders, I found myself at the Ranger Station at Death Valley Center. A special park ranger directed me into a special steel vaulted room, and locked the two of us in. He handed me a sealed envelope with my new orders. He also handed me the keys to a locked gate which was located somewhere far out in the distant desert. He did so in such a familiar manner, I immediately became convinced he knew me by sight, and who I was. We were alone together in the sealed room.

I read the envelope's contents. My new orders said nothing about the Desert Oasis, or the Desert Ranges or its weather shack and park like area. They said nothing about the furrows, the Valley of The Forgotten Lake beds, or training anyone.

"There must be some mistake!", I exclaimed, as I reacted in shock. These orders direct me to drive way out from Death Valley Center, into a desolate section of a far-away desert where I have never been. It's not even in the same direction as I was before. They explicitly state no other human is ever allowed to come past the guard station located just beyond the locked gate, in order to visit me. These orders explicitly state there is an unmarked line next to my mountain weather shack and a gate in a barbed wire fence somewhere out there in the desert and somewhere high up in the mountains. My orders clearly state I am the only human allowed to cross the unmarked line or to go through the gate. It clearly states that any other human who crosses the line or goes through the gate, will be immediately killed, even if they are Death Valley rangers—even if I am dying, and they've only come to save me. How am I going to train any new guys, or show them the ropes , or accomplish anything, with orders like these?"

The special ranger smiled in a fatherly, knowing manner—betraying his obvious training as a Pentagon psychiatrist. He responded, choosing his words carefully,

"There's no mistake in your orders. I'm only a messenger. I'm not allowed anywhere out here other than this immediate fenced and built-up area, and the road you drove in on.

I'm told the Generals are extremely impressed with everything you've already accomplished. The Generals told me you are the only human they would ever ask to go alone into those distant mountains.

I'm told the weather shack you used on your previous climate study when you were out here before, and all of the buildings next to it, have been moved to a new location, far away from where you were—I don't know exactly where you were, or where the buildings are now.

The men who replaced you have been following your instructions very carefully. Word has spread they are your friends. They are now doing better than anyone ever thought possible. They don't need any more training. They are doing so well, they are now training others. I understand they have also made a number of new friends. Thanks to you, the world you knew when you were out here before, simply doesn't exist any more.

I don't know anything about your new mountain climate study. However, the Generals assure me that a place of refuge has been provided for your use only, in addition to your weather truck. They tell me its a kind of old mountain hut. They say it sits on the side of a mountain slope somewhere out there, and it has a beautiful view. You can do anything you want when you are out there. I guess there's an army cot to sleep on, as well.

You are scheduled to spend the next six weeks at your new location. You can come in everyday to Death Valley Center to shower, and shave. You have free use of the facilities. You can do your laundry. You can pick up box lunches, and take your meals at the chow hall. You can put in gas and get maintenance for your truck. You can check out books at the library. The facilities at Death Valley Center are open 24 hours a day, every day. They never close.

If you choose to return to Indian Springs, or go back to Nellis, I suggest you only do so when you are off duty on the week-ends, since it is such a long drive. You're young; you can sleep in your truck, or an empty bunk in any of the barracks.

Currently, the gunnery ranges are closed for the season. The Indian Springs base is almost completely deserted, so you won't find much to do there. If you do go anywhere to rest up, you'll probably want to go back to Nellis. It's closer. You can enjoy the casinos and the shows in Las Vegas.

If you choose to take your weather truck into Las Vegas on the week-ends, the first gas station on this side of the city, is a safe place where you can park your weather truck, and change out of your uniform. It is even safe for you to sleep there in your truck, if you choose to. There's a hidden parking place in the back. No-one will bother you. You can ride the city bus into town from there. I know you'll be sure to carry extra gasoline for your truck with you.

The Generals tell me everyone involved with your new mountain climate study has agreed that no-one but you is allowed inside your mountain hut, or inside your truck—or anywhere in between the doorway to your truck and the doorway to your mountain hut. When you are out in the desert, they are your only places of refuge.

You may go anywhere you want, and do anything you want, whenever you want, when you are out there. Please remember, you are totally on your own. If you get in trouble when you are out there—any trouble whatever—there is no help coming. You have to bring yourself back to the safe area around the guard shack by the locked gate, or die trying. No human will ever be able to come for your body, once you go east of the line.

Every Tuesday at 10:00a.m. in the morning, please bring in your completed weather forms and any other reports to this ranger station. A ranger different from me, will be here to receive them. Make certain the ranger gets a good look at you, close-up, every time you deliver your completed forms. He needs to make certain nothing has happened to you.

Anytime you would like to speak to me, tell the ranger, or tell which-ever ranger is out front. I will come immediately, and meet you in this room. You are free to say anything you want when we are together in this room—anything at all. I give you my word, any statement you make when we are together in this room will never be questioned, rebuked, punished, or criticized. Nothing you ever do or say will ever be classified. You are the only human who will ever know what happens east of the line.

Do you have any questions?"

"No Sir." I respectfully responded. "Thank you, Sir. I understand my orders. I will follow my orders, and perform my duties to the best of my abilities, sir." There was little else I could say.

"I pray God will always go with you, Airman Hall," the special ranger responded. "I pray your guardian angels will always be at your side."

I followed my orders. I took the noon meal at the chow hall before I began the very long drive out into the far-away desert. I tried to keep an open mind as I drove, even though this climate study was not progressing anywhere near the way I had expected. I began by counting my blessings, and remembering how good I had it. These were the days of the Viet Nam War. I thought about how many other young American men my age, were dying heroically and tragically, in the jungles of Viet Nam, while serving their country. None of them were enjoying the special privileges, and the good life I was. I felt nervous, humble, and a little guilty at the time. All I had to do to stay alive was control my fears—and entertain myself. The comparison made it seem reasonable. I recited my favorite prayers, and sang my favorite songs as I drove.

The road out to the far desert had many twists and sharp turns. It changed direction many times, and traversed several mountain passes. One such pass was surprisingly narrow and unforgettably beautiful, as it opened to the west before me.

After a very long time, I came to the turn-off to the locked gate. I didn't recognize it at first. The paved two lane desert road I was on, was paralleling a small stream, which ran along the base of a range of low desert mountains, roughly a mile off to my right. The side road had been intentionally constructed and camouflaged so it looked like an old logging road from perhaps the 1880's.

Even the steel beams on the bridge across the stream had been camouflaged to look like old logs.

An ordinary gate with no lock, barred the bridge at its center. I was forced to stop my truck, open the gate, and close it after I had driven my truck through.

After crossing the bridge, and reaching the base of the low mountain range, the road took an abrupt turn into a small, well hidden valley on my right. A locked gate barred the road roughly a quarter of a mile up the canyon, so whatever happened in the small valley could not be seen by cars passing by on the paved road. The key I had been issued, fit the lock. Once again, I was forced to stop my truck, open the gate, and close it after I had driven my truck through.

I wasn't surprised by the location of the two gates. The U.S. Government is very good at designing shooting galleries.

Roughly another quarter mile up the small valley, the road took another sharp turn to the left, and entered a short shooting gallery-like pass as it crossed the low mountain range into another valley beyond. Once through the pass it took another sharp turn to the left, and continued down along the side of the mountain through another section resembling another shooting gallery—arriving at last at the drive-through guard station. To enter the drive through at the guard station, another abrupt right turn was required. The drive-through itself, was designed like still another shooting gallery.

"Just like the Government," I chuckled to myself as I pulled into the guard station. "One shooting gallery isn't enough. In order to feel safe, they need four of them—because four IS the Government's number."

There were five guards in the guard station when I pulled up. One was obviously the guard commander, two were regular guards, and two were perhaps guards still in training, or on standby. Each of the five guards seemed primarily interested in getting a very good look at me, especially my face. As per my orders, I identified myself to the guard commander as "Teacher's Pet." He handed me an unmarked sealed envelope containing more instructions, and another set of keys.

"There's a ridge three miles up the road from here." he stated. "Don't stop to read what's in the envelope until you get to that ridge. After that , you are totally on your own."

"Do I need to show you more identification?" I asked.

"No." he responded as the gate opened in front of me. "I wouldn't be allowed to look at it if you did. I know you by sight. Anyway, if you are not Teacher's Pet, you will never make it back here alive."

I thanked the guard commander nicely, pulled my truck through the open gate, and set out down the gravel road to the east.

Initially, the gravel road was in good condition. It headed east and northeast into a desert valley which was both unusually wide and unusually long. The desert valley was bordered on all sides by several very tall, tree covered mountain ranges. I estimated the valley was at least 20 miles wide, and more than 50 miles long. The valley seemed to stretch forever into the distance, disappearing finally into a series of jumbled, impassable, interlocked, high mountain ranges. Through the afternoon haze, in the distance, I could identify two passes out of the valley—one to the east, and one to the distant southeast. Unlike most valleys in the area, this one continually sloped gently uphill to the east, and did not contain any dry lake beds. A very small sandy stream flowed the length of the valley, generally following along the southern side of the valley floor.

Several ridges in front of me blocked my immediate view of the road ahead. After a quarter mile, I came to the first low ridge. Beside the road at the top of the ridge, was a large parking area next to a nice picnic area. The picnic area included two wooden picnic tables and a stone lined pit for camp fires. I guessed the area guards were used to having a pretty good time, before turning their trucks around at this first ridge.

After the first ridge, the gravel road was not in very good condition, and appeared to be only lightly traveled. It headed sharply down into a wide arroyo. After three miles, the gravel road came out of the arroyo and topped a second ridge. Another wide graveled parking area was located alongside the road on the top of the second ridge. A very rough and unkempt picnic area sat next to it. This picnic area did not contain any tables or a fire pit.

The top of the second ridge gave a good view of the valley and its surrounding mountains. The two picnic areas were in plain view of each other. Even so, I guessed the area guards were not allowed to spend much time out on the second ridge.

I stopped my truck at the top of the second ridge to read my instructions—like everything else, my instructions were not classified. My instructions did not include a map, or any estimate of the distance to my mountain hut, or any of the details along the way. Like the previous directions out to the Desert Ranges on my previous climate study, these directions read like they had been put together by a child, or a teenager.

However, I noted the instructions were much better written than the previous instructions out at the Desert Oasis. If it was the same person, they were improving, and more polite. The instructions even included the word please, although the writer apparently had not yet learned to use the phrase, "Thank you".

All the driving directions said was keep driving until I reached my weather station. They said my weather shack was sitting up on a slope at the base of the tree line. I decided to wait until I reached my destination before I read the other information.

I expected to be able to see my mountain hut from the top of the second ridge. I was in for quite a shock. I drove a good many miles before the road even began angling to my left, and started to approach the mountain slopes to the north. There was another large arroyo with steep sides to be crossed. The arroyo had a very small stream of water in the bottom, which also had to be driven across. The road was terrible, and just barely passable with my pickup truck. I was certain I was lost and had completely missed the hut, when I finally spotted it up ahead in the distance. It was sitting high on a steep desert slope, almost right up against the base of the tree covered mountainside on the north side of the valley. I guessed it sat more than 2000 feet above me. I was more than 30 miles from the second ridge at the time.

The final two miles or so, were all uphill. The slope was very steep. The dirt road continued on across a wide gently sloping section of land at the top of the ridge, until it ended in a large open area in front of my mountain weather shack. The open area was almost completely devoid of plants and sagebrush. I was careful to turn my truck around, and leave it parked on level ground, facing towards the west, sitting southwest of the weather shack.

I hadn't been driving very fast because my truck was so heavily loaded. By now, it was late in the afternoon. I was quite tired. I unlocked my weather shack, and unloaded my personal belongings. The weather was clear, so I left my equipment in the back of the truck. I entered my weather shack to rest and take stock of my situation.

The site was located at the intersection of a large deep sided valley to the north, and the main east/west valley. There did not appear to be a road anywhere further up either of the two valleys.

The weather shack was somewhat larger than my other weather shacks had been. It was nicely provisioned with a desk, an ivory plotting table, three chairs, some shelves and tables, a couple lamps, an overhead light, a couple waste paper baskets, and a closet for my clothes. A telephone sat on the desk. It had a strong dial tone. There was also a large wooden cot to sleep on. I had brought blankets, sheets, and pillows with me.

The shack was sitting perfectly positioned east and west, with the only door facing south. It had several windows on the northern. eastern, and southern sides of the building. The windows had shades and curtains for privacy. I noted the door closed securely, and could be locked from the inside. The shack was raised. Several sturdy wooden steps led from the desert up to the front door.

The mountain hut weather shack was permanently wired for electricity, and had an electrical heater. The electricity was provided by a permanent power line which reached the shack by way of the side valley to the north. I noted the power line, along with the other facilities out back were all carefully located many feet west of the north-south line formed by the eastern wall of my weather shack. Even the two garbage cans were sitting outside next to the western wall.

Located out back, next to the wall of the mountain, were two supply sheds, a large balloon assembly area with a year's worth of helium and balloon supplies, and a well with an electric pump for drinking water. The drinking water was pumped through an underground pipe to a faucet and a small sink in the weather shack. Otherwise, the site had only outdoor plumbing. The outhouse was unusually tall, and sat highest up on the slope some distance away to the northwest of the shack and the well. There was no water heater, cooking stove, or kitchen utensils. My radio, my watch, and the clock I had brought with me, were my only time pieces.

Roughly one mile to the east was a north-south barbed wire fence with only one gate. The fence came out of the side valley to the north, and continued in a straight line completely across the east-west valley until it finally disappeared into the mountains to the south. The gate was directly east of my weather shack. The gate was closed, but not locked. The fence had only four equally spaced strands of barbed wire. Although a man would not be able to climb over the fence, any child could duck under it. Beyond the barbed wire fence only trees and wilderness could be seen.

Outside, the moon was beginning to rise. I was quite ill-at-ease at the time. Whenever I was outside, I felt like I was being carefully watched by someone hiding over behind the trees.

Darkness was falling, and evening arrived. I locked myself into my shack and turned on the two lamps. After eating one of my box lunches, I carefully said my evening prayers, and turned in for the night. I was very tired. I could see it was gong to be a very long six weeks.

It was approximately 2:00a.m. when I was awakened by some quiet noises coming from outside, in the vicinity of my parked pickup truck. It sounded as if there were three or four children playing in the bed of my truck, where I had left my theodolite and other equipment sitting out for the evening. I was immediately filled with fear when I realized some of the hushed sounds were also coming from the wooden steps outside my front door. There was still some moonlight. However, I was far too terrified to push the curtains aside, and look out the windows. I spent a terrifying 20 minutes or so, laying quietly in my cot, praying, and waiting for the sounds to go away. It's hard for someone to imagine how relieved I was when the sounds finally stopped. Morning would come soon enough. The last thing I needed when I was so far out in this desolate stretch of desert, was to go outside looking for trouble.

Into The Fire

"... And he commanded the most mighty men
that were in his army to bind
Shadrach, Meshach, and Abednego,
and to cast them into
the burning fiery furnace.
... Daniel 3:20-23

The sun was just starting to rise when I woke up that first Monday morning. I had slept very little, and I could have used several more hours of sleep. However, military service is military service.

I was having a hard time deciding what to do next. I wanted to just call off the mountain climate study, and return to Nellis—no-one would ever question my decision if I did so. The events of the night before, left me feeling quite shaken. I had no desire to spend the next six weeks with no other human around out here in these desolate mountain ranges. I mulled it over carefully, as I recited my morning prayers. I ate my second box lunch from the day before, and took my morning vitamin pills. I quickly scanned the requested balloon release schedule. The schedule did nothing to ease my fears.

I had given the Pentagon Generals my word I would perform the mountain climate study duties, whatever they were, for six weeks, only. God expected me to be as good as my word. I expected the same from myself. I decided I would do the study for six weeks only, at any price. Then

I would break off the study, and return to Nellis, for rest and reassignment.

I begin by making the morning balloon release from the southern edge of the parking lot, out in front of my weather shack, as requested. I was careful to stay west of the line. Then I packed my shaving kit and a change of underwear in my truck, and drove back to Death Valley Center for breakfast. There I took a quick shave, brushed my teeth, and showered. Afterwards, I slept for several hours on an empty cot located safely in a small room in the back of the ranger station. According to my orders, they couldn't refuse me.

Feeling like a human again, I took my evening meal early, picked up three box lunches, and a large thermos of coffee. The weather was good. I still had time to make the long drive back out to my mountain hut, and make the requested early evening balloon release—circling to the west of the weather shack to reach the supply sheds and the balloon assembly shed—always staying west of the line. I wasn't yet ready to cross east of the line—and certainly not ready to approach the gate in the fence beyond.

Everything went as expected. However, over the evening meal, feeling better rested, I remembered I had left my pencil out on the theodolite at the end of the morning run. When I returned to the weather shack after evening chow, the pencil was positioned nicely on the top step at the shack's front door. I wanted to be careful to reward whoever had returned it. I placed it in the breast pocket of my work fatigues, and very obviously used it to record the 30 balloon readings which I took during the early evening run—for every child needs to be rewarded for their good deeds.

I got a much better night's sleep that night. I had my six jerry cans full of gasoline, and two spare tires, secured in the back of my pickup truck. There wasn't much there that would be of interest to children.

The winter weather continued to be beautiful the next day. After waking up and completing the requested balloon run, I began feeling more courageous. Sitting on my front steps in the bright morning sun, I finished the second of my three box lunches. I reread the balloon schedule. The close-in runs had been completed. Whoever wrote the schedule, now wanted the balloon runs from much further afield. Today's evening balloon, and tomorrow's early morning balloon should be released from some place up the side canyon to the north of me. The directions provided me said there was a wide place with an electrical sub-station transformer, roughly three quarters of a mile up the northern canyon—sitting just around one of the bends. The location was very obvious because two sets of power lines came out from the transformer. The instructions said I could reach the place by staying completely west of the line, if I chose—however, I wasn't required to. The actual release times didn't particularly matter.

Tomorrow's evening balloon, and the Thursday morning balloons were to be released from some other place, far down in the valley to the south of my location—still staying west of the line if I chose.

Thursday evening, and all day Friday were another matter. I was specifically requested to cross the line to the east of me and work my way up and down this side of the fence. The requested release locations were less than 10 feet from the barbed wire. After next Sunday, all balloon release locations were requested to be on the other side of the barbed wire—east of the fence.

One day at a time, I said to myself. First I needed to reposition my theodolite. In a direct manner, I packed up my canteens, disassembled my theodolite, shouldered the tripod, and hiked up the beautiful, winding side canyon to the north of me. I was careful to stay on the west side of the canyon. The fence continued north up the eastern side of the canyon—although it changed from porous barbed wire to child-proof woven wire.

After locating a suitable spot just beyond the fenced electrical substation, I set up the tripod. Another trip was needed for the heavy and awkward theodolite.

After I had my equipment set up and properly aligned, I took stock of my new location. A more useless location for a climate study could hardly be imagined—and only two balloon releases were requested from this location. Had I wanted to, I could have guessed at the wind measurements and have been just as accurate. I wondered, "Why do they want me to even come up here at all?"

The canyon was only a handful of miles long. It began on the side of some very high and captivating, tree covered mountains to the north. Very large, and very high mountains formed walls on both sides. To the northeast was a long sloping pass to a valley beyond. Even using my theodolite, I was unable to locate any tunnel entrances, buildings, wooden poles, roads, or trails in any of the surrounding mountains.

A twenty foot deep gorge ran down the center of the canyon, and a reasonable size stream flowed down in the gorge. Down stream roughly a half mile, the stream bent sharply to the east and disappeared under ground—I guessed it was probably entering a natural underground reservoir because the inner gorge ended there.

A quarter mile down from my location, a natural barrier on the east side of the gorge, shut off the east side of the canyon. The gap between the sharp cliffs of the inner gorge and the east canyon wall was very small. The fence had been built right up next to the cliffs of the gorge at that point. A large outcropping of tall, sharp rocks, the steeply sloping ground, and some very thick bushes of mesquite made that stretch very difficult—but passable. At the time, it didn't seem like I would ever care.

I found the electrical sub-station to be surprisingly small. It was not as large as the sub-station which served the small Indian Springs Auxiliary Field. It was childproof fenced. The power line coming in, came over the very tall mountains to the north. However two sets of power lines left the station. One was the 120 Volt AC line which continued south to my weather shack. The other crossed the inner gorge diagonally, heading in a southern direction, to the mountain on the other side. Once there, it vanished from sight underground.

I was struck by how small the power lines were which entered and left the electrical sub-station—especially the lines which stretched to the mountain on the other side of the gorge. It meant the sub-station could be supplying electrical power to little more than a small group of dormitories, kitchens, and small appliance repair shops.

I thought about this for a few minutes. I certainly felt totally alone in this canyon. The child-proof woven wire fence on the other side convinced me that no children—human or alien—were ever allowed to play or hike in this naturally dangerous canyon. Even if my balloons, when released, drifted to the north, or over to the other side of the surrounding mountains—so what? I was only requested to release two of them. That's not enough balloons to entertain even a small group of children.

The high pass to the northeast stuck in my mind. The incoming power lines were so small, they couldn't have been expected to carry much electricity from very far away. It meant the next sub-station in the line must be located close-in, just over the mountains to the north. I wondered if I could walk out to human civilization by hiking over the high pass to the north-east. Crossing the pass would be quite simple—whether on foot or by air. I wondered if that was what the planners of this climate study wanted me to see—and why? And if I did cross the pass, what would I find on the other side?

I had plenty of time, and I was curious. So, I set out hiking north up the canyon. I stayed on the western side of the inner gorge. I loved making the hike. However, by the time I reached the head of the winding canyon, it was obvious that in order reach the foot of the pass, I would have to start my hike from the other side of the gorge—and from the other side of the fence. I would have to return back down the canyon to reach the gate, in order to do that.

The day was progressing. I returned back down the canyon. I packed my things in my truck, and headed in to take the evening meal at Death Valley Center.

Returning to my work, things progressed in a routine manner, while I ignored the quiet sounds of someone playing with my tools in the balloon assembly shack out back. None of the buildings out back would lock shut—including the outhouse.

The next morning, after the first balloon run, I brought my equipment back from the northern canyon, and packed it in the back of my truck. I also packed a change of underwear, shaving kit, and other things. I began the drive south into the east-west valley.

I zigzagged south down the slope. There wasn't any road. I had to pick my route very carefully through the open rocky desert, and sagebrush. It took quite a while. In the fullness of time, I found a suitable location down on the northern edge of the valley floor. However, It was a very big desert. I did not feel confident I could find the location again. So I left my theodolite and stand packed in the back of my truck.

I stopped and took stock of the situation. Down on the valley floor, off in the distance, the fence had a second gate. It was a sliding gate similar to the one at the Desert Oasis, but, a very wide one. At the time, it was closed but not locked.

Like the location up in the north side valley, my few balloon wind measurements from down on the valley floor, were obviously going to be totally useless. Yet, the balloon request schedule and locations, had been very explicit. I wondered why anyone would make such a request. I thought about it, and decided whoever put together the balloon schedule, wanted me to see something important from this location, which was not visible from the gravel road back to the guard station.

The valley arced noticeably towards the northeast. I wondered if something was concealed along the intersection of the wall of the mountain above me, and the top of the slope to the northeast.

Up on the slope above me, beyond the eastern fence, and the heavy growth of trees, ran an arroyo with a small spring-fed stream flowing at the bottom. The tree filled arroyo meandered to the east. It defined a large open flat area several miles long and several miles across. The flat open area lay between the L shaped, tree-filled arroyo and the adjacent mountain wall on the north, and was open to the east.

The flat area was so reminiscent of the flat area which lay east of the far-away Desert Oasis, I wondered if the open area was also a landing field—and if there were any tunnel entrances concealed in the adjacent mountain wall on the north. If so, that would mean I was being asked to conduct the mountain climate study from an alien air strip.

Why else, I wondered, would the mountain above me be permanently wired for electricity? I wondered if that was why no other human was allowed east of the fence—as well as not being allowed east of the line—and the noises I had been hearing at night outside my mountain hut weather shack sounded suspiciously like children playing.

Yes, there was a certain logic to the Generals sending me, a weather observer and a low ranking enlisted man, out into this desolate wasteland, to set up a weather station next to a landing field. That is what the generals had me doing for the last many months, back at the Indian Springs gunnery ranges. After all, I thought to myself, these were the days of the Viet Nam war. Even if this open area was only going to be used in the near future for ordinary human activities—such as U.S. Army helicopters on training missions, they would still need close in weather coverage.

I broke off my thoughts, and put my truck in gear. It was time for me to head in to Death Valley Center for the evening meal. It was a long drive, and I had a lot to think about.

Over the evening meal in the Death Valley Center chow hall, I wondered some more. The meal was quite good. It included chipped beef SOS on toast and I took my time—enjoying the feeling of safety.

If my suspicions were correct, I reasoned—if the Gray Aliens have been in this area for several thousand years, they wouldn't need close-in weather coverage at the landing area, because they already had their own. Only if the Generals were planning on having humans visit the landing area, would there be a need for close-in weather support.

But if that was the case, this section of desert was so naturally dangerous, wouldn't the Generals first have to send one weather observer out here alone, and have him establish a safe area—perhaps something such as a mountain hut? Knowing how Generals think, wouldn't they arrange to have waiting for him, perhaps out along one of the trails—a young Gray Alien teenager—presumably a young girl—to establish a brother-sister type relationship of trust and understanding—before any other human could be risked coming out here, to make plans and hold joint meetings?

I wondered. I remembered my days back in boot camp at Lackland AFB, Texas. During one of the private test sessions, one of the civilian interviewers—a middle-aged man—had asked many questions regarding the relationship between me and my lovely older sister Martha. I remembered telling him how proud I was of the close brother-sister relationship that Martha and I had—how we stayed in close touch—and how happy it made my father. I proudly told the interviewer how my father told me once, he considered his proudest accomplishment to be that he had been able to keep Martha and I together.

I remembered the interviewer had taken many notes—I wondered. I decided tonight, after completing the evening balloon run, I would send another letter to Martha.

The remaining balloon runs west of the fence were stunningly beautiful, although routine enough. The read, white, and black balloons generally drifted to the southeast, slowly crossing the valley as they slowly rose into the winter desert sky. A couple of the morning balloons drifted off over the mountains to the northeast before finally reaching the upper level wind layers, changing directions, and drifting once again towards the east and southeast.

However, finding a decent location from which to launch the balloons became an increasingly difficult problem. Coming in close to the fence, as I worked my way up and down the hill, required a great deal of courage—of which I had little. The large trees, thick bushes, and heavy undergrowth on the east side of the fence, began immediately at the barbed wire. I became convinced that someone hidden in the vegetation was watching me intently from close in on the other side. It seemed to be an adult, slowly paralleling my movements. On the late Friday afternoon run, with my theodolite sitting just six feet west of the fence, and a mile down from the top gate, it came in so close on the other side of the fence, and behind me that, in fear, I broke off the balloon run, and returned to the safety of my weather shack. A long time passed before I had the courage to retrieve my theodolite. I left the tripod standing in place until the following Monday morning.

Back at my weather shack, I read and reread the balloon release schedule several times. I finally stopped reading it because each time I became more nervous. It was very explicit. Starting Monday morning of the second week, all balloon releases were to be made, not just east of the line—but east of the fence. What was worse, starting Monday of the third week, all balloon releases were to take place at night—from a location over by the open area out in the high desert—more than three miles east of the fence. I could see that six weeks was going to be a very long time.

I packed my truck, took the evening meal at the Death Valley chow hall, and spent the weekend in Las Vegas—resting in solitude in my empty barracks room at Nellis.

Where To Lay His Head

"... And Jesus said to him,
Foxes have holes,
and birds of the air have nests;
but the Son of man
has not where to lay his head. ..."
... Luke 9:58

To be intelligent, thinking creatures need to naturally take ownership of things. These things are not all physical objects, such as areas of land, or the clothes they are wearing. To be intelligent, they must naturally take ownership of abstract things such as their thoughts, memories, feelings, emotions such as love or hate, their hopes, and dreams. They must learn to proudly express this ownership to themselves and to the others around them.

In short—ownership has to show. Intelligent thinking creatures have to show the things they own. They have to proudly show those things in their thoughts, emotions—and in the very words they use when they are communicating with each other. In their language, they have to have words, such as 'mine'—so different from 'yours'—whether they are human or extraterrestrial.

In the English language many 'be' words show ownership. Many of those words were borrowed from other languages—from other intelligent humans who were proud of the things they too, owned.

For example, in ancient times the emotional feelings shared by every member of the Visigoth tribe were the 'longings' of the tribe. If you joined the tribe and took ownership of a portion of those feelings, then you felt a feeling of belonging to the tribe. The feeling of "belonging" was a feeling of ownership. In ancient times, it was only intelligent to join tribes and feel as though you 'belonged' somewhere. It has been my personal experience, intelligent extraterrestrials are no different. They too, believe every intelligent creature naturally belongs in a group—or a tribe—somewhere. They pay close attention to their groups and their feelings, even more so then humans do. It's only intelligent.

Monday morning of the second week came soon enough. I was quite nervous, and afraid of my own shadow that winter morning. I really did not feel as though I belonged anywhere out in that distant, desolate stretch of desert and mountains. I did not feel I ever would.

I positioned the case holding my theodolite on the ground, a few feet west of the fence, just opposite the top gate. I retrieved my tripod which was still standing a mile or so down along the fence. I gave the section of the fence in-between, wide berth as I did so.

I left the tripod and the rest of my equipment sitting on the rocky desert soil west of the gate as I went alone—and unarmed—through the gate to inspect the area east of the fence. I was singing my songs as I did so. I could tell I was being closely watched with every step I took. There weren't any animals or birds in the wooded area east of the fence, and the winds were nearly calm. There was no other reason for the leaves on a few of the bushes, located down in the valley to the south of me, to be moving the way they were.

There seemed to be rough trail east of the gate, which connected to a small open area at the top of the stream filled valley. That area was possibly a quarter of a mile due east of the gate. From there, the trail appeared to head off towards the mountain wall to the northeast, perhaps 200 yards away. I was quite ill-at ease. I had not originally intended to come that close to the mountain wall—especially since no other humans were ever allowed east of the fence.

After identifying a suitable location in the small open area, I carefully returned to the gate area and one-by-one brought in my theodolite, tripod, and the rest of my equipment. My spot for balloon release was located in-between two very large and very thick bushes. Then I went back to the balloon assembly shack to prepare the balloon.

When I returned, I noticed one of the medium sized equipment boxes had been moved. I knew what it meant. I estimated the box weighed roughly twenty pounds—far too heavy for an alien child to move. Only an alien adult would have had that kind of strength. What was worse, I felt the alien adults must certainly have been watching me for the last several days. It meant when they moved the box, they knew I would notice it—because I had been treating the boxes as if I owned them. It meant the alien guards were intentionally sending me a message. I decided I would live a longer, happier life if I let them know I had gotten the message. I tied the balloon to the nearby bush—then I carefully and deliberately moved the box back to it's original position—praying and singing my songs as I did so.

Then, using only slow smooth movements, I released the balloon, took the wind measurements, and returned to the weather shack. I left all my equipment—and the boxes—sitting in the clearing, and drove in to Death Valley Center. After taking my meals in the chow hall, I did my laundry, and spent a lot of time rebuilding my courage in the library.

I used several map books to carefully study the geography of the area. The geography of the valleys where my mountain hut was located was not actually shown on any of the maps—on one of them, it was just whited out and marked "unexplored territory". However, I was able to determine that a small town way out in the desert, was located only a handful of miles over the northeast pass out of the north side valley.

When I returned from Death Valley Center, it was necessary for me to chose a different location for the evening balloon release. The balloon release requests did not identify any specific sites east of the gate. It only requested the sites be north of the gate and east of the fence. I was nervous about being positioned so close to the mountain wall. The brush was fairly scattered north of me. There was a second larger open area over closer to the fence and north of the gate. The desert grasses in the open area were quite short. The area reminded me of a children's playground, so I moved my theodolite and other equipment over to it for the evening run.

The evening balloon run was routine enough. However, from the point of view of an actual climate study, the results were quite useless—like all of the other wind measurements I had so far taken out in this desolate stretch of desert.

The next morning, Tuesday, it was necessary for me to change the position of my theodolite again. The request was for me to keep moving toward the north, east of the fence, up the side valley. I needed to first identify another suitable place. Leaving my equipment and theodolite in place, I set out to the north, following east along the fence which was also east of the inner gorge. The brush quickly thickened. After perhaps another quarter mile, I reached the line of large heavy bushes which formed a barrier across the canyon, from the canyon wall over to the inner gorge. It stood just this side of the jutted out rock wall.

I expected to just brush my way through the double row of large tall bushes. I was in for quite an emotional shock. In between the double row of bushes was hidden a child proof woven wire security fence. Directly in front of me, hidden in the bushes, was a tall swinging gate. It was latched, but not locked. Although it was overgrown with bushes, and apparently hadn't been opened in a very long time, it was in very good repair.

Since the balloon release schedule had requested several balloon runs be made from the northern valley, east of the gorge, I decided to break off some of the branches and clear the bushes enough so the swinging gate could be opened. I was wearing my heavy work gloves. I had no other tools. Consequently, it was an extremely difficult job. I got the pathway on my side of the fence partially cleared. Because of the bushes, the gate wouldn't open towards me, and one large branch prevented the gate from opening away from me.

I was thinking of just giving up on the attempt. I had been working more or less in a feverish manner, and I needed to take a rest. I was standing back and to the side of the gate looking at the bushes, when I heard something behind me. Before I could turn to look around, my mind seemed to wander for a short moment or two. I remember glancing at the ground, and at the canyon to the west of me. When I was finally able to regain my senses, I immediately noticed the gate was standing completely open. The offending branch had been cleanly snapped off, and was now laying on the ground some distance away. My watch had stopped. It took a while for me to get my watch running again—to say a few prayers—and to get hold of my fears.

I decided for my own safety, I needed to go through the open swinging gate and set up my theodolite on the other side. I hardly needed to offend anyone out in this desolate stretch of desert by refusing to accept gifts when they were offered. I nervously went through the now open gate, and continued on up the canyon for another quarter mile. It took several trips before I had my equipment set up at the new site.

The land sloped sharply towards the cliffs of the inner gorge at the gate. The gate would very obviously be dangerous to use during bad weather. The balloon releases went routinely enough, as did my trip in to the chow hall.

The Wednesday morning balloon run was near disaster. The weather had turned colder. A storm had blown in. It rained heavily that evening. In the morning, it was still raining lightly, and the ground was muddy. The cold rocks were as slippery as ice. I took a bad fall coming through the swinging gate, losing the balloon in the process. Bruised, but otherwise unharmed, I decided to immediately retrieve my theodolite, tripod, and equipment, and move it back south of the cross fence to safer ground. Another release attempt would simply have to wait.

I will always remember how difficult that morning was. The last six foot stretch of sloping, polished rocks before the gate were covered with slowly forming ice, and I was unable to walk across it. I had to virtually crawl and slide my equipment in front of me. At one point I had to press my forehead down against the top of the theodolite case to steady it, while I moved the equipment case forward with my left hand. Only when I reached the swinging gate was I able to grab onto the cross fence and pull myself to a standing position.

Once everything was through the swinging gate, I could position it in a nearby place where the land was level, and the footing was greatly improved. I closed and latched the gate behind me. I quickly picked a new safe location some feet away, and completed the morning run, vowing to never use that gate again.

When I came back in the late afternoon, after going in to the chow hall at Death Valley Center, the rain had stopped, and the weather was clearing. However, up on the slopes of the mountain, and in the canyons and valleys, it was still very gloomy.

As per the release schedule, I needed to once again, change my release location. I decided to carefully check for a safe location next to the inner cross fence, and closer to the mountain wall. Carefully, I worked my way east along the cross fence, through and around the bushes.

I finally got my first view of the base of the mountain wall when I broke out of the last set of bushes. Shock hardly describes my reaction. Recessed into the mountain wall, some distance away, was a large dark brown colored, rough surfaced, metal door. A layer of rock overlaid the door's edges, so the door could only be opened from the inside. The door was roughly 8 feet wide, and 12 feet tall. The corners of the opening in the rock were smoothly rounded, like the doors on ships. I could see immediately I was looking at an opening to a tunnel entrance, and the door was its pressure seal. The opening was so perfectly concealed that in the gathering gloom and the evening mist and haze, I almost didn't see it.

Fearful that I had crossed some kind of unseen line, and afraid of what might follow, I did not stop to inspect any further. I quickly returned to my current release location. In hurried fashion, I packed up my theodolite, tripod, and equipment and moved it back south to a level spot just inside the eastern fence, directly next to the gate leading back to the refuge of my weather shack.

I used the location next to the refuge gate for the evening run, as well as the next morning's run. As usual, after completing the next morning's run, I gathered my belongings and headed in to Death Valley Center.

I had just taken a seat in the chow hall when the duty park ranger came in to the chow hall, and walked over to me. He greeted me politely, and made certain I was feeling OK. He told me to enjoy myself, and take all the time I wanted for chow. He said when I had finished, there was a friend of mine over at the main ranger station who was hoping to speak with me.

I thanked him kindly, and said I would be over as soon as I finished my meal.

His request left me feeling quite nervous. I supposed whoever had come to talk with me was carrying orders to cancel my mountain climate study and send me back to Indian Springs or Nellis. On the one hand I wanted very much to be re-assigned back to Indian Springs or Nellis. On the other hand, I had given my word to the Generals that their faith in me was justified. They had granted me numerous special privileges. As I saw it—so far, I had accepted the privileges—and accomplished nothing in return—and this with other young men my age heroically serving their country and dying on the battlefields of Viet Nam—young men who surely could have done better than me on this assignment, had they been given the chance. To date, I did not have so much as a single balloon wind measurement that was worth the paper it was written on.

So it was with considerable trepidation that I finished my meal, and made the long walk back over to the main ranger station. I checked in to the special room in the back, and sat down in a comfortable chair next to the sofa and a small end table. I waited for someone else to join me.

After a few minutes, the door to the room opened, and the special ranger politely greeted me. "Good afternoon, Airman Hall" he said, closing the door behind him.

"Good afternoon, sir." I responded in military fashion—duty weather observers never salute indoors.

He took a comfortable chair next to one of the other end tables, and began, "I wanted to make certain, and see for myself that you were still OK. They told me you took a bad fall, so I was concerned for your safety. I know you are the kind of airman who never likes to come in for sick call."

"Yes, Sir." I responded. "I still have some bruises from the fall I took yesterday. However, I'm young. I'm healing fast. I'll be completely over my bruises in another day or so. God takes care of me."

"That's good to hear." he responded. "The first thing I need to tell you is how impressed the Generals are with everything you have accomplished so far on this mountain climate study. You have accomplished more during these past ten days than the Generals ever thought could be accomplished during the first two years. Back at headquarters, we are all just stunned at how well you are doing."

"Thank you, Sir." I instinctively responded. Privately I was in quite a quandary. So far, I didn't feel as though I had accomplished anything. On the other hand, rangers as high ranking as the special ranger seldom, if ever, passed out compliments to low ranking enlisted personnel such as myself. Yet his body language clearly showed he meant every word he was saying. I sat quietly and waited for him to continue. I could see he was choosing his words carefully.

"I wish to remind you that when you are out there in the desert, you are completely and totally free to go anywhere you choose, anytime you wish.

No one will ever stand in your way, or ask why you've come.

Even I am never allowed to ask you any questions. I am only allowed to listen to anything you may wish to say to me.

Nothing you do is or will ever be classified. Only you will ever know what actually happened out in the deserts and mountains where you have been sent.

You are totally free to reject any request made of you for any reason. You never have to give a reason for anything you do, or any decision you make, or any request you reject.

The only requirement is that you always be totally by yourself—totally alone.

If you ever did take anyone else out to where you are, you would not be in any trouble. Whoever was with you, or whoever you encountered would be totally on their own." he said. "I am told they should not expect to come back alive."

"Yes, Sir." I answered. "I understand that." By his body language I could see he wasn't satisfied with my answer. I waited while he chose his next words carefully, before he continued.

"I have never been out where you are. I don't know anything about the place, and I don't know where it is. But for example, they tell me there is a beautiful canyon, surrounding mountains, and a mountain pass you might enjoy climbing and exploring. If you wanted to, you could even release balloons from up in the pass."

From his body language, I could see immediately what he was wondering about. I had been awfully timid about going north of the cross fence, even during the good weather.

Defensively, I responded, "Yes, Sir. There is such a pass. However, getting there is quite difficult."

Still thinking carefully before he spoke, he said, "They tell me the slope up into the pass is so gentle that an older child could easily make it up to the top of the pass and back down."

I could see immediately what he was getting at. The balloon release schedule had requested several balloon runs to be taken from the northern head of the canyon, maybe even from the pass itself. I had done something similar on my first climate study. Yet, right at the minute, I had no further plans to ever again progress north of the cross fence.

"Yes sir" I answered him. I remembered the children playing in the back of my truck at night—and that he was obviously a high ranking and a highly trained psychiatrist. I continued, speaking carefully and distinctly, "The slope up into the pass is quite gentle. Older children can easily make it both up and down the slope. However, the entire route is quite dangerous in bad weather. Even older children would need some young adult man who knew the trail to accompany them, in case they slipped or fell.

Of course, if an older child could make it both ways, so could a middle aged man or woman if they also had a young man who knew the route, to act as a trail guide. The distances are not very great."

I could see by his body language that my statements had hit a target. He was thinking thoughts he had never considered before. So I continued while he listened intently, "Of course, I suppose on their own, they would have to get prior approval of the guards, in order to enter the canyon or the area.

The canyon has a nicely formed wall. If they encountered anything unexpected or frightening, they could just stop and stand with their back to the inner canyon wall and wait until things clarified themselves—the way I frequently do. That way, whatever happens has to happen in front of me where I have the best chance of dealing with it.

The technique always works. Sometimes I stand with my back to my truck, or to the security fence, or to any one of the large bushes which are out there. It is not at all unusual for me to stand with my back to something sturdy for ten minutes or more. When I hear something moving, I stand and wait to see if anything is going to happen. In order to safely handle any of the trails out there, you have to be very patient. You have to let whatever you encounter out there along the trail, come out into the open in its own time.

The only real dangerous part of the trail is where it gets down near the area where my weather shack is. There is a cross fence blocking the canyon with only one gate. That gate is right up next to the edge of a sharp cliff with very slippery footing. That's where I fell yesterday. Once a person makes it past that gate, it is very easy to go the last two miles and get down to the refuge where I am."

"But there's a second gate," he exclaimed without thinking. "They tell me there's another gate hidden over at the other end of the fence."

I could see by his body language he was telling the truth. For my part, I reacted in shock.

Defensively I responded, “A second gate over at the other end of the fence?” I exclaimed. “But that end of the fence is fixed to the mountain wall just a few feet away from the tunnel entrance. The tunnel entrance is sealed by a large metal door. I don’t have the courage to ever go over there. It’s probably one of the tunnel entrances the children are using.

Even if there were a second gate over there, what would I do if I went to use the gate and the tunnel entrance was open?”

His smile and his body language showed he had just accomplished his goal, as he answered my question politely and calmly, “Well, Airman Hall. If the tunnel entrance were open, if you wanted to, you could just go in. Your orders allow you to go anywhere.”

I sat silently in shock as his words sunk in. I listened as he continued professionally, “So I believe you told me that a safe hiking route exists between the top of a mountain pass, down through a beautiful canyon, through a safe gate in a fence located safely next to a mountain wall. The gate is located directly next to a tunnel entrance, to a set of children’s living areas. The tunnel’s security door may or may not be open.

You also clearly stated that in your opinion, a middle-aged man, or a middle-aged woman, or an older child, could easily make the trip both ways, if they are properly escorted by an experienced trail guide, preferably a young man.

The trail is not long. The hikers could safely stand with their backs to the canyon wall and study the situation if anything unexpected happened.

The middle aged man or woman would first, on their own, have to obtain permission from the guards because everything you just described is located east of the fence."

"Yes, Sir." I answered, stunned. "You heard me correctly, Sir. Of course, I, myself, will have to personally check that the second gate exists. Otherwise, the gate I used yesterday can only be used during good weather."

"I can't tell you what an incredibly good job you have been doing." he stated finally. Then he bid me good-bye, and left the room—leaving me, as always, free to come and go as I pleased—as long as I did so alone.

I rushed to complete the rest of my business at Death Valley Center, and hurried back to my mountain hut weather shack. I felt for my own safety and piece of mind, I needed to take possession of the northern side canyon and the safe route into it. I felt I needed to show I was intelligent, and I wasn't failing at my assignments—I felt I needed to show ownership of a few things. I wanted to accomplish that goal while I still had reasonably good weather and some daylight to work with.

Consequently, as soon as I had my truck parked and unloaded back at my weather shack, I grabbed my canteens and work gloves, and hurried over through the gate to my current theodolite location. I picked up my equipment box and set out for the second gate in the cross fence.

As expected, the tunnel entrance was closed. The second gate was located exactly where I had been told it was located. It opened easily and smoothly. The trail running right next to the wall of the mountain was an excellent all weather trail, and safe even during a light rain.

I picked a location some distance up the canyon, opposite the electrical transformer on the other side of the gorge. In successive trips, I repositioned my theodolite and took the evening balloon run from the new location. I recorded the winds, as I always did, but hardly cared where the balloon went.

I felt quite satisfied with myself as I hiked back to my weather shack. I felt I had finally accomplished my first personal goal of the mountain climate study. I felt I had established my ownership of the northern canyon. Even today, as I remember the beautiful surrounding mountains, the artistic, captivating canyon with its rocky walls, the enchanting cliff-lined deep inner gorge, the spring fed stream at the bottom, the beckoning, sloping pass to the northeast—even today, I think of it all as mine.

Moments To Remember

"... And the LORD said unto him,
This is the land which I sware unto Abraham,
unto Isaac, and unto Jacob,
saying, I will give it unto thy seed:
I have caused thee to see it with thine eyes, ..."
... Deuteronomy 34:4

I could hardly wait until Friday morning. I moved my theodolite and equipment to the head of the northern canyon for the morning balloon run. After I had taken the requested 30 numbers, I closed up my equipment and began the careful hike up the long slope of the pass to the northeast. I probably had to hike up roughly 2,500 feet to reach the top of the pass. I brought my last box lunch with me. When I got to the top, I found some rocks to sit down on, enjoy my lunch, and take in the view.

It was a cloudy chilly hazy day. However, the visibility was pretty good, and the scene before me was one I will always remember.

Off to the northwest, several miles out, ran an ordinary woven wire security fence. There was a locked gate and a small, poorly hidden guard station. Just inside the distant fence was another electrical sub-station. The power lines from it ran to the substation in the canyon.

In the distance, a few miles beyond the security fence, sat the small desert town, as I had expected.

A narrow dirt road, which looked as if it was never used, started at the poorly hidden guard station. It ran across the level desert, and connected to a large, level, open parking lot type area at the northeastern base of the pass. From the pass itself, the land sloped gently down on both sides. A large four wheel drive truck or a jeep could probably have been driven from the parking lot up and over the pass into the canyon. I was glad to see the information I had provided to the special ranger was correct.

The shock I felt came when I looked east, and carefully studied the desert floor and the base of the north side of the east-west mountain range below me—the one with the tunnel entrance back at the second gate to the canyon. I was looking for a large Gray alien base with many more tunnel entrances—or, at the very least, some secret USAF base testing new aircraft.

To my shock, there wasn't anything unnatural, or civilized in view. Stretching as far as the eye could see, there was nothing—nothing but ordinary uninhabited deserts, untouched rocky mountainsides, and mountain wilderness. After studying the desert floor and the sides of the mountains east of me, I was forced to conclude the north side of the mountain range simply did not have hidden tunnel entrances, Gray alien bases, any secret USAF air fields, facilities, or anything. There was simply nothing man-made—or Alien made—on the north side of the mountain range. There was simply nothing out east to be seen. It came as a terrible shock.

I finished my box lunch, and returned back into the canyon from where I'd come. I left my theodolite in place, and headed back for morning chow at Death Valley Center.

Along the way, I struggled with the facts I was certain of. I was certain the tunnel into the south side of the mountain east of the fence must have had a few small rooms—probably small dormitory areas and classrooms. They were probably being used by a handful of Gray Alien children. The Generals must have designed my mountain climate study as an excuse for me to periodically release a few weather balloons to entertain the children.

Something didn't seem to be making sense. "Why don't the Alien parents entertain their own children?" I asked myself. "After all, they must have been doing so for several thousand years." I really didn't see where either the Generals, or the Aliens, needed me for anything.

I was feeling shaken and humbled. I had previously thought my work was going to eventually be of some importance—but how? The children were growing daily. The day would soon come when pretty colored weather balloons rising into the desert skies no longer interested them. What would the General's plan be then?

I shrugged. "They also serve who stand and wait. I am only a low ranking enlisted man. Orders will always be orders."

I finished the Friday evening run, packed my truck, and headed in to Nellis and Las Vegas for the weekend.

Point Man

"... Then Nebuchadnezzar the king was
astonished,
and rose up in haste, and spake,
and said unto his counselors,
Did not we cast three men bound
into the midst of the fire? . . ."
. . . Daniel 3:24

For the next week, the balloon release directions requested I enter the lower tree filled valley with the spring fed stream. I was to slowly work my way south down the valley, following the winding, tree shrouded stream. Eventually I would break out of the trees and heavy foliage, into the desert on the other side. I would have to make my own trail.

The forested valley floor was much wider than the stream. There were many fully grown trees, and large bushes overhanging the stream for most of its length. However, there were a handful of places open enough for a balloon to be released. One was of special note. It was located roughly three quarters of a mile down along the gently sloping trail, at a small bend in the canyon. I named the place "nostalgia point". It was a natural place for a hiker to stop for a few minutes, and rest. From that spot, both ends of the trail were visible. In addition, in the distance to the north, could also be seen the tunnel entrance and the second gate.

There were a number of stream filled arroyos flowing down into the valley from the east. The east side was the uphill side. Consequently, those side canyons were quite steep and rocky. By comparison, the western side of the valley was nearly level with the downhill slope of the desert to the west. Only the thick trees and other vegetation—and the parallel barbed wire fence a short distance off in that direction—prevented me from taking shortcuts to my weather shack on the hill.

Even on my first day in the valley, I noticed a second narrow and lightly used trail winding between the stream and the barbed wire fence. That trail had numerous natural stopping points which allowed a hiker to remain hidden while being able to view both the stream and the desert to the west.

I ignored the second trail, because someone else had made it—so presumably someone else might be using it. Instead, I marked out a trail of my own. The trail I marked out stayed right next to the main stream bed for its entire length. It was roughly a mile and a quarter long—maybe longer. It was as naturally beautiful as any hike in a valley, along a stream could be.

The problem I faced wasn't the length of the route, or the cold stream at the bottom. The problem was, there was only one way to enter or leave the north end of the valley. The valley was roughly 25 or 30 feet deep. A long steep down hill slope connected the small level open area at the top of the valley, and the valley floor. The small open area was east of the main gate in the fence. The footing on the slope during wet weather was obviously going to be treacherous. Yet the balloon release schedule specifically requested I make extensive use of the route. It pointed out I was free to make as many improvements to the trails I used, as I desired. Even though the trees and other foliage were already quite thick down in the valley, my instructions made it clear I was free to plant as many additional plants, presumably down along the stream, as I desired. I was, of course, free to visit the valley, any time I chose.

Without further ado, bright and early on Monday morning, I retrieved my theodolite, tripod, and other equipment, from the north side canyon, and descended into the lower stream filled valley. For my first release, I chose a place at the bottom of the slope. I did so, but, not without a great deal of trepidation. The bushes and trees in that area stretched west to the fence, and were especially thick. In days past, I had become certain an older adult lady Gray would frequently take up a standing position hidden in the dark shadows of the trees. She would study me carefully from a distance. The second trail coming in from the south certainly made it easy for her to do so.

The following two days passed easily enough, as I worked my way down the valley. The balloons were fragile. If a weather balloon touched even a small tree branch as it was rising out of the stream filled valley, it generally broke. Consequently I had to make several additional round trips through the valley, and back to my balloon assembly shack, to replace broken balloons.

Nostalgia Point was the easiest location to release from, so I quickly moved my theodolite and other equipment down there.

During those two days, I quickly became convinced that in addition to being frequently observed closely by the older, Gray Alien lady, she was joined by the young girl and her younger brother. The adult lady would stand hidden in the trees along the second trail, generally paralleling my movements. The children would generally stay hidden behind bushes on the bluffs and in the side arroyos on the east side of the stream filled valley. They were the same two children I had previously seen months before on my first climate study.

The two children had grown noticeably and were now somewhat more muscular. The older lady was always wearing a breathing device of some type. Sometimes when I would become convinced they were out there watching me, hidden behind the trees, I would turn slowly to look. I would get short glimpses of them and sometimes a tiny handful of others, before they stepped back behind the heavy foliage. Now and then they seemed to be intentionally slow at doing so.

Consequently, I did not idly walk into the valley. By Wednesday morning, I was quite happy when I finally broke out of the valley into the desert on the other side. I picked a new release location in the desert to the southeast, probably 50 feet from the south entrance.

Late Wednesday afternoon, as I was returning from evening chow at Death Valley Center, the guard on duty at the main "shooting range" gate stopped me for a moment. He handed me a sealed brown manila envelope. As usual, he asked me not to read it until I reached the ridge at three miles. I complied.

Inside the envelope was a modified balloon release schedule. The new schedule requested I begin making two evening balloon releases, one at 7:00p.m., and a second at

9:00p.m., starting tonight. The schedule requested I remain on station out at the release point for the time in between, recording the temperature and observing the sky and the stars every half hour.

In return, the morning run could be taken as late as necessary. After completing a balloon run of 30 readings, and hiking the valley, I could be back in my weather shack by 10:15p.m. , and still get a good night's sleep.

The moon was just past the first quarter, and the desert winter weather remained good. The schedule seemed simple enough to a highly trained weather observer such as myself. The Wednesday night runs were so easy, they seemed like child's play. However, I couldn't help noticing through it all, I was alone—obviously, totally and completely alone out in the desert.

I certainly didn't mind being alone. I felt much safer, and happier when I was alone—"But still", I remember wondering, "doesn't anyone know I am out here?"

After finishing my balloon run, and recording the final weather report, I began the nostalgic hike back to my weather shack. There was plenty of moonlight, so I did not use my flashlight. I was enchanted by the shadows in the moonlight along the trail. When I reached "nostalgia point", I was surprised to see, in the distance, soft lamplight flooding out from the tunnel entrance by the second gate. I had never seen the tunnel entrance open before. I expected there were other tunnel entrances into the mountain, so I had come to suppose the one by the second gate was never used.

The lamplight was not particularly bright, but, I was also able to determine that the second gate was open. I paused for a few minutes and studied the scene in the distance. Nothing else seemed to be happening, so I went back into the shadows under the trees, and into the shadows along the trail, and continued the walk back to my weather shack. I was equally surprised, when I finally reached the northern end of the valley and climbed out to the high level ground. The light in the distance was now turned off, and the tunnel entrance was closed, as was the second gate—and I was still completely alone outside in the evening. There was nothing left for me to do, except return to my weather shack, and turn in for the night.

The next night, Thursday, the desert was once again bathed in beautiful moonlight. Once again, I found myself obviously completely alone in my balloon assembly shack, alone along the trail, and alone in the enchanting night-time desert. At 8:00p.m., in between the runs, my curiosity got the best of me. I just had to know if, once again, the tunnel entrance was open. On a whim, then, I hiked back to nostalgia point to have a look. As before, the tunnel entrance was open, the lamplight was on, and the second gate to the north canyon was open. Nothing else could be seen, so I returned back south to the desert, to my balloon release point for the remainder of the evening. At 10:00p.m., when I was returning to my weather shack, the tunnel entrance was closed, as was the second gate. I was more than a little curious.

Colder winter weather moved in during the evening. All day Friday the weather slowly deteriorated. The sky was gloomy overcast, and the air filled with light hazy mist.

I wanted to take my truck in to Nellis and Las Vegas for the weekend. I decided to spend the entire day resting and cleaning my weather shack, picking up, sweeping the floor, and cleaning around the buildings. As soon as I completed the 9:00p.m. balloon release, I could just return to my truck, and drive in to Death Valley Center—with its 24 hour chow hall—and on in to Nellis, and to the shows and casinos in Las Vegas. I had planned ahead and brought an extra box lunch from the chow hall the evening before.

Late afternoon arrived. I finished my janitorial duties by re-stacking the new, current, department store catalogs which I had brought from Las Vegas the week-end before. They contained the latest winter fashions, and fit nicely in a corner on the shelf across from my bunk. Without thinking, I stacked them in a precise order, with the thickest one on the bottom.

The sky was still heavily overcast and gloomy. I prepared my two balloons more than a half hour before sundown. Collecting my things, I set out for the release point. With evening coming on, I wanted to make it through the dark, misty, stream filled valley while there was still some daylight. I felt completely alone as I descended the northern slope, and entered the valley.

I was just reaching "nostalgia point". In the distance, the southern entrance to the valley had just come into view when, once again, I began to feel I was being carefully observed from the final thick grove of trees which stood on the right hand—western—side of the southern valley entrance. The feeling was so strong, I stopped along the trail for a few minutes to get hold of myself.

The visibility wasn't particularly good in the rapidly darkening valley, and in the gathering gloom, and mist. I waited a few minutes, and nothing seemed to be happening.

So, having little other choice, I cautiously resumed my walk towards the south entrance, carefully choosing my steps and studying the grove of trees, as I did so.

After a few minutes, I had slowly cut the distance to the south entrance by half. Up ahead on the trail, as if on command, the young girl and her younger brother stepped carefully out from the grove of trees on the right side of the trail. With the younger brother, five feet or so in the lead, the two of them proceeded to walk slowly across the trail in front of me.

As soon as I saw them, for my own protection, I stopped walking completely, wondering what was going to develop. I could still feel the older adult lady watching both me and the children from back in the same grove of trees.

The children obviously knew I was standing there. However, both of them were only looking down at the trail in front of them. Neither were looking in my direction. The darkness, the gloom, the distance, and the generally poor viewing conditions obscured most details of the children's faces. However, it was immediately apparent both children were wearing new clothes and new shoes—apparently purchased from one of the major department store catalogs—such as the catalogs I kept back in the weather shack.

The boy appeared to be wearing sturdy outdoor play clothes and shoes. The young girl appeared to be wearing a full winter skirt, a winter long sleeved blouse, and a new pair of ski boots—of which she appeared to be quite proud. Under her skirt and blouse, she appeared to still be wearing the protective Gray slacks and gray under clothes, as she always had before. Her short hair hadn't changed. However, it did appear to be somewhat fluffier, and as usual, well combed.

As if on command, the young girl came to a standstill when she reached the middle of the trail, and waited for her younger brother to finish crossing. When the boy reached the other side, he smoothly slipped behind the foliage on the other side, disappearing out of sight. He appeared to intentionally go down on his hands and knees as he did so.

The young girl waited in the middle of the trail for another few seconds. Then, in quiet, reflective fashion, she resumed her slow, deliberate walk. She was gazing down at her new shoes, and slowly taking full strides—obviously showing off her new skirt and shoes as she did so.

She continued after reaching the other side of the trail, also disappearing out of sight behind the foliage on the left side of the south desert entrance.

I did not immediately resume walking. I still felt I was being closely watched by the older adult lady from behind the western grove of trees. Alone, out here in the desert as I was, I did not wish to cross any unseen lines. I preferred to wait and let her cross the trail in her own good time. After waiting for perhaps ten minutes, it felt like she was no longer hiding behind the grove of trees, and I felt completely alone again. With night coming on, I cautiously resumed my walk, until I reached the south entrance.

Through the south entrance, in the distance I could see the older adult Alien lady out in the desert. I stood and watched as she descended the south slope until she reached the bushes along the sharp eastern bend in the stream near the fence southwest of me. Once there, she turned east, following the foliage along the stream until she finally disappeared into the onrushing darkness. She appeared to be heading toward another entrance into the bushes and trees probably two miles or so, southeast of me at the time. Despite her obvious age, as she walked, her gait appeared to be normal enough for an adult Gray Alien. Still, her body motions were noticeably different than those of a human. As she walked, her motions were reminiscent of a working oil derrick.

Very carefully, I exited the south entrance, stepping out into the desert beyond. I was expecting to see the two children somewhere. However, they were nowhere to be seen. The desert floor in that section was damp, and covered with the usual desert gravel. It did not preserve much in the way of footprints. However, some small stones had been disturbed to the northeast. It was easy for me to conclude the two children must have circled around north-east, staying out in the desert, and returned to a tunnel entrance in mountain north of my position.

I noticed a place just inside the edge of the foliage where the soil and pebbles had been disturbed. I concluded I had been correct about the little boy playfully going down on his hands and knees for a foot or two. The sight of the disturbed soil caused me to wonder about what I had just witnessed. I had already spent many months watching the Tall Whites and their children, at Indian Springs. I had never seen alien children play on their hands and knees the way human children naturally do. Tall White hands and knees are too fragile to permit it.

The balloon runs proceeded as planned. Although it was generally a very dark, gloomy night, a few breaks developed in the clouds. Some moonlight was able to illuminate various places in the desert. I stayed close to my theodolite the entire time. The trail back through the stream filled valley was so dark, for my own safety, I did not wish to use it any more than necessary. Consequently, I did not check to see if the tunnel entrance—or the second gate—were open.

At 9:30p.m., after completing the second balloon run, I packed up and made the hike back through the valley. It was going on 10:30p.m. when I arrived at my weather shack. My truck was already packed. I needed only to place my clipboard, weather forms, and other equipment inside the weather shack, and close up. Then I could immediately head into Death Valley Center, Nellis, and Las Vegas for the weekend. Being alone, so far out in the desert, for my own safety, I had taken to never locking the front door.

This being the end of my duty week, I was quite eager and in something of a hurry to get on the road. There was a new show playing on the Las Vegas strip which I wanted very much to see.

I quickly mounted the front steps. With a practiced hand I opened the front door, turned on the light, and placed my clipboard and other things on the kitchen table sitting in the eastern half of my unoccupied shack. Almost without thinking, I noticed all of the chairs in my shack had been moved slightly during my absence. At least one of them had been turned to face my bunk.

At first, I didn't actually think much about it. During the many months I had spent at Indian Springs, I had gotten used to people entering my weather shacks, and barracks during my absence, and rearranging the furniture—and, at the time, I had weekend plans on my mind.

Instinctively I checked my stack of department store catalogs, and the blankets on my bunk. The catalogs were still stacked neatly. However, their stacking order had changed. The largest one was now on top.

The blankets still lay neatly on my bunk. However, the bumps in the mattress, and the manner in which the top blanket had been rearranged caused me to wonder if two people had sat on my bunk.

I remembered, back at Indian springs, how much the young Tall White extraterrestrial mothers enjoyed shopping my catalogs for women's clothing. Like human women, the young Tall White women could do so until it could just drive a man up the wall. I wondered. I probably had the only complete set of current winter catalogs in at least 50 miles.

Without thinking much more about it, I closed up, and headed out. The desert road back to the main "shooting gallery" gate was wet and in bad shape. To drive safely, I had to give it my full attention.

When I was through the main gate and back on the paved highway, I had several hours of driving to do—and a midnight meal at the Death Valley Center chow hall. First I thought extensively about my plans for enjoying the shows and casinos in Las Vegas over the week-end. There were so many of them—for a young man like myself, there was much to be considered.

However, now alone in the emotional safety of my truck out on the paved highway to Las Vegas, I still had plenty of time to think about the events of the past week. For my own safety, there was much I needed to consider.

To begin with, there was the matter of the catalogs. The catalogs were too thick and too heavy for either Alien women or Alien men to lift and carry across the room to my bunk—or to re-stack. At Indian Springs, I had the catalogs on display on an easy to reach shelf. I had them sitting open to women's fashions, and to children's play clothes. Neither the Tall White women nor the Tall White men ever moved them. Only a human woman—or a human man helping her—could have moved the catalogs in my mountain hut weather shack.

As I drove, I remembered the week before when the special ranger had reviewed my orders with me. He had explicitly stated that no other human was allowed in the climate study area except me—implicitly exempting himself—and his high ranking friends. Only he and his high ranking friends could—on their own—deal directly with the guards. I wondered.

I thought some more, as I drove on. Between the two climate studies, the young girl and her younger brother both had long since gotten used to being around me, an adult human man. Now, both of them were no longer afraid of being around other humans like me.

The young girl was certainly reaching an age where she would naturally be learning to choose her own clothes. However, if she was expected to choose human style clothes, wouldn't she need an adult human woman to help her get started? Considering the young girl must have spent the last several years out here in the desert with her younger brother, wouldn't she need the help of a human lady to make that transition? It would now be a simple matter for the two children to get used to being around humans trained in child psychology—especially if the other humans introduced themselves as my friends—and proved it by showing the two children the catalogs in my weather shack—and used those catalogs to purchase new clothes and toys at U.S. Government expense.

I wondered. What had happened in my weather shack earlier tonight? The only scenario which made any sense to me, left me feeling quite stunned. I was forced to ask myself: Had the special ranger, along with a lady child psychologist, and two or three specially trained wilderness guards, hiked out here by way of the north side canyon? The weather was still good enough to have permitted it.

The group could have met the young girl and her younger brother at the tunnel entrance, and brought them over to my weather shack. With the young girl, they could have shopped for clothes, make-up, and shoes. With her younger brother, they could have shopped for toys and play things. When finished, they could have returned the children to the safety of their tunnel entrance, and bid the children good-night.

All they would have wanted from me, would be for me to stay out of sight and out of the way, acting as point man, releasing weather balloons far out in the desert.

There was a certain logic to it. However, I still had one problem. It had been my experience at Indian Springs, that Extraterrestrial mothers were extremely protective of their children, and extremely proud of their abilities as mothers. If an extraterrestrial child—whether Tall White or Gray—needed new clothes or shoes, the Alien mother would proudly handle everything entirely by herself. For a human man or woman to try to bypass the Alien mother for any reason, without first obtaining the mother's permission, would simply be a quick form of suicide.

So why would any Gray alien mother permit her two children to shop for clothes without her, by meeting with other humans in my weather shack? Alien women always came well armed. Why wouldn't the Alien mother simply show up and take matters into her own hands?

I wondered. Is that why the Generals wanted me specifically on this climate study? Is it because I had learned to recognize each child individually—and the children had learned to recognize me individually from other humans? Therefore, I could tell the children apart—and when I came, any of the special children could recognize me and respond by separating themselves from the crowd. No-one would ever have to tell me anything—or talk to me about anything. The special ranger and his friends could now tell which children they could become friends with, and which ones they couldn't. And the children could now tell which human they could become friends with and which ones they should shy away from. No wonder my orders said if I brought any other human out here with me, they would be killed.

I still had one problem. Why that specific young girl and her younger brother? What made them special? So far they were the only two children that had cleanly separated from the crowd.

I checked into my empty barracks room at Nellis, and rested. Saturday evening came. I found myself enjoying an evening dinner show at one of the major casinos down on the Las Vegas strip. The price of the meal and the show included two free post cards. I was planning to send one to my sister Martha.

The memory of the young girl walking across the trail in front of me, and showing off her new skirt and shoes stuck in my mind. It reminded me of a late summer afternoon many years before when I had walked over to my grandparents farm to visit Martha. I found Martha happily strolling out in their apple orchard, wearing a new skirt and blouse which our grandmother and one of our aunts had just purchased for her. As she was walking over to greet me, Martha, also, had made a similar happy motion as she was walking, in order to show off her new skirt and shoes. I wondered. I wanted to tell my sister Martha about my memories of that happy day in the orchard. However, I couldn't find the words.

After a while, the show began. Soon the stage was filled with young dancing girls wearing pretty skirts, comedians, and headliner performers. As expected, there were dancing girls of several nationalities, including Asian and Chinese. At the close of one of the dance numbers, one of the young Chinese dancing girls, wearing a medium length skirt, danced herself off the stage to the left. As she did so, she showed off her pretty skirt and shoes by making the same dance step like motions which both Martha and the young alien girl had made.

Suddenly, I finally realized, the young Gray girl had to be human. Only a young human lady could make those dance-like motions. Since her skin had a slight yellow tint, she had to be of Chinese descent. She probably had never spoken to me because she hadn't yet learned to speak English—and I didn't speak Chinese. The same had to be true for her younger brother.

Yes. Now I saw it. The mountain climate study was all so shockingly simple.

The ancient human people, Native Americans,—and the Gray aliens—expected humans to begin thinking for themselves when they reached the age of 12 years old. Humans were considered to have reached the age of adult-hood when they were 15 years old. The young Chinese girl was already in that age range.

Both she and the little human boy had probably adopted each other, for their mutual protection on the playground. Now they weren't just growing older, they were growing physically stronger—physically much stronger than any extraterrestrial adult could ever be.

Adult humans are expected to go out into the world, and take care of themselves, completely on their own. Parents, grandparents—and Guardians—who love them, have to prepare their human children for that eventuality—and then, painfully, stand aside and let the children leave on their own.

My grandparents kept my sister Martha living with them for fifteen years. Then they had to let her go out into the world wherever she wanted.

The older Gray Alien adults were in a similar boat. Considering their advanced age, any of their own alien children—if they had any—would already be fully grown, and would have already left home. The numerous famines, diseases, natural disasters, and wars, out in the deserts of central Asia, during 1950's, had tragically created many homeless and starving orphans. The older Alien couple had apparently rescued two of them.

The young Chinese girl could not have been living with the two older Gray adults for much over 6 or 7 earth years—the young human boy not much over 2 or 3 earth years. The two Gray older adults saw the handwriting on the wall. The time had now arrived when the two older Gray adults, whether they liked it or not, had to prepare—and return—the two human children they had adopted and fallen in love with, back to human civilization. The growing physical strength of the two human children left the Gray Adults with no other choice.

However, The older Grey Alien couple did not wish to return the two human children they loved, back to the starvation and hardship of the deserts in Central Asia. Instead, the older Alien couple presented the Generals with an immense opportunity, where everyone could win—including the older couple. They wanted to release the two human children into American society, with the help of the U.S. Government. If the plan was successful, the two children would be able to live a normal life in our culture. The Generals could handle the rest of the arrangements.

I stopped thinking about it, and returned my attention to the show. The dancing girls were beginning their grand finale.

The Smart Hunter
. . . Never Pursues

" . . . And the boys grew:
and Esau was a cunning hunter,
a man of the field;
and Jacob [was] a plain man,
dwelling in tents.
. . . Genesis 25:27

The weather was much colder on Monday. The wind out of the Northwest was quite a bit stronger, as well. Winter was making itself felt. However, the hiking trail in the north side canyon was still usable.

I was in the middle of a late breakfast at Death Valley Center, when the duty ranger wandered in and informed me there was another manila envelope waiting for me over at the ranger station. I thanked him nicely. After I finished my meal, I walked over to pick it up.

The duty ranger was in an unusually talkative mood. He picked up the envelope, and while he held it in his hands, started up a conversation. I decided he must be doing so in order to deliver a message to me. Normally, the duty rangers always stayed out of my way.

In the next few minutes which followed, in a brotherly fashion, he related how much he enjoyed the state of Indiana, especially a University town which he named. He said the town was a great place for a family to raise children, and send them to the nearby University. He especially enjoyed springtime walks in the historical parks, and walks along the Wabash river. The flowers, he said were so beautiful. He had the highest praise for the schools, colleges, and Universities throughout the state.

I thanked him kindly and promised to remember every word he had spoken. I said I was looking forward to visiting the town he named, once I got out of the service. He seemed both pleased and relieved as he handed me the envelope. He requested I not open it until I was out at my duty station.

I readily agreed. I was in no hurry. The envelope was obviously empty. As I drove back to my weather shack, I said to myself, "So that's where they intend to relocate the two children—to the town the duty ranger named in Indiana."

The balloon release schedule requested I move my theodolite a large distance to a broad rounded hilltop southeast of the southern stream valley entrance. The distance out there was quite substantial. I estimated it to be between two and three miles. The entire large area between the stream valley to the south and the mountain wall to the north was open, featureless, and bare. There was absolutely no cover from the winter wind, or the weather. The location did give a near perfect view of the entire valley to the south, to the east—and to the mountain wall up the slope above, and north of me. I could see three more tunnel entrances hidden in the mountain wall, all of which were closed. There was also another set of jutted out rocks opposite the center of the apparent landing field. The northern mountain arced around to the northeast, concealing the far northeastern part of the valley.

I could not see the north side canyon, or anything back in the direction of my weather shack. The view in that direction was uphill, and entirely blocked by the trees and foliage along the stream filled valley. I could not see the second gate, or the tunnel entrance next to it. I could see immediately that when I was at the release point, I would not have any way of knowing if the children were having visitors or if they were alone.

I was starting to get another cold/flu again. My health was beginning to concern me. All future requested balloon releases were at night. They were scheduled for every two hours starting at 10:00p.m. and lasting until 4:00a.m., with hourly temperature measurements in between. The runs would begin weekday evenings, Monday through Friday.

As I reviewed the requested balloon release schedule, it was apparent to me the Generals were quite serious about wanting to relocate the two children before my promised six weeks were up. The Generals obviously wanted me to stand lookout, and otherwise stay completely out of the way. I wondered if my health would allow me to stay on duty that long.

I picked up a dozen or so cans of a paraffin like camping fuel at the Death Valley Center supply post. They looked like double sized cans of tuna fish. They were great for camping. I just opened the top of the can, set it in a fire pit, and set the paraffin on fire. The resulting small cooking fire could be put out at any time by replacing the top, and could be restarted later. One can of fuel would burn for perhaps three hours. The fire would even burn in the rain. I used the camping fuel cans to provide heat and light at my new release location. Unfortunately, the fire they provided couldn't be used for roasting marshmallows.

The first week passed routinely enough. The weather was harsh. My cold got worse, and my cough returned. Some nights, shortly after 1:30a.m., a small number of child sized Gray shadows would come out from a place along the tree filled stream valley perhaps a mile southeast of my release location. They would always stay some distance away from me, and just watch me prepare, release, and track the 2:00a.m. balloon on schedule. I was sick, typically had a headache at the time, and had difficulty focusing in on the Gray shadows. However, I was quite certain the young Chinese girl and her younger brother were never among them. I never saw the young girl or her younger brother south of the northern head of the stream filled valley any more. The few distant glimpses I did get of them, they were always by themselves, usually talking. Always, they were wearing new human clothes.

By comparison, I noticed almost all of the short Grey shadows always stayed south of the invisible line which connected the south entrance to the stream filled valley, with my release location. I first noticed it when two or three of them crossed the line east of me, and headed diagonally towards the eastern boundary of the wooded area northwest of me for a little ways. They watched me from that location for a few minutes, before returning southeast to rejoin the other shadows. Older children seem good at establishing tribal like boundaries.

The weekend arrived. I was not feeling well enough to drive in to Las Vegas. I needed to nurse my cold. I decided to spend the weekend resting in my mountain hut, and taking things easy at Death Valley Center. I did go in to Death Valley center for Sunday Mass.

Sunday afternoon, I was feeling stronger. I was wondering what I could do to provide myself with some type of protection from the wind out at the new release point. I wondered if I could possibly make myself a wind break down by the tree shrouded stream due south of the new release point.

The afternoon was clear and sunny. I assembled my hiking supplies, and set out on a pleasant afternoon walk. The air was fresh, cool, and clear. Both the tunnel entrance and the second gate were closed. I could tell immediately I was going to be completely alone on my hike. The hike through the stream filled valley was one of the most pleasant I ever had. Alone as I was, I enjoyed every minute of it.

As I walked, I remembered the beautiful flowering plant which I had seen back at the distant Desert Oasis so many months before. It was too late in the winter for there to be any flowering plants of that type growing in the stream filled valley.

However, I wondered if that type of plant was native to the deserts and mountains of western China, as well as being native to the deserts and mountains of northwestern Africa. The climates and growing conditions in both places were very similar—and the two places were connected by the ancient camel caravan trade routes.

If that was the case, I wondered if the young Chinese Girl had brought a plant of that type with her to America, to keep alive her memories of her human parents. I found myself wondering what the Chinese name for that particular flowering plant might be.

After reaching the new release location on the hill, I turned straight south. I followed downhill, as the gravel covered slope got successively steeper. I was singing loudly at the time. By the time I reached the stream, I was roughly a mile south of my theodolite on the hill.

That stretch of stream had only short grasses and other short bushy desert vegetation along it. Turning east, I began following along the north side of the stream for perhaps 500 feet. I was heading towards another large entrance into another tall, wide region of large trees and unusually thick vegetation. This second region began like a wall which enveloped both sides of the stream filled valley. The region filled the valley and continued along the stream as it flowed slowly downhill for perhaps another three miles.

I could see the tree filled region would make a perfect refuge from the winter weather, day or night, rain or shine. I stopped suddenly, still outside in the sunlight, probably 50 feet from the pitch dark entrance. It wasn't the sunlight which caused me to stop. It was the sudden realization that an older Gray Alien man was standing inside the pitch black entrance looking straight at me. I noticed he had to be standing inside the entrance to a weather proof shelter which did not have any windows or open doors. Not even the bright sunlight penetrated through the tree leaves into the darkened interior.

I was in shock. It was all so simple.

The mountains north of me were made of rock. Tunnels could safely be dug into the rock at the base of the mountain. Those shelters were only intended for temporary short term use because they did not contain hangers or repair facilities for the Alien scout craft.

The hill between the stream filled valley and the mountain was composed of the usual unstable desert gravely soils. Tunnels could not safely be dug into those soils. They turn into mud in the rain.

The adult Gray Aliens had built above ground shelters and hidden them in this valley—easily covering them with soil to protect them from the weather. All of the shelters undoubtedly included kitchens, bedrooms, drinking water, and sewage facilities. Since the Aliens were plant eaters, this set of shelters probably included greenhouses for winter use, as well.

However, like the living areas up in the mountain, these were also intended for temporary short term use. They, too, did not contain hangers or repair facilities for Alien scout craft.

It was all so simple. Of course, the Grey Aliens would choose a desolate desert valley and a set of empty agricultural facilities such as these, and the facilities in the mountains above me. It was a perfect place where they could safely return rescued human children back to human society. Once the Grey Aliens left the area in their scout craft, there was nothing whatever non-human about the entire valley—and there never had been. The plants, trees, fences, electricity in the mountain above me, the writing on the tunnel walls and on the walls of the shelter—everything had always been perfectly American—and perfectly human.

As long as a human man could tell the difference between a human child and a Gray Alien child, he could wander around anywhere he wanted to. Gray Alien mothers and grandmothers do not care if a human adult touches or talks with a human child—they only care about their own.

I was in shock. I slowly backed away from the darkened entrance, and returned to my theodolite on the hill.

Of course the Generals wanted me to establish a lookout post out in the open on the top of the hill. They wanted me to periodically release pretty colored balloons with lights, and attract the children. They wanted me to show myself to all of the children, and see which of them were willing to show themselves back to me because they looked like me. No matter what language the child might happen to speak, every child knew what he looked like.

I decided to let the Generals do the rest of the math.

I spent a few minutes polishing and adjusting my theodolite. I gave up any thought of constructing a make-shift shelter at my release point. I decided I was going to be a lot safer staying on the hill, out in the open, where everyone could see me.

Once my theodolite was clean, I made the long walk back to my weather shack. Through it all, I was completely alone.

Monday evening came. The winter weather remained good. I was going out somewhat early to my release point. I wanted to be able to easily find my theodolite out in the desert while there was still some twilight.

When I reached the south entrance to the stream filled valley, in the gathering twilight, in the distance off to the east, I could see the older Grey Alien lady walking alone from the greenhouse shelter across the desert straight north across the middle of the landing field open area, towards the rocks jutting out from the mountain wall.

Although she was probably two miles away, I did not want to frighten her. I remained standing behind the foliage by the entrance. I waited patiently for her to complete her journey. After all, she and the older Grey adult man who frequently accompanied her, seemed a pretty decent, charitable, older couple. When the young Chinese human girl and her younger brother had come into the couple's guardianship, both she and the older man must have engaged in a great work of love and charity to have been working so hard and so long to return the human children to American human society.

I wondered how old the lady was. I knew the Tall White extraterrestrials back at Indian springs typically lived something like 600 to 800 earth years—perhaps longer.

I also knew the aliens whom I dubbed "The Norwegians with 24 Teeth" who were coming here from a colder, near twin of the Earth orbiting one of the very nearby stars—perhaps Bernard's Star or perhaps Wolf_359—have a life expectancy of 140 earth years.

Watching the older Gray alien lady walking in the gathering twilight, I wondered if her life expectancy might be something between that of the Tall Whites and the Norwegians with 24 teeth, perhaps 200 to 300 earth years. Since the couple's values of love and charity were consistent with those of human Grandparents perhaps 50 years old, I arbitrarily guessed the Gray alien couple to be roughly 150 Earth years old.

I reasoned the young Chinese girl and her younger brother would be able to share their bond of love, charity, and trust with their Grey grandparents for the rest of their lives.

The two human children could grow and educate themselves to became highly educated adult humans within only 10 to 15 Earth years. They would almost certainly want to have their family reunion picnic right where I was standing—right on the trail where the young Chinese girl had first showed off her new human clothes. I wondered what we would all be like then.

The older Gray alien lady reached the jutted out rocks by the mountain. She went behind the rocks and disappeared out of sight. The rocks obviously concealed a tunnel entrance. With the evening advancing, I resumed my walk out to my theodolite.

Time passed. It was going on 10:00p.m. and I was preparing for the first balloon release. Off to the northeast I was surprised to see a large scout craft with its headlights on coming down along the base of the mountains from the northeast. It appeared to be coming in to make a landing opposite the jutted out rocks. It was more than two miles away from me at the time.

I wasn't in any actual danger. However, the craft did certainly seem out of place, and its landing pattern seemed somewhat unusual. I knew that when such craft are fully powered up, they are surrounded by force fields of immense strength. Such fields can easily extend more than a mile and a half out from the craft. Considering my exposed position, I was afraid that no one knew I was out here. If the alien craft were to power up suddenly, and head in my direction, I would seriously injured.

I was sick, and running a slight fever. Consequently, I wasn't thinking very well. I instinctively turned on my flashlight, and began double timing uphill towards the distant scout craft—shouting and still holding my balloon as I did so. The scout craft reacted immediately. Without landing, it tightly circled back to the northeast, behaving the way an airliner does when it has been waved off in its landing attempt. Several minutes later, I saw the craft come in for a smooth careful landing roughly four miles to the southeast down in the stream valley east of the shelters.

Later, as I was tracking the balloon, out in the darkness, I could just make out the older lady walking quickly down across the desert to reach the craft sitting on the desert waiting for her. She had several miles to cover.

I felt so ashamed of myself. There wasn't any reason why I couldn't have just let the craft land, and waited until she was safely on board. Then I could have turned on my flashlight to make sure they avoided me. I wanted to run over to where she was and apologize, but that was obviously impossible. The best I could do was be sorry and ask God to forgive me. I also prayed the older lady would understand. I knew I had acted stupidly, and I was sorry.

The remainder of the week progressed as expected. However, the weather was getting colder, and I kept getting sicker. I continued to feel completely alone through it all.

Thursday night, however—a short time before midnight—I was out at the release point, sitting on my equipment box. I had lit a can of paraffin camping fuel for heat and light. There was also some moonlight. I was extremely sick at the time and wondering if I was going to be able to track the balloon after releasing it.

Out in the darkness north of me, I could hear a large adult approaching. He took up a standing position probably

70 or 100 feet away, still far enough, to remain hidden in the darkness. He seemed to be quite large, perhaps 6 feet 3 or 6 feet 4 inches tall. He was also quite muscular. I noticed immediately, whomever it was, he walked the way a human man would walk. Hearing him periodically shift weight from one foot to the other convinced me he was human. I knew from experience, Gray Alien men didn't have to move around when they were standing and watching me from out in the darkness.

After watching me from a distance for perhaps an hour, including observing my balloon release, he retreated into the darkness to the north.

I didn't go after him. I understood the rules. I was on my own, the same way my replacement was.

I wasn't surprised when he came again on Friday night at the same time, from the same place to the north—by the mountain wall—and maintained the same distance out in the darkness. To be a special ranger, I reminded myself, you have to know how to tell time—and how to order replacements to show up at the right place at the right time.

The weekend arrived. I was still too sick to drive in to Las Vegas. So, once again, I spent the weekend in my mountain hut weather shack. This being my last weekend on the climate study, I rested and made certain my weather forms had been completed properly. I reasoned, not without some humor—since my wind measurements were virtually worthless, the least I could do was have them written down properly for government use.

Sunday, as I was finishing my noon meal, once again, the duty ranger informed me I had a visitor waiting to talk with me. I wasn't surprised. I was very sick, and this was going to be my last week on the mountain climate study. I completed my meal, and walked over to meet my visitor.

I was sitting in my usual chair by the small table when the special ranger opened the door, and entered the room. The kind of respect he showed me when he came in, can hardly be described. As a low ranking enlisted man, I was quite taken aback.

He took his usual chair, and began in near amazement, "I don't have words to describe what you have accomplished, Airman Hall. You make everything look so simple. The way you are willing to analyze everything—plants, flowers, catalogs. All of us-the Generals, everybody—are in shock. The entire project is at least two years ahead of schedule."

I didn't think of myself as having accomplished much of anything, except, perhaps, having taken emotional ownership of the north side canyon. My wind reports, although accurate, were otherwise of no use. I still felt ashamed of myself because of the incident with the older Gray lady on Monday night. "I hope I did not upset anyone by shouting and waving my flashlight", I reacted defensively.

The special ranger chuckled. "No. Not at all. I am quite certain everyone is just ecstatic with everything that has happened."

"Everyone, Sir?" I responded.

He chuckled, some more. He continued in guarded fashion, "Everyone. You are the only human allowed to look at everything out there."

I saw immediately what he was saying. The replacement weather observer must certainly have started his training duties on Monday night, hiking out with the special ranger's party. The older Gray lady would certainly have wanted me to see her and the other Grays vacate the facilities before the ranger's party arrived, and the new replacement began his training. Once she and the scout craft departed, everything else out at the site, including the two human children, was perfectly, harmlessly and innocently human.

However, for some reason, the scout craft had come late, and the eager humans had come early. The Gray lady and the scout craft were in danger of being seen by the replacement or the human guards. I had warned them off in time.

Now I understood. Neither the replacement nor any of the guards in the ranger's party were ever supposed to see or know anything relating to the Gray Aliens.

It was obvious. I sat quietly for a few minutes.

The two children had grown rapidly, and were now ready to be relocated to a new life back in Indiana. The special ranger was certainly planning on relocating the two children into their new life, by the end of the week.

In addition, The mountain climate study project had outgrown my mountain hut weather shack. A new reception and medical screening facility was going to be built west of the fence, and west of the line. The results of my mountain climate study would be needed to justify architectural decisions and the resulting costs passed on to the government, when building the facilities. The fact that my wind measurements showed nothing out of the ordinary in the way of winter weather, would mean a great deal to government lawyers and regulators.

The facility would not be particularly large since probably only a handful of children would be processed through it at any one time. It would, however, provide much needed medical screening, clothes shopping, and processing facilities, prior to relocating the human children. Since all of the children would be human, the facilities could easily be dual purpose.

Everything east of the fence would be designated as the receiving area. The handful of humans working at the facility would be told the receiving area was quarantined, and off-limits to local humans, supposedly in order to control the spread of diseases, flus, and the like. They would be told the weather observer was posted over there because some diseases are airborne.

The humans at the facility would be told the facility was being used to receive Chinese and Asian children who had been orphaned by wars and other natural disasters in China and Asia. The weather observer would be told the children who came at night to watch the balloons were all Chinese or Asian orphans. None of the children over there could ever be touched or spoken to.

The Gray Alien children would be told to never cross north of the east-west line marked by the theodolite at the hill-top release point. The Gray Alien children would also be told to always stay well east of the fence.

By contrast, the human children would be told they could go anywhere they wanted. However, once the human children crossed north of the invisible east-west line, the Alien mothers will no longer protect them from other humans. The human children, for example, could check themselves into the dormitories tunneled into the mountain. Only human children would be allowed to use the tunnel facilities.

Once the new reception and medical facilities were completed, The Gray Aliens would have no reason to stay in the area. Alien mothers could just stop by at night, drop off their older human children, and leave.

Human children had always been free to go west of the fence, and west of the line. No Alien would ever pursue them into those areas. The human children could be escorted into the new receiving area, the clothes shopping area, or into the new medical facilities, at anytime. When the individual human children were ready for their new lives, they would be transported to new homes elsewhere in America.

The small number of human personnel in the receiving facility would be told they could safely talk or interact with any child who came west of the line, or west of the fence. Only a tiny handful of humans, medical personnel, and the like would be allowed to enter the buffer zone/ playground area for human children in between the line and the fence.

Yes. It all made perfect logical sense. Only special human children would be returned to this new facility. The Generals already had the facilities at the Desert Oasis to use, in the unlikely event that a Grey Alien child needed to be returned to their parents.

I wanted to make certain I was seeing things correctly. So I said respectfully to the the special ranger, "I see some snow fell in the north side canyon over night. It will probably be there for several days. I hope it doesn't surprise anybody."

He showed surprise.

I continued respectfully, "Snow levels in the canyon do not show up on any of my weather reports. Anyone building a new set of buildings in the area would probably want to include a consideration for snowfall in the design."

The special ranger smiled, and said, "You sure are good. You have the entire project figured out, don't you?"

I smiled, as I was coughing because of the cold I was suffering from.

The special ranger continued, "Before I go, I have one last request to make of you. You do not have to make any of the Friday night balloon releases. However, please leave your theodolite and other equipment out at the release point, and please wait until Saturday morning to retrieve it. Also, and this is very important. Please stay out at your weather shack, or close by in the area, until at least 4:00p.m. in the afternoon on Saturday. Promise me you won't leave in your truck until at least 4:00p.m. Saturday."

"Yes, Sir." I answered, coughing.

The last week seemed to crawl by. The weather grew successively colder. My cold and fever grew steadily worse. By midweek, based on the shadows I was glimpsing out in the desert to the north of me, I became convinced that a two man team would be replacing me. It made sense. Out in this desolate section of the desert, two men together are much safer than one.

At last Saturday morning came. It was wet and cold. The temperature hovered at 33 degrees Fahrenheit. It had rained and snowed some the previous night. Mud and snow covered the trail from my weather shack to the release point. I didn't go in for breakfast. I was much too sick and feverish.

After finishing my morning box lunch, I packed up my things, and loaded them into my truck. I wasn't in any hurry, since I couldn't leave until 4:00p.m. Off in the mountain to the northeast, I noticed the tunnel entrance was open, and the second gate was still shut. It was obvious the two children were also packed and waiting. I was certain all of the Gray Aliens had already left several days ago. I had come to believe the Grays had permanently relocated somewhere else, and now might only stop by once in a while when they had human children to drop off.

Only the two children and I remained on site. I was therefore determined I would not leave until I was certain the special ranger and his team had come to move them to their new home.

When 10:00a.m. arrived, I decided I would go get my theodolite and other equipment from the release point, and load it in the back of my truck. Then, I could rest and wait patiently until the two children were picked up.

Sick and feverish, I made the long hike out to the release point. After disassembling and packing the equipment, I began carrying it back. I needed to make three trips. First I moved the equipment to the south entrance to the stream filled valley. Then I rested.

Then, in three trips, I moved the equipment up the valley to the bottom of the north slope. Now exhausted, I began the brutal task of moving the equipment up the slope to the level area on top.

The young Chinese girl and her young brother came out from the tunnel entrance to watch me from just beyond the two large bushes. They were dressed in warm winter clothes, ready for travel. It was obvious they would have helped me if they could have. However, that was impossible.

Sick, and feverish as I was, it never occurred to me that I could have just waited for the special ranger and the three strong trail guards he was bringing with him. Rules or no rules, they undoubtedly would have finished my work for me. However, my orders did say, ". . . even if I was dying . . . ." I resumed my work alone.

I began bringing the equipment box up the hill. The slope was mud covered, and very slippery. However, that trip wasn't too bad.

Then with great difficulty I brought the heavy theodolite in its case up the slope. It was just barely possible. By the time I got to the top, I was exhausted.

Finally I went back for the tripod. On the first and second try, I was unable to make it back up the slippery slope. I found myself laying face down on my forearm in the cold mud, praying, and afraid I'd gambled wrong on my ability to persevere. On the third try, I was just barely able to make it up the slope with my tripod.

Then fighting exhaustion, and still using three trips, I moved my equipment to the back of my truck. I brought the theodolite back last. I was able to lift it up into the back of my truck. However, I was too exhausted to push it all the way forward in the truck bed.

On the final trip, the young Chinese girl followed me as far as the fence gate. Her younger brother followed me half way to my truck, before they both turned back, and returned to the open tunnel entrance.

Sick, and exhausted, I climbed into my truck, closed the truck door, and laid down on the front seat and went to sleep. It was now almost 1:30p.m.

I slept until almost 4:30p.m. I awoke still feeling sick, but well enough to drive. However, before I could leave, I had to be certain the children were gone. Carefully I got out of my truck onto the muddy soil outside. I called to the children. There was no answer.

In the mud, I could see the footprints of another, larger human. While I was sleeping, he had moved my heavy theodolite to a more secure position up to the top of my truck bed, and carefully closed the truck's tail gate. Even though I felt totally alone at the site, I wanted to be sure it was OK for me to leave.

I walked part way back to the gate in the fence to see if the children were still there.

The tunnel entrance was now closed—and the second gate stood open.

Postscript

The preceding true account of my time among the Grays may leave some readers confused about what was going on.

I concluded: The Way-station, was built and maintained by humans. The adult Greys were returning two human children, who had spent time among the Grays, to our culture. The way-station appeared capable of receiving and processing displaced, orphaned, or otherwise special human children. In addition to human children who had spent time among The Greys; the planned facility would also be capable of receiving special children of diplomats, war casualties, spies, or others; who for one reason or another, were taken from one environment, and now needed time and interim care before being placed in a new home environment.

BOOK TWO

DISASTER AT ROSWELL

Introduction

I hope readers will find my account of the events of early July, 1947, to be a refreshing and compelling look at something which has been written about and discussed endlessly in the years since. I feel I have come to a more complete understanding, not just because of things I have heard mentioned, or articles I've read, but, more importantly, because of my own experiences while working in the Valleys of the Greys, as well as my experiences with the Tall Whites at Indian Springs, and also my experiences with the Norwegians with 24 teeth.

Over the course of my lifetime, I have traveled extensively throughout the entire American West. During those many travels, I have personally studied and observed in detail, the West's geography, geology, and climate.

My account includes my own personal observations which I made during those many travels.

Because my Roswell account is such a stunningly different take over everything that has preceded it, I am including a Bibliography, primarily URLs, on which people may find direction to other reading materials regarding various related subjects.

July 1947

In the first week of July, 1947, three extra-terrestrial flying disks crashed to earth in the deserts and mountains north and west of Roswell, New Mexico. There were 15 extra-terrestrial children and young extra-terrestrial teenagers on board. They were members of the alien race called the Greys. None of them survived.

Some died immediately in the crashes. Some died within a few hours from their wounds, and from the injuries which they sustained during the crashes. Any children who may have initially survived the crashes, still in shock, dazed and confused, may possibly have gone to seek help from the nearby humans. Not receiving any, in all probability, they would have tried to return to the crash site—only to die later from exposure.

One child was taken alive by the U.S. Army, only to die later in captivity. The remainder died during the days and weeks which followed. The remaining alien children and the young teenagers perished from their injuries, or from hunger, thirst, and overexposure to the earth's cold, harsh elements, waiting for rescue at their crash sites. For the extra-terrestrials—for members of the alien race—The Greys, Roswell was an unmitigated disaster.

The Grey parents love their children dearly—and the children love their parents. When notified their children were missing, the parents did everything physically possible to find the children and to rescue them. However the deserts of the American southwest are vast, desolate, brutally harsh, and unforgiving places—especially for non-humans, no matter how intelligent they may be. The Grey children are very frail. They injure—and perish—very easily. Being only flesh and blood creatures, the alien children do not have the natural reflexes, mental reflexes, physical strength, or the durable, fast healing physical bodies which they would need, in order survive for more than a handful of days at a crash site here on the surface of this earth. Unfortunately for the parents and for the children, through no fault of their own, all of the alien rescue attempts failed. Even today, the surviving parents, who, I believe, live 200 to 300 earth years, are undoubtedly still in mourning. Even today, the surviving alien parents undoubtedly consider the alien pilots and co-pilots and the children on board the three craft, to have died tragically—and as heroes.

Grey Aliens

As I have personally witnessed, The Grey Extra-Terrestrials have men, women, and children—just as we humans do—just as the "Tall White" Extra-Terrestrials do—and just as the Extra-Terrestrials which I have named "The Norwegians with 24 Teeth" do.

While I was stationed as a weather observer in the U.S. Air Force at Nellis AFB, Nevada, back in the mid 1960's, I personally encountered members of each of these three extra-terrestrial races—both their adults, and their children.

I am certain that for each of the three alien races, the parents love their children and the children love their parents, even more so then we humans love our parents and our children. Like humans, each alien creature is a unique individual. Each one, has their own unique, individual personality—sometimes good—sometimes bad.

I am also certain each of the three alien races enjoy and appreciate Beauty, The Fine Arts, Truth, and Careful Logic. All three of the alien races can be very emotional and, like humans, they enjoy sharing and expressing their emotions—both good and bad. It was my personal, direct observation all three of the alien races enjoy different types of entertainment, different types of food and different types of clothing. They also enjoy various types of humor. All three types of alien children greatly enjoy playing.

The Tall White adults and their children, The adult Norwegians with 24 Teeth and their children, and of course, human adults and human children, can easily breathe the earth's cold, thin air. By contrast, The Grey adults can not breathe the earth's cold, thin air without the help of a breathing device.

Only the Grey children and their young teenagers can directly breathe our air. This is because, for the Greys only, the physiology of their lungs and hearts is much different than it is for humans. The Greys have only one organ which performs the same physiological functions as the Heart and the Lungs do in humans. As humans grow physically larger, both their heart and lungs grow larger in corresponding proportion. However, as the Greys grow physically larger, their lung functions do not grow correspondingly larger. This is not a problem on the Grey's home planet, because the Greys come from a planet much larger than the Earth. Their home planet has a much stronger surface gravity and also a much higher surface air pressure than the Earth does. The atmosphere on the Grey's home planet also has a somewhat higher percentage of oxygen than the earth's atmosphere. Thus adult Greys are well suited to live on the surface of their home planet. However, by the time they have grown to the equivalent age of older teenagers, they can no longer breathe the Earth's thin, cold air without the aid of a breathing device. This breathing device and The Earth's thin atmosphere, places limits on their physical activity.

This means Grey children who may have been born and raised here on this Earth, are—to a certain extent—trapped in a miserable desperate situation. For many such Grey children, this Earth is their childhood home, containing the only happy playgrounds which they will ever know. The Earth also contains a gravitational field which their bodies have become adjusted to. Like highly intelligent children everywhere, when they go out to play on their favorite playgrounds, and to enjoy their childhood, they want their parents to accompany them. Their parents can not easily accompany their children—or discipline them—when they are here on the surface of the Earth. For this reason, many times, when a human does encounter a Grey Alien, the human finds himself having to deal with a very undisciplined teenager. It is very common for the Grey parents not to accompany their children when they go out to play. So it is not surprising that a number of Grey teenagers can be quite malicious—even dangerous to be around.

As the Grey children grow into teenagers, the day comes when they can no longer directly breath the Earth's thin, cold, air. For each Grey teenager, the day comes when they themselves must start wearing the uncomfortable breathing devices. No Grey child wants to face that day. No Grey child wants to grow up. No Grey Child wants to face Childhood's End.

Yet, if a young Grey adult leaves this Earth—and leaves all of their happy childhood memories behind—and travels back to their home planet, or to some equivalent planet where they can freely breathe the air, their bodies must make the long painful adjustment to a much stronger gravitational field. Either way—whether they go or stay—their childhoods all come to a painful end—with only years of emotional hardship and adjustment ahead of them. If some of the Greys are abducting humans to help them here on this Earth, or are trying to mutate themselves, or are trying to create a hybrid race—perhaps Childhood's End is the reason.

When the time came for me to leave Nellis AFB , Nevada, and transfer to Viet Nam in the first week of May, 1967, I had come to the personal conclusion there were relatively few adult Greys here on the surface of the earth. By comparison, I had personally seen a significant number of Grey children and young teenagers playing at night by themselves, out in the desolate wastes of the western deserts. That difference in numbers is very significant to understanding the Disaster At Roswell in July, 1947.

Grey Alien Bases

The Natural Laws of Economics, as well as the Natural Laws of Military Science, apply everywhere throughout the galaxy—even to extra-terrestrials and to their children coming to earth from distant planets. By the natural laws of economics, I never encountered enough adult Greys, to perform all of the tasks which would be needed to maintain a large, well protected base for "Deep Space" capable vehicles here on Earth. Logically, because of the presence of the large number of children, the Grey adults had to have a main base for their "Deep Space" vehicles, located somewhere nearby within The Solar System. The Earth's moon comes naturally to mind.

By the first week of May, 1967, I had come to the personal conclusion that logically, the Greys probably had their main Deep Space base dug deeply into the inside of a crater located on the near side of the Earth's Moon. I became certain the Grey adult scout craft could make the crossing from a base on the Earth's Moon, to a scout craft base on the Earth in 15 minutes or less, anytime they felt like doing so. Logically, the main living areas at the Moon base would have to be located on the crater's floor and well dug into the inside of the crater's wall.

Of course, in order to maintain a thriving moon base, many resources such as food, water, and building materials, must be collected from here on Earth.

The alien parents greatly prefer the unaccompanied children, playing outdoors, only play here on the earth's surface. Playing on the Earth's surface is many times safer for the Grey children, than playing out in space, or playing on the surface of the moon. In addition, the alien Grey children, growing up and playing here on the surface of the earth are many times more comfortable, and grow up much stronger, and much healthier than would be the case on a moon base. This is because the laws of biology, biochemistry, sunlight, exercise, and good nutrition are the same all over the galaxy.

The Grey children and the young teenagers commonly form up into small playgroups, entirely by themselves. Without an accompanying adult, the group goes out to play and to entertain themselves on the Earth's surface. When they do so, for their own safety, they always take at least three scout craft.

By comparison, when the Tall White children in Indian Springs Valley, Nevada, went out to play, they were always accompanied—and disciplined—by well armed Tall White adults.

It is rare to see the Grey adults outside together with their children, on the surface of the earth. A human who had never personally encountered a Grey adult and a Grey child together, could easily remain completely unaware that the small "Little Grey" extra-terrestrials are the children of the adult "Tall Greys". A human who had never personally encountered an alien adult and an alien child together might, unknowingly, classify The Little Grey children and The Tall Grey adults as two different types of extra-terrestrials.

The children of the Greys behave much differently than their adult counterparts. For example, the children are obviously very interested in playing with objects—such as trucks, airplanes—weather balloons with radar reflectors—and Project Mogul balloons—to entertain and educate themselves. By comparison, their adult parents have little interest in playing with anything—objects, games, balloons, airplanes—or with humans.

Many of the Grey children, because of their youth and in-experience, have no idea how to relate to humans or how to respond to threats from humans. They are, after all, children—frequently very young children. For example, during the early 1950's, many Grey children thought humans enjoyed playing the game "Chicken"—as depicted in a number of famous movies back in the 1940's and the 1950's. During the 1940's, Adult humans happily played Chicken all of the time when driving their cars and passing trucks on America's many two lane highways. For this reason, it was common for the alien children to use their high performance scout craft to play Chicken with airplanes. They did not think of themselves as being malicious teen-agers. Many of the young teen-aged aliens undoubtedly thought the humans on board the airplanes were enjoying the experience.

Equally important, when threatened by a human, the young Grey children typically become very agitated and greatly prefer to just run away. Most, if not all, of the young children are not actually armed.

The Grey families here on Earth, normally live in comfortable, underground Scout Craft bases, typically tunneled deep into isolated mountains located in desolate places far out in the western deserts—and also far away from The Tall Whites and the Tall White base near Indian Springs, Nevada. It was my personal observation the Greys and the Tall Whites do not trust each other. Although I personally never saw the two groups fight openly, it appeared to me back in the mid 1960s, the two alien groups were natural enemies.

Grey Children's Play Areas

Because of their longer life expectancy, alien children spend many more earth years playing and enjoying themselves than human children do. It is no surprise then, both Tall White parents, and Grey parents consider locating safe playgrounds for their children to be important to their life style.

When the Greys first arrived here on earth, the deserts of the American west must certainly have reminded them of their home planet. When they first arrived, those deserts were virtually uninhabited. So the aliens naturally picked a few strategic locations out in those deserts for their Scout Craft bases and, for their children's playgrounds. At least a few of these locations were in the western portion of The North American Continent.

Arriving here on earth, at least Three Thousand years ago, the Greys would have been arriving at a time when there were no "Lines" on the Earth. They could set up their system of base areas and playgrounds virtually anywhere—and anyway—they wanted to.

When the Grey parents were studying the North American continent from space—or from the surface of the Earth's moon—the alien parents must certainly have noticed a handful of very strategically located natural mountainous areas whose locations perfectly suited their needs. One of these areas is the area of mountains and valleys which surrounds the modern day city of Bishop, California. This area includes The Owens Valley. Before the completion of the Los Angeles Aqueduct in 1939, The

Owens Valley was an ideal place to raise crops of every type. It had been that way since the last ice age. To the Grey Aliens, it would have looked something like an earthly paradise.

A second naturally strategic location, which would have perfectly suited the needs of the Grey Aliens, is the area of mountains and valleys, which surround Green River Utah. A natural geologic system of long, generally straight, low, level desert valleys with neighboring high mountains, connects the Bishop and the Green River areas.

In the American desert southwest, the air temperature and the air pressure down on the valley floor is much higher than the colder, thinner air found higher up in the nearby mountains. A decent barometer for example, can measure a difference in air pressure when the barometer is taken from a table top and placed on the nearby floor. Here on Earth, adult Humans typically notice differences in air pressure due to changes in altitude of as little as 1000 feet. Grey adult aliens are at least as sensitive to changes in air pressure as humans are.

Therefore, the alien parents chose their children's playgrounds accordingly. They wanted some of the playgrounds to be on the valley floor so the higher air pressure and higher air temperature would allow the older children to play out doors without yet having to wear the cumbersome breathing devices. The older children were always expected to watch over and protect the younger children on the playground. Alien Children have always been taught to play together in groups for their own safety.

The alien parents wanted each of their playgrounds to be adjacent to at least one fortress-like mountain with places to hide. Such fortresses naturally provide the Grey Alien children with protection from humans and from other animals. The animals here on earth, have always been quite dangerous to frail aliens of all ages. It is not just humans the Grey Aliens have always found naturally threatening. It is Earth's animals, as well.

The parents wanted the playgrounds to be easily accessible from the parent's protected Scout Craft base areas because the alien children would be traveling between the base areas and the playgrounds on a routine basis. The parents positioned their underground scout craft bases and children's playgrounds at places where the long, low, desert valleys generally connected with one another. Those valleys form natural highways from several base areas to several playgrounds areas.

The natural geologic system of hot, desert valleys, protected by nearby mountains, forms a system of highways which are shockingly easy for alien children use. It is simply alien child's play for them to pilot their high performance scout craft up and down the inter-connecting desert valleys between their home base areas and their protected playgrounds. When the Grey alien children go out to play in groups, their alien parents naturally prefer, their younger children keep their high performance scout craft close to the surface of the earth, for their own safety. Frequently, the older children are still learning how to pilot the high performance scout craft.

The system of natural alien highways stretches much farther out from the base areas around Bishop, California and Green River, Utah, than most humans would ever notice. These natural highways connect the alien base areas with numerous distant playground areas perfectly suitable for the alien children. One such playground area is the area around Muroc Lake, California—now Edwards Air force Base. Another very special group of natural, beautiful, playground areas, next to the protection of nearby fortress like mountains, is the area around the San Rafael Swell located just west of Green River, Utah.

Two additional very special natural alien refuges and playgrounds are the two areas named the "El Malpais" and the "Carrizozo Malpais" which are located in modern-day New Mexico. The Malpais were given theiir names by early Spanish explorers in the late 1500s'.

The Western El Malpais with its protecting mountains and mesas, is located south of Grants, and Zuni, New Mexico. The Eastern "Carrizozo Malpais" with its protecting fortress-like mountains, are located west of The fortress-like Capitan mountain—and located north and west of Roswell, New Mexico.

Grey children may well have been playing in the two regions of New Mexico's "Malpais" since before some of the lava flows formed. One of the lava flows in the Western "El Malpais" is believed to have formed roughly one million years ago. However, according to the U.S. National Park Service, one of the lava flows in the Eastern "Carrizozo Malpais" may possibly have formed as recently as the time of the Great Crusade in 1095 A.D. Some of the lava flows are still warm to the touch. The Greys who were here on Earth at the time, may have actually watched the Eastern Carrozozo Malpais form.

Undoubtedly, the Grey children greatly enjoy playing out in the desolate, jumbled lava flows of both the Eastern Carrozozo Malpais and also in the Western EL Malpais. The entrances to the children's refuges are hidden in some of the many eroded sandstone formations and lava tubes. For an adult human, hiking in the lava flows is so difficult, even a modern day National Park Ranger wouldn't be able to find the entrances to their underground alien playgrounds and refuge areas.

The events of the Disaster of 1947 form a pattern around the Grey Alien Children's Playground areas located at Green River, Utah, and the two areas of the El Malpais. Those events do not from a pattern around Roswell, itself.

Grey Children's Equipment

As was common on the hot summer day of Wednesday, July 2, July, 1947, the Grey alien children and the young teenagers chose to use a short range scout craft, for their excursion out to their favorite playgrounds. Such scout craft had obviously been specifically designed for use by children. The scout craft are constructed in a number of different sizes, as well as a number of different shapes. As I personally observed back in the mid 1960's, most of the scout craft, and especially the larger ones, are actually ellipsoidal in shape. Ellipsoidal shaped craft offer the occupants better protection than the disk shaped craft. Only the smallest of the Grey alien craft are actually disk shaped. One size scout craft which the Grey aliens commonly use, has seats for 5 children and has little, if any, room for the much larger adults.

The Grey alien children would have taken time to prepare. Their parents would have insured they were properly clothed. Even so, the shoes and clothes which the Grey alien children were wearing, were not designed for emergency outdoor survival—and only humans have physical bodies built strong enough to enable them to survive emergency conditions, here on the earth's harsh surface.

The gray colored suits and helmets which the Greys wear, are very non-reflective at all wave lengths of light. Direct sunlight does not glint off the gray suits or gray helmets. This is an important protective feature of the design of the gray colored suits and gray colored helmets.

For example, when a group of the Greys are walking together in bright sunlight, if sunlight glinted off one of their helmets, it could easily interfere with the vision of other members of the group. Because of this fact of nature, back in the mid 1960s, I frequently wondered if the home planet of the Greys had a much brighter sun, and therefore had much brighter sunlight, than the Earth does. I also wondered if the brightness of their sun is why the Greys natural skin color is not gray. Their natural skin color is yellow-orange.

Major Limitations of Alien Children's Scout Craft

The scout craft used by the Grey alien children was a simple design with little if any frills or luxuries. It was designed to operate reliably in the cold emptiness of space—and also high up in the cold upper regions of the earth's atmosphere.

However, the propulsion system on the alien scout craft, was not designed to operate with that same high level of reliability in places such as the hot desert floors of Death Valley, Owens Valley, or of Panamint Valley, California. On the fateful day of Wednesday, July 2, 1947, those western desert valleys, including the deserts and plains of New Mexico and Utah, were as hot as furnaces. Only occasionally were they cooled by a few widely scattered thunderstorms.

The alien children can have fun playing all day out in the desert heat. The alien children can safely spend the entire hot summer day outside, down on the desert floor. However, as I personally observed as a USAF weather observer, back in the mid 1960s, down on the desert floor, the alien children's scout craft has a propulsion system which is subject to over-heating, sudden melt-downs, and catastrophic failures. On hot afternoons in the summer, the temperature of the fiber optics propulsion coils had to be carefully monitored. Of course, traveling at night or hiding in a rainstorm, would help the propulsion system coils cool down.

The scout craft on which the Grey children flew was a standard alien construction. Structurally, the craft was designed to be very durable, to survive a great deal of wear and tear, and to be used for a very long time—provided the fiber optical coils which comprised its propulsions systems and its protection systems, were well cared for and did not ever overheat.

As I personally observed out in those desolate and deserted desert valleys, back in the mid 1960's,The alien scout craft was capable of tremendous performance. It could travel easily to and from the Earth's moon at velocities as high as one million miles per hour. Further out in space the scout craft could easily reach velocities as high as 20% the speed of light. It could travel from the Earth's South pole to the Earth's North pole in less than 15 minutes. It could journey to the Earth's moon in the same amount of time. It could generate accelerations greater than 10,000 times the force of gravity—easily reaching accelerations so high that steel itself would liquefy were it not protected by the craft's all surrounding force fields—while the children sat quietly and safely in their seats on board. When fully powered up, the alien craft's all surrounding outer protective force fields protected the children and the entire craft, from every form of cosmic radiation, radar beams, small rocks, missiles, bullets, and all projectiles.

However, the craft had its limitations. The First and Foremost major limitation of the alien children's scout craft is the alien craft of that design can only engage in high performance flight when their outer protective fields are turned on and fully powered up.

Only when their outer protective fields are turned on and fully powered up is the craft and its occupants protected from debris, projectiles, radiation, and the extreme "G" forces generated by high performance maneuvers.

In the mid 1960's as a USAF weather observer at Indian springs, Nevada, on numerous occasions, I personally witnessed Tall White scout craft of a similar design in operation. In every case, when the outer protective force fields were powered down or turned off, the craft had to be flown slowly and as carefully as a human would guide a baby buggy.

The second major limitation of the alien scout craft was—it was only a short range craft. As such, it very obviously lacked important backup safety equipment—such as emergency locater beacons. Incidentally, as I personally observed close up on many occasions in the Indian Springs Valley, Nevada, back in the mid 1960's, even the very technologically advanced Tall White Ellipsoidal scout craft, lacked emergency locater beacons.

The Grey children's scout craft had other important limitations. It was not designed to be taken on long deep space journeys, and therefore did not have much in the way of storage facilities for emergency supplies such as food, water, medical supplies, extra clothing—or repair and replacement parts. It also did not have any special safe areas such as beds or hammocks where injured alien children could rest, sleep, or bandage their wounds. In those cases, they were expected to communicate to their home base and request that an ambulance or other rescue vehicle be sent. Thus, a craft traveling alone, which experienced any type of malfunction, was in a very serious emergency situation.

An equally major limitation of the Grey children's scout craft design was when the craft was flown higher than the surrounding western mountains with its outer protective fields turned off, the craft would show up on Army Air Force Defense radars. Whether or not the Army Air Force Defense radars had any direct effect on the alien craft or its operation, when the alien craft's outer protective force fields were turned off, depended entirely on the specific details of the craft's design.

In general, radar does not have any effect on alien scout craft. However, American Defense radar of that era might possibly have introduced noise on the craft's communication channels. This is especially possible because the three alien craft involved in the 1947 Disaster at Roswell must certainly have been older craft which had been in use for a number of years. After all, on the day when the alien children left their home base, they were only intending to go out to play on what—for them—were a few nearby children's playgrounds. They certainly intended to stay inside of the earth's atmosphere, and usually stay—for them—close to the surface of the ground. As such, the Grey parents would certainly have told the children to use the older craft of the simpler design, to play with. These older craft, the children would naturally be the most familiar with. This, obviously, was not their first trip to their favorite playgrounds.

In any case, in 1947, American Defense radar development was still in its infancy. The three alien craft must certainly have been designed and constructed at a time before the American Air Defense Radar System was developed.

Most, if not all of the craft's communication systems, were "Line of Sight" only. If a damaged craft were traveling alone, once it dropped out of sight below the western mountains and into the desert valleys below, it was typically out of communication with its home base. Out in the vastness of outer space, everything is in sight—so there was little need, if any, for any other form of communication.

A lone, damaged craft, here on the surface of the earth, faces a quite different reality. Mountains and nearby valley walls cause many "Communication Shadows". Only if the Grey parents sent a deep space craft out into space and positioned the deep space craft 100 or 200 miles over some special place here on Earth, such as Green River, Utah, or perhaps Roswell, New Mexico, would a group of alien children, forced down in a damaged scout craft, have any hope of communicating with their alien parents, or with their home repair base, possibly located on the Earth's Moon.

Weather here on Earth can also interfere with the communication systems on a Grey alien child's scout craft. A damaged craft trying to cool it's damaged propulsion coils by hiding in a thunderstorm is unable to communicate effectively with its home base. Bolts of lightning within the thunderstorm would certainly interfere with the transmission. In addition, if the damaged craft were forced to turn off its outer protective force fields, bolts of lightening from a thunderstorm could easily strike the craft itself. Bolts of lightening, of course, would do immense damage to an already damaged scout craft.

It is certain the Grey alien scout craft typically carried radio equipment which permitted the occupants on board to listen in on the Army Air Force radio communication frequencies. In addition, many young alien teenagers, and adults, in 1947, certainly understood spoken English. However, the children on board seldom, if ever, transmitted in English—even on UASF frequencies—even if their lives were in danger.

One of many important facts relating to The Disaster at Roswell in July 1947, is, to the best of my personal knowledge—throughout the entire series of related events, The alien children themselves, whose lives were in danger, never once transmitted any distress calls in English using the same Army Air Force communication frequencies which they had obviously been listening to. This fact is all the more surprising when it is remembered an electric circuit designed by humans to receive radio signals is nearly identical to an electric circuit designed to transmit those very same signals on the very same frequency.

Alien Children Go Out to Play

On Wednesday morning, July 2, 1947, the first group of Grey alien children to experience the tragedy was apparently the last to leave their home base. We may never be certain which of their various bases they left from—or exactly when they left their home base. However, a logical, and reasonable hypothesis is they left from one of their bases hidden in the mountains which surround Bishop, California, early in the afternoon of Wednesday, July 2, 1947. It appears the other two similar scout craft, each with a group of five alien children and teen-agers on board, left from a different, although similar base in the same area, also to go out to play. Thus logically this third scout craft—the third in the play group—was leaving alone and probably much later than its two companions. All by itself, it would be unable to recover if it suffered a coil meltdown. Logically then, this third craft must have been expecting to join the company of at least two other similar craft for its own general protection. Remember, the alien parents understand the craft the children are flying,. The parents know the craft have limitations.

Grey aliens—adults and children—whose natural life expectancy is 200-300 earth-years—are naturally very schedule conscious. Intelligent beings have to be naturally schedule conscious, in order to travel accurately between the ever-moving stars and other bodies out in space. This implies the last scout craft, leaving significantly after the other two have left, was leaving on schedule. This implies the last scout craft was carrying the youngest group of all of the children on board the three scout craft—and therefore—the most helpless.

On Wednesday July 2, 1947, it is not certain which of their many playgrounds, the three groups of alien children were headed towards when they left their home bases near Bishop, California. However, it seems certain their parents believed the last group of children was heading generally east—towards the vast, empty, beautiful, and desolate valleys in and around Green River Utah, located some 600 miles away. There are many beautiful, natural playgrounds for alien children in the area.

One such natural playground in the Green River Area, is the stunningly beautiful geologic feature known as The San Rafael Swell. It can easily be found by following a large and beautiful canyon system—and therefore of a natural alien highway. The canyon approaches the San Rafael Swell from the west and southwest—i.e. from the general direction of Bishop California. The San Rafael Swell itself, is just west of the city of Green River. It is another area which could easily remind the Grey Parents of their home planet. When the children arrived at their playground, they were undoubtedly landing alone in a place where afternoon surface air temperatures would already be reaching 110 degrees F.

The children's high performance scout craft was easily capable of making the 600 mile desert crossing between Bishop and the San Rafael Swell at more than 10,000 miles per hour, if it chose to rise up above the many western desert mountains. Thus, when they arrived, the alien children could return home in less than five minutes if they wanted to—and if their craft were operating correctly.

Based on subsequent events, logic dictates that well before this last group of alien children left The San Rafael Swell area, the other two scout craft full of alien children, had already gone on ahead to the alien playgrounds in the Carrizozo Malpais near Carrizozo—and Roswell—in New Mexico—possibly to watch the Project Mogul Balloon flight #4. The alien children were very obviously taking up perfect Mogul Balloon viewing positions north and west of Roswell. The Carrizozo Malpais set of playgrounds is only another 600 miles—and therefore another five minutes south east of The San Rafael Swell. These alien children too, could return home to their Bishop bases in just a handful of minutes if they so desired—and if their scout craft were operating correctly.

For the alien children from Bishop California—out in their high performance craft, they are all still just out having fun in their parent's backyards. All they were trying to do, was enjoy themselves until the planned launch of Mogul Balloon Flt #9. The balloon launch was scheduled for sun-down on the following day.

The alien children would certainly have been playing only in areas where they had their parents' approval. For alien children with a high performance scout craft, The San Rafael Swell is a natural fortress as well as a safe playground. There are plenty of plants to eat, water to drink, and sandstone or lava caves to take refuge in. No human could ever bother them or surprise them there. Similar statements could be made for both sections of New Mexico's "Malpais".

Because of the earth's rotation, and the human population distribution, leaving the Bishop base and heading east towards Green River makes it easy for the children to play safely by themselves. If their parents allowed them to, they could also safely take their high performance scout craft high up into the earth's atmosphere, play a while among the clouds—and the Project Mogul balloons—and return home to their base east of Bishop, without becoming lost. The alien children, as well as their parents, very obviously know the Deserts and Mountains of the American West in great detail.

Project Mogul Balloons

The Project Mogul Balloons were being released from the desert west and north of Alamogordo, New Mexico. Because of the prevailing winds, each Project Mogul balloon train would rise high up into the atmosphere and drift slowly across the deserts of New Mexico, in full view from the ground. The balloons could be seen from both sections of The "Malpais"—west and north of Roswell, New Mexico. The Project Mogul balloons were some of the most beautiful balloons that mankind has ever created. How could any group of alien children with a high performance scout craft at their disposal, playing on their traditional playgrounds, have resisted the balloons' appeal?

These unusual and beautifully constructed balloon trains would have been of tremendous entertainment and educational interest to the Grey children. Since the large balloon trains contained at least three Signal Corps ML-307B RAWIN radar reflecting targets, it would have been a simple matter for the alien children with their high performance scout craft, to locate the balloons and follow them high up and up close. Their scout craft did have windows. Loving Alien parents would never have allowed their children to fly blind.

The protective force fields which surround their high performance scout craft can easily extend for as far as three miles out from the craft when the craft is in flight, and the corresponding coils are operating at full power. The alien scout craft can easily use those same force fields to push on a Project Mogul balloon train, as it floats in the distance.

That's Correct. The alien children in their high performance scout craft can do more than merely follow and watch the Project Mogul balloons drifting high up in the earth's atmosphere—the alien children can play with the large, beautiful—and fragile—neoprene balloon trains in a manner that no human could in July 1947—and in a way that no human could possibly have anticipated. From a distance, the protective force fields which surround the alien craft, can push directly against the fragile balloons, and directly against any portion of the fragile balloon train. Thus, the alien children—if they chose—with their parent's permission—could safely play with the balloons high up in the earth's cold atmosphere—too high to be bothered by defending U.S. Jet fighters—with no fear of experiencing a coil meltdown in the thin cold air. The alien children could play with the large balloon trains just as human children play with a beach ball on a sunny day at a Pacific Beach.

. . . . And a number of the fragile balloon trains did crash for unknown reasons.

Of course, playing with such a large, tall balloon train is more fun if there are three scout craft in the game. The protective force fields have a spherical shape and the rules of geometry apply everywhere.

However, on the late afternoon of July 2, 1947, only two scout craft were in position, waiting for the launch of the next Project Mogul Balloon. A third scout craft carrying young children, would make the game much safer—and a lot more fun. This third scout craft had not yet arrived from the playgrounds at The San Rafael Swell west of Green River, Utah. The third scout craft was already out of communication—and overdue.

First Alien Scout Craft Crash
Roswell, 1947

Alien children in a high performance craft, would be expected to follow along one of the natural valley routes when traveling from the playgrounds of The San Rafael Swell area near Green River, Utah, to the playgrounds in the western Malpais and the Eastern Malpais. The children would have kept their craft down in the valleys—as their parents would certainly have taught them—so their craft would not show up on the American defense radar network. Of course, on July 2, 1947, the air outside of the craft was very hot, so by the physical laws of thermodynamics, the coils on the scout craft would have also run very hot.

In any case, on that fateful hot late afternoon day of July 2, 1947, the optical fiber windings overheated on the simply designed scout craft which the Grey children were flying. The coils began melting down long before the children arrived anywhere close to the western most "EL MALPAIS". The full coil meltdown must have begun slowly, as soon as the craft entered the furnace like valleys along the route. The heat buildup must have begun first in the many propulsion coils. It must have begun as soon as the craft slowed down, and came close to the ground. The heat buildup had to have started slowly because throughout the resulting disaster, this craft never exploded. Except for the obvious coil meltdown, there is no reason to believe the craft suffered any other mechanical failure.

Although proceeding slowly, the full coil meltdown would have taken the alien children pilots by surprise. The coil meltdown, if severe and sudden enough, would have caused a huge explosion within the coils. Therefore, the pilots, as soon as they noticed a coil meltdown in progress, were forced to attempt an immediate emergency landing.

The pilots would certainly have transmitted calls for help to their parents back at their base if the overheating equipment permitted it. In that emergency transmission, the Alien children would certainly have identified the playground refuge they were hoping to land at. The pilot—an older child himself—did, after all, have nearly helpless younger alien children on board.

However, a high performance scout craft of the Double-Hulled type, off course and out of control, can cover an enormous amount of ground in just a handful of minutes. The children obviously were not able to tell their parents the exact location where they were attempting a forced landing. There are many deserts and many mountains in Utah, New Mexico, Arizona, and Southern California. They could have crash landed almost anywhere.

Based on my personal experiences during the Two "Climate Studies" in the mid 1960s, and my first hand observations of Southwestern geography, and terrain, I believe the Young Gray pilot was trying to crash land in a soft sandy area near the southern tip of the western "El Malpais" lava flow. It is my well formed belief there must certainly be at least one well hidden refuge, out in those broken, nearly impassable lava flows.

Had the young pilot succeeded, he and the other alien children would have stood a good chance of surviving, relatively uninjured, until their alien parents could find them. At the very least, the pilot was certainly hoping help would arrive immediately, since the Gray Alien parents would certainly begin by searching the alien playgrounds in the area of The San Rafael Swell and the Western Malpais first.

However, the children's hopes for reaching a safe playground refuge were soon dashed. With the coils over heating, and the scout craft off course and nearly out of control, the alien pilot was forced to crash land in the first open area along his path.

Looking at a map of the American southwest, for an alien scout craft traveling from the San Rafael Swell in Utah, towards the Western El Malpais, in all likelihood, the craft would have been traveling from the northwest towards the southeast when the crash landing occurred. Thus, if the scout craft pilot was a mere 50 or 60 miles off course, he would have been over the level open Plains of St Augustine, New Mexico, with the Luera Mountain peak in front of him.

Once the coils begin overheating, turning the craft from side to side in a controlled manner, becomes extremely difficult, if not impossible. In desperation, the pilot would certainly have attempted the emergency landing there. Even on any piece of level ground, any crash landing of a stricken Double-Hulled scout craft would have required great skill on the part of the young alien pilot.

In any event, it is logical to believe this first craft crash landed somewhere south of Grants, south of the Western El Malpais, south of the Zuni pueblo, and somewhere south of Datyl, in New Mexico.

When the crash landing occurred, the craft would have been heading towards the Eastern Carrizozo Malpais and towards the balloon launch site at Alamgordo, New Mexico. It seems certain the pilot was able to shut down the propulsion system prior to the crash landing, so the craft did not explode or catch fire. If the actual crash landing had resulted in an explosion or a large fire, it would have attracted the attention of ranchers and fire watch observers in the area.

However, the craft was heavily damaged, and most of the occupants were severely injured. The pilot and co-pilot were certainly injured so badly they were unable to be of any help to the younger children. Worse, there were no emergency locater beacons and there was no emergency power to communicate their actual location back home to their anxious parents. Their actual location was much too far away from the western Malpais for the injured children to walk back to the shelters and the alien refuges located there. Any injured children still able to move around would have had no choice but to remain within walking distance of their damaged craft.

Alien Parent's Desperate Search

By late afternoon on Wednesday, July 2, 1947, It is certain The Grey parents back at their home base had come to believe this craft was missing and overdo at its playground destination. To the Grey parents, it was obvious the craft had either made an emergency landing or had crashed somewhere. However, it is also certain the alien parents did not know where the craft had actually come down. An extensive—and desperate—search would be necessary.

The desperate alien parents set out to search the playground areas of The San Rafael Swell, west of Green River, Utah. Not finding the alien children on the mountain, the parents continued on—searching the surrounding river valleys and nearby mountains. Not finding the children, the parents began searching the city of Green River itself. The Grey parents were perfectly willing to come into the city in broad daylight to retrieve their missing children, if that was necessary. Unfortunately for the alien parents, their missing children were not anywhere near Green River.

The alien parent's desperate search was quickly expanded to cover other desert valleys and other dry lake beds in the American southwest, such as the dry lake bed at Muroc Lake, California.

At the same time, the parents ordered the two scout craft, which were waiting at a playground refuge in the eastern Carrizozo Malpais, north and west of Roswell, to break off their playground activities. These two Gray scout craft, each with five children and young teenagers on board, where ordered to begin searching for the missing scout craft. These two scout craft were ordered to backtrack along the route the first scout craft had been expected to follow. The two craft were to work as a team, searching the route back from the Carrizozo Malpais to the Western Malpais. From there, they were to continue searching back along the route to the Saint Rafael Swell west of Green River, Utah. To be on the safe side, the two craft were ordered to start the search somewhat further east of Roswell, just in case the missing children had overshot the Eastern Carrozozo Malpais before crashing.

Unprotected, Double Craft, Wide Area Search Pattern

As ordered by their parents, in the late afternoon of Wednesday July 2, 1947, the two alien scout craft, each with five alien children and young teenagers on board began a standard search and rescue flight plan. The plan they chose—or were ordered to use—was the unprotected, double craft, wide area search pattern. The alien children were obviously searching for the missing scout craft and its five missing alien children and young teenagers. The two scout craft started their desperate search by quickly accelerating to a point somewhere southeast of Crossroads, New Mexico. Crossroads is located east of Roswell, New Mexico and south of Clovis, New Mexico.

Roswell at the time was home to The Roswell Army Air Base and home to the 509 Bombardment group. At the time, the 509 was the only Air Force Bomber group armed with nuclear weapons. For that reason, in the days of The Cold War, the base would certainly have had one or two of America's first operational jet fighters—the P-80—sitting outside a pilot's ready room somewhere, fully armed and ready to scramble on a moment's notice. In the days, following the end of World War II, every American General remembered Pearl Harbor.

As part of their search and rescue mission, the two young alien pilots—mere older children by alien standards—brought both of their craft to level flight at an altitude of 10,000 ft, and slowed to 185 knots (roughly 213 Miles Per Hour.) At this altitude, under perfect viewing conditions, their viewing horizon would have been roughly 100 miles in every direction. However, on a late summer afternoon, through the sun's glare, with dust and heat waves rising off the furnace-like desert floors, the lava fields, and distant mountain sides, seeing the wreckage of a downed scout craft even as far away as 30 miles would have been a major challenge.

To improve their viewing conditions, both scout craft turned off their outer protective force fields. When they did so, they immediately began showing up on the Army Air Force defense radars. The two craft closed up into a tight diagonal formation. The lead craft was on the left (and southern side) of the trailing craft. The trailing craft was on the right and on the northern side of the lead craft. The sides of the two scout craft were separated by less than 10 feet of air space. The two scout craft were so close they were almost physically touching. In this formation, the two scout craft now appeared as only a single blip on the defense radar screens.

These two scout craft, maintaining that same tight formation, then began a standard search pattern by weaving slowly from side to side over a flight path roughly a mile or two wide. From the point of view of the alien children on board the two scout craft , they now appeared to be as large and as obvious as possible to any of their alien friends who might be stranded on the ground below. If the searchers on board the craft can't see their friends stranded on the ground, perhaps their friends on the ground can see them and show themselves. The Grey children's eyes are as good as those of a cat's when it comes to spotting motion.

The alien children on board the two scout craft are conducting more than a visual search for their missing friends stranded somewhere on the ground below them. They are conducting an auditory search as well. With the outer protective coils powered down, the alien scout craft are running in near perfect silence. The alien children on board have hearing as good as that of a dog, and they can hear every sound coming up from the earth below. The alien children can hear—and make—sounds too high for a human to hear. If so much as one alien child, stranded on the ground below, gives out a loud, high pitched shout, or otherwise makes a large noise using the same audio frequencies as a dog whistle uses, while the two scout craft pass overhead, the stranded alien child will be immediately heard and discovered. This search pattern which the alien children have started, will not be stopped at sundown. This search pattern can be continued all night long.

The occupants on the lead craft were obviously searching forward and to the south of the formation's flight path. The occupants of the trailing craft were obviously searching to the north and behind the formation's flight path. In this fashion, and in this search formation, the two scout craft began searching a wide path leading directly towards The Western Malpais. Then they expected to turn slightly towards Green River, Utah and The San Rafael Swell. On this day, the alien children on board the two scout craft cared nothing about the 509 Bombardment group stationed at Roswell. On this day, they cared only about finding their missing friends and playmates.

If the two scout craft had continued searching in this fashion, with only minor deviations in their flight path, they would have been able to search the natural alien highway between the two Malpais. Once they arrived at the western "El Malpais" they would have been able to slightly arc their search route to the west, and continue searching along the obvious natural alien highway which leads back to the San Rafael Swell and Green River, Utah.

However, "if" is a big word—and they might still have missed locating the actual crash site of their friends.

P-80 Jet Fighter

Once the two scout craft had fully powered down their outer protective fields, the American Defense radar could now track them. A Base commander somewhere was notified, and asked to proceed immediately to his control Tower. Simultaneously, a P-80 jet fighter was scrambled and the pilot was ordered to give chase. The P-80 quickly and easily closed in behind the two saucers. Then the pilot of the P-80 quickly and easily brought America's best fighter at the time, into firing position. The P-80 was carrying six 50 caliber machine guns loaded with live ammunition. The P-80's armament was not visible from the outside. The six machine guns were well hidden inside of its wings. There was no way to tell from the outside if the P-80 was actually armed or if it was carrying only gun-sight cameras.

The pilot of the P-80 had no way of knowing the two alien scout craft were carrying only children on a search and rescue mission. The pilot's orders were to protect the nuclear capable heavy bombers of the 509th sitting on the tarmacs at The Roswell Army Air Field below. The officers and men who proudly serve in The American Military have always proudly taken their sworn duties and their orders with a life-or-death seriousness.

Weaving slowly back and forth with the P-80 following, the two alien scout craft continued to follow their planned search pattern. It is entirely possible the alien children on board the two scout craft did not at first realize the P-80 behind them was carrying live ammunition because this important fact had never been mentioned in the pilot-to-tower communications. In addition to ordinary flight details, the pilot-to-tower communications only mentioned the pilot was trailing two alien craft. Some in the tower, undoubtedly did not believe the P-80 pilot, and showed it in their responses.

On board the two scout craft, the alien children may well have believed the P-80 was there to help them with their search efforts because the three planes together made a still larger object in the sky, and would immediately attract the attention of any alien children who might be stranded on the ground below them. In addition, the jet engine of the P-80 did make a lot of noise, and would certainly have attracted the attention of any alien child stranded on the ground below. It is no surprise, then, the alien children on board the two scout craft, did not at first appear to care they were being closely followed by the P-80.

It was already late in the afternoon. All three pilots were looking into the soon-to-be-setting evening sun. Traveling at 185 knots, the alien scout craft were progressing directly towards Green River, Utah at roughly 3 and a half miles per minute. At the rate they were traveling, it would have taken them almost 3 hours to reach Green River Utah. However, it would take them only less than 10 minutes to cover the distance from the Roswell Army Air Field to a point roughly 35 miles northwest of Roswell. The sun would be setting in a few minutes. The pilots of the two alien scout craft appeared determined to continue their search pattern. For the alien pilots, after all, the lives of the missing alien children depended on them continuing their search pattern. It was now the pilot of the P-80 who had to make a decision.

The P-80 had a maximum speed of 558 miles per hour at sea level, a service ceiling of 45,000 ft—and a range of at least 780 miles. At the rate at which the entire formation was traveling, the P-80 could have continued the pursuit all the way to Green River, Utah. However, within a few minutes, the setting sun and the gathering darkness would have forced the pilot of the P-80 to break off the pursuit. A decision had to be made.

If even one of the two alien scout craft had its outer protective coils powered up, the pilot of the P-80 would have been committing a form of suicide to have come in as close as he had.

If even one of the two alien scout craft had its outer protective coils powered up, the P-80 would have been helpless against them. However, the occupants on board the scout craft were, after all, only children—and even for young aliens, making mistakes is part of being young.

Top Cover
Protected Search Pattern

In my opinion, based on my personal experiences among the Grey Aliens back in that cold Late Winter of the mid 1960s, all of the occupants on board the two scout craft had to be children. In my opinion, based on my own personal experiences, if even one of the two alien scout craft had a single Grey adult on board, the adult would almost certainly have ordered only one of the two scout craft to power down its protective coils and enter the search pattern. The other scout craft would have been ordered to stay fully powered up, and take up a "Top Cover" position, high up and behind the first craft. High up in the earth's cold atmosphere, the protecting scout craft could be certain its propulsion and protection coils would have been running cold. Had that been the case, it would have been literally "Alien Child's Play" for the children in the protecting scout craft, surrounded by the craft's fully powered up force fields, to force the pilot in the P-80 to break off the chase. In their high performance scout craft, fully powered up, even a child at the controls could have immediately forced the P-80 pilot to stand clear and give up any thought of interfering with the alien search and rescue mission which was in progress.

In my personal opinion, within less than a week, the alien parents, would change to sending search craft out in teams of three. These teams of three craft would switch to using this Top Cover protected search pattern at places such as Muroc Lake, California.

However, at Roswell, on Wednesday, July 2, 1947, the occupants on board both of the alien scout craft were, after all, only children—still using the unprotected, double craft, wide area search pattern—and even for young aliens, making mistakes is part of being young.

Fatal Radio Communication

Unnoticed at the time in July 1947, for the entire 10 minute long pursuit by the P-80 fighter, even though both alien scout craft were obviously listening in on the communications which were taking place between the pilot of the P-80 and the pilot's control tower, and understanding the English words which were being spoken, neither one of the two alien scout craft chose to transmit anything in English using those same communication channels.

As the formation was approaching a point roughly 35 miles north west of Roswell, the pilot of the P-80 made a fateful decision. The pilot of the P-80 radioed his control tower and requested permission to make a live firing pass on the two alien scout craft which he had in his sights at near point-blank range. It was the first time the pilot had mentioned that he was carrying live ammunition during the entire chase.

Back at the Control Tower, the Pilot's Commander had just arrived. Speaking clearly and distinctly into the microphone, the commander gave the pilot of the P-80 permission to make a live firing pass on the two alien scout craft which he had dead ahead in his sights.

On board the two alien scout craft, the children were obviously listening in on the communication channel and fully understood the communications which were taking place in English. Apparently, for the first time, the children on board realized that the P-80 behind them was armed and carrying live ammunition.

Panic and Disaster

On board both scout craft, instant panic ensued. In desperation now, before the P-80 could began the firing pass, both alien scout craft began immediately powering up their outer protective coils. The result was disaster for the 10 alien children on board. The two craft were much too close for either craft to power up. The two craft should have separated first.

The protective fields of the leading, southern most, alien scout craft began coming up first. As they did so, those fields blew a large bite shaped hole into the side of the trailing, northern alien scout craft. The coils of the trailing, northern most scout craft, still only partially filled with radioactive subatomic particles, exploded, blasting hot, molten fiber optic aluminum shrapnel and other debris into the side of the leading, southern alien scout craft. Both of the alien scout craft were now mortally wounded.

The trailing, northern craft, now in a death spiral, losing altitude rapidly, and wobbling essentially out of control, arced off to the north and back to the east, entering into a nearby thunderstorm as it did so. The alien pilot, I believe, while escaping from the pursuing P-80, appeared to be trying desperately to return to the safety of the refuge in the children's playground area located in the Eastern Carrizozo Malpais, located down on the desert floor below. As the alien pilot was doing so, he would be passing behind, and below—and out of sight of—the pursuing P-80 fighter. The Eastern Carrizozo Malpais and The Capitan mountain were now located south of the P-80's flight path. When the alien pilot of the scout craft reached a point east of The Capitan mountain, he was able to turn the damaged scout craft back towards west. The alien pilot was turning back towards The Capitan mountain and towards the Eastern Carrozozo Malpais located to the west of the mountain. Unfortunately for the alien children on board, the northern scout craft was too damaged to make it to a safe refuge. The alien pilot tried desperately to keep it aloft and moving. Sadly, The alien pilot failed. Too soon it crashed, still desperately trying to return to a safe refuge. Its wreckage formed one of the debris fields. Four of the children on board were mortally injured. One perished immediately. Three more were injured and unconscious. They perished within a few hours. One of the very young children, probably a very young girl, badly injured, was taken alive when the U.S. Army soldiers finally arrived. That child undoubtedly died later in captivity. You see, in July, 1947, no "Desert Oasis" had yet been established where injured Grey Alien children could be returned to their parents.

The leading, southern alien scout craft, also mortally damaged, wobbling heavily, was obviously having serious control problems. However, most of the scout craft was still structurally intact. It rapidly accelerated straight ahead in the same direction towards Green River, Utah. When it was out of range of the P-80's guns, it arced slightly towards the south, intentionally heading directly towards the disk of the setting sun. The pilot of the P-80 was following the closer, northern scout craft at the time, as it arced towards the north and east and entered the outer clouds surrounding the thunderstorm. The events had transpired too quickly for the pilot to comprehend all of the details. The pilot thought the northern craft was intentionally hiding from him in the storm. Seeing his fighter could not keep up with the northern scout craft, especially with night falling rapidly, the pilot stopped following it. He turned his head back to look for the leading, southern scout craft. By now the southern scout craft was many miles away and was hidden by the disk of the setting sun. The pilot supposed the southern craft had crashed immediately—there was, after all, a small field of aluminum like debris on the ground behind him. With the weather to the north possibly closing in, the pilot decided to break off the chase and return to base.

The leading, southern alien scout craft, mortally damaged and out of control, I believe, was also trying to make it in to a soft crash landing near the refuges in the children's play areas which were hidden in the Western El Malpais. However, it too, soon veered further off course still more to the south. That scout craft crashed on a mountain peak somewhere out in desolate west central New Mexico. A number of years passed before this third crash sight was accidentally discovered. When it was discovered, all of the Grey children on board were dead. All of them had apparently survived the crash. They had apparently lived for perhaps another two weeks, trying to survive in the thin, cold mountain air—trying desperately to survive the strong winds, and the bad weather high up on the mountain side. Several of the alien children had injuries which they had suffered during the crash. Their suffering must have been enormous.

Making things even more tragic for the Grey alien parents, the alien parents mistakenly ended their search efforts too early. The alien parents had been monitoring all American public radio transmissions out of Albuquerque, Roswell, and other cities in central New Mexico, and western Texas. The alien parents had ended all search and rescue efforts by the morning of July 9, 1947. They had been listening in on American Public radio broadcasts. The alien parents had come to believe the wreckage recovered at the debris field, 35 miles northwest of Roswell, contained the wreckage of both of the scout craft which were conducting the search mission near Roswell. In reality, it did not. The alien parents had also come to believe the reports that the debris field near Corona was the wreckage of the first missing scout craft. In reality, it was only the wreckage of a Project Mogul balloon train.

At the time the alien parents ended their search efforts, I believe the five alien children still waited on the mountain peak—waiting to be found and rescued. By then they were past desperation, near death from their injuries, starving, and thirsty. However, I believe they were still alive. Even so, because of the desolation of their crash site, and the vastness of the American west, it is not likely they ever had a chance to be rescued alive by their parents, or to survive if found by humans.

Credible Updates

We continue to receive many credible updates from people all over the world. Unfortunately, this section is much abbreviated, as we suffered a massive computer meltdown, losing most of them. We hope you will find the few printed here, to be as interesting as we did.

. . . .

Many newspapers around the world, quoted an article carried in L'OSSERVATORE ROMANO, the official Vatican newspaper on May 16, 2008. The article virtually conceded that aliens exist. It featured an interview with Father Jose Gabriel Funes, who became head of the Vatican observatory in 2006. He said the existence of other intelligent life-forms would not contradict Christian belief. Father Funes is the Vatican's chief astronomer and one of his quotes is as follows:

> "As there exist many creatures on earth, so there could be other beings, also intelligent, created by God," he said. "This doesn't contradict our faith because we cannot put limits on the creative freedom of God. To say it as St. Francis [of Assisi], if we consider some earthly creatures as 'brother' and 'sister,' why couldn't we also talk of an 'extraterrestrial brother'? He would also belong to creation."

In November of 2009, the Vatican sponsored a week long conference on Extraterrestrial life.

. . . .

Dear Marie,

. . .

More detail: When I was twenty one years old, It was October, full moon night. My brother and I went to an area that was called by the locals, Zero Mountain—Charles might be able to find out or already knows of this facility, around Fayetteville Arkansas. It's actually outside of town, in a smaller town, can't remember the name now.

We were going to sit atop this mountain and watch the moon, talk, ect, have a few beers.

Down below the mountain is a cold storage facility that is or was at that time, heavily guarded. Supposedly they keep food in case we are ever hit by some sort of war. Understand that this cold storage facility was created in a huge Cave. When I say huge, I mean you can fly an airplane into it.

My brother was out of the Air Force by then, and home.

The hillside next to this cave was the only place you could view Zero facility, and there was a little gravel road that led halfway up it. Further up it was another small road, leading halfway around it, with no apparent end point, just ended in a sharp drop off. So we were on the first plateau.

My brother had left me in his car, radio on, dark except for October moon, to do something away from the car.

I was minding my own business when I looked to my right and saw them. There was a slant on the hill in front of me, leading to the next plateau, this hillside which was very tall., about 20 feet?

Okay, they were descending this hillside, yet their heads almost met the top of the hillside, but not quite. There was a group, in a formation. I can't remember now the exact amount, but I remember thinking they looked like a military group, because they were either in a set, like 3 in the front, two in the middle, three in back, not sure now.

One in the front, appeared to speak? to another one in front, and then the first one lifted out its arm to me, as if to point. I was terrified, literally. I never saw a hand, because it was dark and they were wearing white cloaks or robes with hoods, very large sleeves.

I remember that time seemed to slow down, and I felt I knew they were coming to get me, take me with them or something. Their robes were fluorescent white? I never saw their feet because they were standing in tall grass. They seemed to flow together, not really bounce when they moved. You know how some people when they walk, they sort of jerk , well they didn't. On the white robes was some kind of gold filigree along and down the front, but not on the hooded part or sleeves. I have looked up every sect I can think of and no of them match this, as well as the fact, as they were HUGE!

When I saw them pointing? at me, I called out to my brother, "THEY ARE THERE!" It's all I could say. He came running to the car. They slowly turned around in unison, as if in slow motion. Each one of them was perfectly in unison, I can't state this enough. They took about three large steps? and disappeared at the top of this next plateau. I figured that there was a small drop off that they landed in. My brother insisted me go check it out, and I was so scared, but too scared to stay by myself and went with him. No one was there. The tree's leaves had fallen, and not a sound was made in the crisp October night. We looked as far as we could see on that moonlit night, but nothing. It really appeared as if they were wearing robes, not a suit, but they were probably 30 feet from me, so not extremely close.

. . . I'm glad to share my story with you, just not sure this was what Charles encountered.

Update: since then, I have encountered a small mercury colored object in my living room, and wonder if its related. It looked liquid like and yet not shiny, it appeared to be a flame, but not flame like. Thank you for reading my response, and if this sounds like it could be the Tall Ones, I would love to know I've found the answer, but as I've lived without the answer for over 20 years, I can live with that too.

Wishing you abundance in your life,
H. J. Irwin

. . .

Date: Sunday, June 10, 2012 9:46 AM
Dear Marie,

. . .

Please do include my story and as I'm a writer also, I would be honored for you to use my name and any more detail that I can provide regarding my story.

It feels some what validating, as this has been a life long search and I feel finally I have found some truth.

Heart to heart, we are one!

H. J. Irwin

. . .

My experience happened in Timmins Ontario Canada, I was asleep in the basement with my two small girls, one on each side of me.

I had slept down in the basement as it was cool and quiet down there, I was a single mom and my three older children slept upstairs and the two little ones in my big king size bed with me. I did not have a husband at that time.

For about a week, the lights kept flickering on and off, or the light would go on, etc.

On this night , I woke up, sat up and looked to my right , a little guy was looking at me. then he slid to the end of the bed, then to the left side. I saw something at the corner of my eye as he slid so I looked back to the end of the bed and to my right, he did not slide, there was one, at my right, one at the end of the bed, and then two to my left, one of them was beaming love to my youngest fifth child, I screemed and they disappeared.

About a week later, my fifth child, a girl, went with her aunt and uncle to visit a few hundred miles away . . . . During the night, i awoke again to this little alien looking guy again, sliding up to me and saying without words, where is she,! I got so scared that I screemed at him and called him the dumbest alien , I had ever met, then he disappeared . . . I called my sister to check on my child and sure enough, there was a fight with the relatives and she was in a bad storm traveling in the middle of the night with my relatives, that was around two in the morning.

That all happened in 1998, prior to that I was a sheep farmer, and found myself many times walking the property in the middle of the night, I would just go in and go to bed where my husband and young babies would be sleeping, that was in the early 80's, and i was about 18 or 19 yrs old . . . the aliens were the size of a ten yr old child.

Your husbands story gave me the validation that they really have feelings and when I yelled at the one, he was scared and upset, and one beamed love to my daughter, I have been searching for many years for answers and have found nothing at all, until I watched your husband speak on T V . . . thank you and sincerely, Arlene, also, my daughter and I are both O negitive blood types,

Arlene Elizabeth Salo Roy
Timmins, Ontario, Canada

. . . .

APPENDIX A

A Technical Discussion Of The Double-Hulled Alien Scout Craft Design and The Many Coils of Optical fibers

The scout craft the Grey alien children were using, was designed with a double hull. Back in the mid 1960's, each one of the many Tall White scout craft and the Tall White deep space craft, , as well as the Grey scout craft, which I personally observed close up, out in the deserts of Nevada and California were designed with very extensive double hulls and fiber optic windings. In between the two hulls, each alien craft had perhaps a thousand miles of optical fiber windings.

In the case of the Grey Alien children's scout craft, most of the outer hull is not particularly strong. All by itself, the outer hull is actually quite weak. In many places, it is little more than a thin flexible weather covering for the many coils of optical fibers which are located between the two hulls. However, the force fields where are generated by the optical fiber coils are of immense strength. The various force fields are generated by radioactive sub atomic particles traveling inside of the fiber optic coils.

When fully powered up, the outer protective force fields, are so strong they permit the craft to perform huge accelerations, while flesh and blood intelligent beings sit calmly on board. When fully powered up, the outer protective fields would easily stop 50 caliber bullets fired at point blank range.

The outer protective force fields can easily become many times stronger than steel. The fields, all by themselves, can easily cause furrows in the ground if they are still powered on and the craft is crashing. When the craft is within a few feet of the ground, if the optical fiber coils are overheating, the combination of the intense heat and the power of these same force fields, can easily melt rock and cause a fast moving craft to skip on the ground as a flat stone skips on water.

However, when these same fields are turned off—or damaged—well, that's another matter.

The strands of optical fibers are wound into many separate coils located within the double hull. As I have personally observed, the individual strands are as thin as a piece of human hair. They are constructed from special ceramics and coated with special elements and compounds which give them their optical properties. Back in the mid 1950's, when I was still in grade school in Wisconsin, I was personally shown a 3 foot long piece of one of the original optical fiber bundles salvaged from the Roswell debris. The strand was a flexible, complex ceramic section from one of the propulsion coils. It clearly bent a beam of light from a flashlight. It appeared to have been coated with a dark coating of undetermined composition. It looked very nondescript. I was told at the time, the fiber had been recovered from one of the debris fields associated with the Roswell crash. The fiber which I was shown, could not possibly have been constructed by humans at that time.

The optical fibers are formed into coils and conduits for specific sub-atomic particles. As I have personally observed, back in the mid 1960's, the specific sub-atomic particles are generated from particle generators located in the back of the craft. Exactly which sub-atomic particles the aliens use is still a mystery. What is certain is the particle generators and their associated optical fiber coils form the propulsion system for the craft.

Similarly designed particle generators and their associated optical fiber coils also form the protection, shielding, and control systems for the craft. Altogether, they generate several different physically real force fields—all of which were unknown to Albert Einstein. One of the fields also streamlines the craft for velocities greater than the speed of light—thereby making travel between nearby star systems both possible and practical.

I am certain, based on my personal experience, there exists at least five force fields which were always unknown to Einstein. These first five force fields are quite stable and are very easy to generate. There exists two more force fields which are unstable and at least two more which are very unstable. Every alien craft is designed to make use one or more of these nine force fields. Most use at least three of the stable fields. Deep Space craft are sometimes designed to use all five of the stable fields.

The existence of these physically real force fields is why Einstein was wrong when he formulated his theories of relativity. In essence, Einstein was trying to piece together a puzzle without first having assembled all of the pieces.

A key point is the sub-atomic particles used by the propulsion system coils are themselves subject to the ordinary physical laws pertaining to radioactive decay and thermodynamics. Once created, the particles undergo radioactive decay rather quickly. For this reason, when in use on the Grey alien scout craft, the fiber optic coils are always running hot. If the coils become too hot, they melt—thereby destroying the propulsion system, and forcing the craft to immediately dump the molten material by making use of one or more of the ordinary access doors located on the bottom of the craft. The access doors are designed for use in just such emergencies.

Coil meltdowns are very common for craft of the Grey children's scout craft design. It is very common for coil meltdowns to cause the craft to lose control—and to force the pilot to immediately make a forced landing. Such molten fiber optic material is typically 49.6 % aluminum. To a human such material could very well appear to be metallic slag from an aluminum furnace. If physical samples of the melted fiber optic coils were analyzed, the scientific report might reasonably classify them as aluminum furnace slag which had been heated to about 2,000 degrees Fahrenheit.

Incidentally, any location where a UFO crash may possibly have occurred, should be searched for pieces of such aluminum slag. The aluminum slag might well be in the form of pieces of aluminum shrapnel embedded in old trees near the suspected crash site.

Ceramic based optical fibers, in addition to typically being composed of 49.6% aluminum, are also composed of nearly 50% silicon dioxide. Silicon Dioxide is the same material that composes more than 90% of ordinary desert rocks. Desert sand is also composed almost entirely of this same silicon dioxide. When an alien scout craft suffers a coil meltdown, if the temperature at which the meltdown occurred rose into the proper range, a puddle formed by the melted fiber optical coils can appear to be a puddle of melted rock or of melted desert sand. A person who is not a geologist—or a child at play—stumbling across such a puddle of material, might never notice it.

Most types of ceramic optical fibers lose their ability to transmit beams of light very suddenly as they heat up—and therefore, they very suddenly go from normal operating temperature to hot or extremely hot—and therefore melt suddenly and catastrophically—easily reaching temperatures in the vicinity of 2,000 degrees Fahrenheit—temperature also hot enough to melt rock. Therefore, the pilot of an alien scout craft which is experiencing a coil meltdown, can easily be taken by surprise—especially if the pilot is a young teenager or an older child.

An extremely important point is that one of the outer force fields protects the occupants of the craft from the forces of acceleration. It also protects the occupants from bullets and other debris thrown at the craft. It also protects the occupants from cosmic radiation when the craft is out in space.

However, these same outer protective force fields, do themselves interact directly with light itself. When inside of the Earth's atmosphere, they stop sounds from coming in from the outside world. For this reason, when the outer protective force fields are powered up, these same force fields interfere to a certain extent with the view of the earth below.

For example, these force fields tend to fuzz over many of the distant, finer visual details. When powered up, these force fields—together with the heat waves rising from the hot afternoon desert floors, would make it very difficult for children on board a search and rescue craft, to locate children waiting next to another such damaged craft on the ground.

For this reason, alien children on board one of their scout craft, searching for another such damaged craft on the ground, would greatly prefer to begin by placing their craft in a slow level search pattern. Then they would turn off the outer protective force fields, while they proceeded with the search.

On a hot day in the deserts of the American Southwest, the children on the search craft would also want to turn off this outer protective field to lower the rate of heat generation in the optical fiber coils on their own craft. The last thing they would want would be a coil meltdown of their own. Their parents would have made certain all of the children had been taught that simple important fact of life.

Because of the ever present danger of a full coil meltdown, based on my personal experiences back in the mid 1960's, groups of Grey children seldom took just one of the double hulled scout craft when they went out to play. They almost always went out in groups of at least three such craft for safety—each craft capable of holding a group of five children and young teen-agers.

The reason the alien parents prefer their children go out in groups of at least three scout craft is very simple. The coils surround the entire craft and by the rules of geometry, every craft has exactly two sides. If one craft loses control because the coils are over-heating and beginning to melt down, that craft can shut down the damaged coils while the other two craft can come alongside—one under each side.

Then the two working craft, using their outer force fields, can stabilize and guide the first craft to a safe landing or can return back to a safe harbor. Back in the 1960s, out in the deserts of Nevada, on several occasions, I have personally seen two Tall White ellipsoidal scout craft of a similar double hull construction, stabilize a third in exactly that manner, and for exactly the same reasons. It always required two rescue craft to do it.

APPENDIX B

ML-307B Rawin Radar Reflector

According to published reports by the USAF, in June and early July 1947, numerous Project Mogul balloon flights were launched from the Alamogordo Army Air Field in New Mexico. These flights consisted of very long trains of neoprene sounding balloons, radar reflectors, and other equipment all attached to a long cable. Typically, each balloon train had a total length of more than 600 feet.

It was common for each balloon train to be trailing three ML-307B Rawin radar targets. The ML-307B Rawin radar target was quite fragile. It consisted of a collection of pieces of aluminum foil, and an assembly of short, small I-beams constructed from aluminum and plastic. It was an off-the-shelf item and the manufacturer shipped it disassembled. Consequently, It had to be carefully assembled at the launch site, just prior to launch time. With the help of tape and glue, it could be assembled into any one of several configurations.

Each different configuration reflected the incoming radar waves differently. For each particular configuration, the reflector also reflected incoming radar waves differently in different directions. This was not necessarily an undesirable property for the radar reflector. If a Project Mogul balloon, trailing three such reflectors, were drawn into a storm with high winds, it could still be tracked on ground radar because its radar reflection would appear to pulse on the operator's radar screen. This pulsing radar signal would therefore allow any nearby aircraft to safely avoid the balloon, even if it were obscured by darkness, rain, or by thick clouds. The balloons, after all, were trailing steel cables.

Thus, in July 1947, any ground radar station reporting a pulsating radar reflection, coming from an object hidden in a thunderstorm, could easily be describing a Project Mogul balloon with its three flimsy radar reflectors being torn apart by the heavy rain, lightening, an d high winds.

The strength of the peaks and valleys of the pulsating radar signal could also be used to support the corresponding scientific analysis of the atmospheric qualities, the winds, and level of ionization of the air surrounding the balloon, and of the cloud in which the balloon train was floating.

To support this routine scientific analysis, the radar reflecting qualities of the ML-307B Rawin radar target had been carefully measured during the design stages, as part of establishing the Military Specifications. If the military had wanted an un-calibrated radar target, they could have just as easily used off-the-shelf aluminum foil gum wrappers of that era.

Since the reflector could be assembled into several different configurations, the results of the calibration studies were summarized into a series of advanced mathematical equations. These equations were stamped directly into the reflector's aluminum, wood, and plastic I-beams.

These equations describe the percentage of the incoming radar signal which the reflector reflects back to the transmitting antenna. This percentage depends on the direction from which the incoming signal is coming.

This percentage also depends on the direction the reflected signal is traveling.

Consequently, the equations are quite complicated. The equations were stated using the standard mathematical and Greek symbols in common use at the Ph.D. Level by scientists studying Advanced Physics and Electromagnetism.

Such mathematical equations and symbolism could easily be misunderstood by everyday farmers and ranchers. Such equations could easily appear to everyday humans as alien writing, which, of course, it was not. This is especially true if the imprinted equation is faint, faded, or otherwise hard to read. This is especially true, for example, if the I-beam containing the equations has been broken in half, or otherwise damaged, so that part of the equation is missing or being viewed upside down and backwards.

If we were to read aloud the first few symbols of these relatively ordinary equations, using English, we would be reading a complicated mathematical equation which might read something like:

"The gradient of the derivative of the contour integral of the incoming radar radiation over the surface of the reflecting radar antenna is equal to the tensor product of the surface normal vectors which describe the angle between the transmitting antenna and the radar reflector, summed over all of the antenna-s surfaces".

Thus, the equation is a concise mathematical way of using a very few mathematical symbols to say something which is very long and very confusing when stated in English. It is saying, for example, how the strength of the reflected radar signal decreases as the balloon travels away from the radar transmitter and as the balloon lifts the radar reflector higher up in the atmosphere.

Early versions of the ML-307B Rawin radar target were imprinted with only the equations. At balloon launch sites out in the field, interpreting the equations and using that information, when assembling the radar target, was admittedly very challenging for ordinary bachelor level engineers and technicians.

In order to make the target easier to use, later versions of the ML-307B Rawin radar target were imprinted with small butterfly like icons which showed the relative radar reflection strengths and reflection patterns for various standard configurations and orientations. Like the equations, these icons also could be confusing to interpret. Like the equations, these icons could also be misunderstood, and mistakenly interpreted as alien writing—which, of course, they were not.

In essence, these complicated equations and confusing icons were simply the Ph.D. Level Physicists at the ML-307B Rawin radar target factory, communicating with similar Ph.D. Level Physicists out in the field who would be using these same radar targets in their studies. There was nothing alien whatever about them.

Thus, in my opinion, any debris field which includes pieces of an aluminum I-Beam containing unusual markings, one of which appears to be the Greek letter Delta, or an icon shaped like the wings on a butterfly, is unquestionably the wreckage of the ML-307B Rawin radar target. In my opinion, this makes every such debris field the wreckage of a weather balloon, or the wreckage of a Project Mogul Balloon. For this reason, it is my personal belief the aluminum like debris publicly displayed by the US Army Air Force, which was reported to have been found near Corona, New Mexico in July 1947, is the wreckage of a Project Mogul Balloon train.

Here are a few more examples of perfectly ordinary equations and mathematical identities from the field of Vector Calculus, which use some of the same symbols which where were routinely imprinted on the I-Beams of the ML-307B Rawin radar target:

(Note: the div operator was commonly symbolized by the symbol /)

(Note also the use of the Greek letter Delta)

$$\operatorname{div}(\operatorname{grad} f) = \nabla \cdot (\nabla f)$$
$$\operatorname{curl}(\operatorname{grad} f) = \nabla \times (\nabla f)$$
$$\Delta f = \nabla^2 f$$
$$\operatorname{grad}(\operatorname{div} \vec{v}) = \nabla(\nabla \cdot \vec{v})$$
$$\operatorname{div}(\operatorname{curl} \vec{v}) = \nabla \cdot (\nabla \times \vec{v})$$
$$\operatorname{curl}(\operatorname{curl} \vec{v}) = \nabla \times (\nabla \times \vec{v})$$
$$\Delta \vec{v} = \nabla^2 \vec{v}$$

Additional examples using Stokes Theorem, Contour Integrals, Surface Integrals, Maxwell's Equations, or the Divergence Theorem could easily have been included.

Bibliography

In addition to the previous four books in the Millennial Hospitality series, a great deal of interesting related material can be found through the URLs listed below.

Millennial Hospitality, Millennial Hospitality II, The World We Knew, Millennial Hospitality III, The Road Home, & Millennial Hospitality IV, After Hours can all be ordered from AuthorHouse 1-888-280-7715, Amazon, through any bookstore in the world, or for autographed copies, via our www.millennialhospitality.com

The International UFO Museum and Research Center
http://www.roswellufomuseum.com/

Mailing Address:
International UFO Museum and Research Center
114 North Main Street
Roswell, New Mexico 88203
Phone: 1-800-822-3545(Toll Free Worldwide)
FAX: 1-575-625-1907

Open Seti Initiative, authored & maintained by Gerry Zeitlin
http://www.openseti.org

UFO Crash At San Augustin
Art Campbell
http://ufocrashbook.com/index.html

El Malpais National Park
http://www.nps.gov/elma/index.htm

San Rafeal Swell, Green River Utah
Utah State parks
http://stateparks.utah.gov/

Biblical quotes are taken from the original King James Version of the Bible.

About the author

Charles James Hall is a physicist and Information Technology professional. He had been writing his memoirs for his grandchildren in his spare time, for over eighteen years, before his wife became aware of it. Charles and Marie Therese, his only editor, married 43 years, live in Albuquerque, New Mexico. Their six children are grown, most married, and when they are not busy enjoying their thirteen grandchildren, find time to accept invitations to speak at conferences, and appear on talk radio all over the world.

United States Air Force
Certificate of Enlistment

This is to certify that

CHARLES J. HALL

has been accepted for active duty in the

UNITED STATES AIR FORCE

As a member of America's Aerospace Team, he will serve in a position vital to our defense effort. Both he and you can be proud of his choice to serve his country in an organization dedicated to maintaining our peace and freedom.

Detachment Commander
USAF Recruiting Service

Department of the Air Force

CERTIFICATE OF TRAINING

This is to certify that

A3C CHARLES J. HALL,

has satisfactorily completed the

WEATHER OBSERVER COURSE (ABR25231)

Given by

3345TH TECHNICAL SCHOOL, USAF, CHANUTE AIR FORCE BASE, ILLINOIS

16 MARCH 1965

ROBERT D. MONTAGNE
COLONEL, USAF
COMMANDER

AF FORM 1256 FEB 64

Honorable Discharge

from the Armed Forces of the United States of America

This is to certify that

CHARLES J HALL [redacted] SGT USAFR

was Honorably Discharged from the

United States Air Force

on the 19TH *day of* JULY 1970 *This certificate is awarded as a testimonial of Honest and Faithful Service*

JAMES O. WALKER, JR.
COLONEL, USAF

DD FORM 1 NOV 51 256 AF PREVIOUS EDITIONS OF THIS FORM MAY BE USED.
THIS IS AN IMPORTANT RECORD – SAFEGUARD IT!

California State University, San Diego

The Trustees of the California State University and Colleges
on recommendation of the Faculty
have conferred upon

Charles James Hall

The Degree of

Master of Arts
in Physics

with all rights, privileges and honors thereunto appertaining.

Given at California State University, San Diego, this
eighth day of June, nineteen hundred seventy-three

Chairman, Board of Trustees

Governor of California and President of the Trustees

Chancellor of the California State University and Colleges

President
California State University, San Diego

THE CALIFORNIA STATE UNIVERSITY AND COLLEGES
VIR VERITAS VOX

CITATION TO ACCOMPANY THE AWARD OF

THE AIR FORCE COMMENDATION MEDAL

TO

CHARLES J. HALL

Sergeant Charles J. Hall distinguished himself by meritorious service as Weather Observer, Detachment 13, 30th Weather Squadron, Binh Thuy Air Base, Republic of Vietnam, from 11 May 1967 to 11 March 1968. During this period Sergeant Hall endured 15 mortar attacks and demonstrated outstanding poise, devotion to duty and technical skill in the performance of observing and Security Police Augmentee duties. His efforts contributed significantly to the safety of the base and of combat aircraft operations in the IV Corps Tactical Zone. The distinctive accomplishments of Sergeant Hall reflect credit upon himself and the United States Air Force.

Lightning Source UK Ltd.
Milton Keynes UK
UKHW010259190520
363456UK00001B/225